PROLOGUI

'What's for breakfast?'

'Toast, same as it always is on a Saturday. Toast and strawberry jam, same as it has been every Saturday since we got married and same as it will be on a Saturday until our dying day.'

Willie Arkenthwaite stared at his wife Thelma. 'But I'm in training.'

'What do you mean you're in training?'

Willie sighed. "I'm in training for the trip breakfast next Saturday.'

'Oh, that.'

'Yes, that! And I need a giant breakfast today to prepare myself for the big feast next week.'

'So, I know some of the details, because I helped you plan them, but what's the full itinerary?'

Willie belched. 'The what?'

'Oh, for crying out loud! And give over making those foul noises. Now what is the plan of the day? What's going to happen?'

'Oh, that's easy, breakfast at eight at The Grapes, then off to Blackpool for the day.'

'What time will you be back?'

'Well that's for me to know and you not to worry about, but not too late. The coach has to leave Blackpool by six, so if we stop on the way home for a quick one, it'll probably be about eleven when we get back.'

'And the rest,' muttered Thelma under her breath. 'Anyway,' she said, 'you've got two choices, you can have toast or you can get up off your behind, go along to the village, buy the bacon, sausage and whatever else you desire, bring it back, fry it yourself and do your bit of training. I have the washing and ironing to do so you'll have to do it all for yourself.'

'I'll have toast.'

Stephen Bailey

*

    This particular Saturday morning, this scene was being repeated in forty seven other households in Grolsby village. The men folk trying to get a big breakfast, and some of them succeeding, with the womenfolk trying to extract as much information as possible from their reluctant to tell husbands about next Saturday's trip.

Murgatroyd's Mill Trip

BY

Stephen Bailey

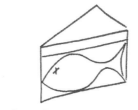

Murgatroyd's Mill Trip

Published by Fishcakes Publications
Huddersfield

www.fishcakepublications.com
ISBN 978-1-909015-34-0

Paperback Edition

Cover Illustrations by Michael D Garraghan

About the Author

Stephen Bailey

Well here we are again: still tall, still handsome, still thin, still sophisticated and of course still very modest. Still living in the fantasy world and, as those of you who know me are aware, still a physical medical and mental wreck.

So you see I have put pen to paper once again, Yes, and even pressed the keyboard occasionally we're rapidly running out of suitable feathers to make the quills.

This time it's about a mill trip. Now those of you whose education has been sadly neglected, by not partaking in a mill trip, do not know what fun and what a shambles they have missed. Perhaps this can fill in some of the gaps.

Anyway start reading at the prologue, because the fun starts there.

This is the second book in a trilogy (which, for those whose education was neglected, means three books).The third one will be along the same lines and appear sometime in the future, if I live that long!

I must reiterate (that's a big word for a Monday morning!) that any reference to anyone alive, deceased, or somewhere in between is purely coincidental.

So do please enjoy reading.

Stephen.

'Are you going to run the Christmas club again this year, and if so, can I please join?'

'Yes and no,' Arthur replied quickly.

'It's not fair, not at all fair.'

'Harry, you know full well that it is only for the employees of Murgatroyd's Mill and no one else.'

'Yes, but I'm almost an employee of the mill. I look after all you lot, morning, noon and night; I might as well be on the mill payroll. It's just not bloody right.' Harry decided to change the subject. 'So you're all off to the match then are you?' he enquired.

'That's right.' The five friends knew what Harry was wanting.

'Have you got tickets for the stand then?'

'Aye, that's right.'

'Are they all reserved seats?'

'Of course.'

'Which end are you going to sit at?'

'The gasworks end, like we always do. Anyway what's it to you? Why all these searching questions?' asked Arthur.

'Well I were just wondering, like, you know, if it were possible, like, you know, if you'd consider…'

Willie cut him short, "Oh for heaven's sake, go and get your coat, we've got you a ticket. You can come along subject to the time honored customs and practices.'

'You what?'

'You know what.'

'Oh aye, I do.' Harry poured six pints, free gratis to the football crowd. 'My treat,' he said.

'Thank you,' chorused the others, knowing full well that the drinks had come out of club funds and not out of Harry's pocket.

'Shall we get going then?' asked Harry.

'No rush, no, no rush at all, time for another round yet,' said Dick.

CHAPTER 1

It had all started at Christmas. Boxing Day to be precise, early one afternoon in the Grolsby Working Mens Club, Affiliated.

The terrible two, Willie Arkenthwaite and Arthur Baxter, with their two other friends Dick Jordan and Lewis Armitage, plus one other hanger on cum friend in the form of Eustace Ollerenshaw, were enjoying a convivial drink before walking to the station to catch the train to the big city to watch the Boxing Day football derby. A tradition which had remained unbroken for more years than anyone cared to remember.

It was the first time that all five of them had got together for a drink since the success of their Mill Christmas Club social evening in the Club almost a week earlier.

Arthur and Willie were revelling in the praise that rained down on them for organizing such a brilliant event as the social, and the Christmas club itself.

Eustace was continuing the praise, because Thelma and Jess, the respective wives of Willie and Arthur, had verbally attacked Eustace's wife Joan for publicly and physically attacking Eustace in full view of everyone at the social. Their single act of selfishness had relieved Eustace of years of aggravation at the hands of Joan the Dragon and now here he was, living a slightly improved life with Joan and enjoying both it and her a little bit more than he had done previously. In fact he'd enjoyed his Christmas more than he had done for many a long year.

There was also a further side effect. Eustace had for years stammered and stuttered his words and that had got just a little bit better with the lessening of the persecution from Joan.

Fat Harry Howard, the club steward, was in deep conversation with them, as ever, leaning on the bar and polishing it with those parts of his anatomy that were in contact with it as he slid backwards and forwards serving the drinks.

Contents

'Nay, steady on,' said Willie. 'I'll be in the bog more than I'm in the stand at the match if I sup any more; you all know what my bladder's like.'

'Yes, yes. Unfortunately we do,' they all nodded in agreement.

'Come on then,' said Arthur, 'get locked up and let's get going.'

Eustace came out of his trance and took stock of the situation. Here he was, going to the football match with his friends without Joan having shouted at him to make sure he fastened his coat and put his hat on and watch what he spent and didn't get lost and she had wished him an enjoyable day out, which before today would have been unheard of.

'Are you coming to the match, Harry? Are you? With us? To the match? Are you? Good, good I am pleased, I am Harry, I am.'

For once, because he was happy with his lot as well, Harry did not shout at Eustace and replied to him in a suitably happy tone.

'Well? Are you coming or aren't you?' Willie enquired of Harry, who was locking his cupboards, bar, safe and doors and getting his coat and generally checking that everything was in order.

'As Steward, I have a duty to ensure that everything is one hundred percent ship shape and in order before I can leave the premises.'

'Crap.'

'Yes, I know, but it sounds good. Anyway, here I am so let's get going. Have you had your dinners? I haven't had mine.'

'Of course we've had us dinners,' said Lewis.

'Oh well, I'll get something on the way. I don't suppose the station buffet will be open today.'

'No, I think not with it being Boxing Day,' said Arthur, 'mind you, if it were up to Evans it would never open again.'

'Well let's go and find out,' said Harry.

*

The station was at the other end of the village and the six friends walked the half mile or so through the almost deserted streets, the only exception being other like minded people going to the match. They were not long arriving at the station and each of them, except Eustace, was preparing himself for the verbal battle ahead with their old adversary Evans the Station Master, cum porter, cum ticket clerk, cum buffet manager, cum parcels superintendent, cum anything else that might be needed in a not too busy small station.

They trooped into the booking hall making as much noise as possible on the bare wooden floorboards. Willie was the first to arrive at the booking office window.

'Da y bore. Oh, it's not you!' Willie stared in amazement. 'Who are you then?'

'Relief.'

'Relief what? Where's Evans?'

'Not on till two. You've a quarter of an hour to wait for him yet. Yes?'

'Yes what?'

'Yes, where do you want to go to?'

'To the match. Return.'

'Where's the match?'

'What?'

'Where's the match?'

'What do you mean where's the match?' asked an incredulous Willie. 'Everyone knows that the Boxing Day match is at the ground not far from the middle of the Town. What sort of an ignorant wally are you?'

'That ignorant that I'll come round there and alter the shape of your face if there's another remark like that in the near future.'

'Now, now,' said Willie, 'its Christmas you know, good will to all men, peace on Earth and all that. Where are you from then?'

'Leeds.'

'Leeds?'

'Yes, sorry, best British Rail can do at Christmas, relief all the way from Leeds.'

'Is the buffet open?' roared Harry from the back of the crowd.

'No it isn't, what do you think I am?'

'Evans would have had it open.'

'Well by the time your train's arrived, he'll be here, so you can wait for him, miss your train and the match, and have a good cup of hot tea.'

'We've got one here and no mistake,' Dick said to Lewis.

'Aye, he's almost, but not quite, another Evans.'

They bought their tickets and filed onto the platform where it was bitingly cold as the East wind whistled straight through the Station.

Eventually the train puffed its way up to the platform, pulled by an old tank engine. The passengers boarded it, as did the relief station master on his way back home. The guard blew his whistle, waved his flag and the train went on its way.

Willie looked out of the window across the up line to the booking office where he observed Evans watching them and gesticulating a not altogether seasonal gesticulation.

*

When they arrived at the station in the town, Harry immediately made a bee-line for the buffet.

'This'll hold us up, won't it?' observed Arthur.

'Not for long if I know Harry,' Willie replied.

'Where's Harry gone? Harry? Where's he gone? Where to? Why? Has he? What's he gone for?'

'Shut up Eustace, he's only gone to get some dinner.'

'Hasn't he had his dinner yet? Hasn't he? Yet? His dinner? Why? Why hasn't he? His dinner? Why not?'

They all ignored him and left him to mumble to himself as they followed Harry to the buffet.

Arthur's observations had been very wrong, as Harry met them at the buffet door with a full mouth, a wide grin and an armful of paper bags.

'B…g…p…t…g…h.'

'What's he saying?' asked Dick.

I think he said 'B…g…p…t…g…h,' said Willie.

'What did you say?' asked Dick of Harry.

'R…s…o…i…p…y…l…a.'

They stared at him as he swallowed hard, emptied his mouth, opened it to explain, decided against it, stuffed the remains of the pie in and began to chew again with a wide grin.

'T…y…i…w…a…b…g…p'

'Come on,' said Arthur, 'or somebody will be sitting in our seats.'

They joined the other thousands of regular Boxing Day match goers and walked the mile or so to the ground, greeting people they knew, and mixing with the away supporters, directing them to the ground.

At the Goalkeepers Arms just outside the ground, they pushed into the already overcrowded bar to try and get a drink. There were so many people in there that it was either a case of wait for a drink and miss the kick off, or catch the kick off and miss the drink. As time went on, and they made no progress towards the bar, the latter became the favourite, although they had the utmost difficulty in prizing Harry away from the young lady he had somehow managed to become entangled with.

As they emerged into the daylight to walk the last few hundred yards to the turnstile, they met up with another crowd of younger people from Murgatroyd's Mill and they walked along with them.

Willie got talking with Ned Bennett who worked in the blending department and who suffered frequently from epileptic fits. To those who knew him, this was no problem; he just lay down for a couple of minutes, got up, rested for another couple of minutes, and then went about his business again. On a bad day it could happen three or four times, and frequently did. As he was saying to Willie how much he was looking forward to the match, he slowly stopped talking and slumped into a heap on the pavement. The lads all stopped and formed a shield around him, waiting for him to come round again.

Unfortunately events took a backward step in the shape of the long arm of the law, as a young, fresh, out of training college, inexperienced, Constable ran across the road, through the throng, to see what was happening.

'Right, what's going on here?' he shouted in his most commanding voice as his size eleven boots landed at the side of Ned, almost crushing him. This was his first big case and he was all alone. 'Right we'd better send for...'

Willie cut him short. 'Send for nowt lad. He's only had a bit of a fit, he'll be right as rain in a couple of minutes and then we'll go to the match.'

'No sir,' said the policeman remembering his training. 'Undo his top shirt button, cover him with a warm coat and I'll send for an ambulance.'

'No need, he'll be better in a minute.'

However the PC was having his glory, except that he didn't know which way to go and find a telephone, so he was practicing the noble art of trying to go both ways at the same time, and in the process, staying where he was. Being a lad with an active brain, he quickly reassessed the situation and blew his whistle long and loud.

Within twenty seconds a huge posse of police and onlookers were at the scene and an ambulance was called. The ambulance station was nearby and, although Ned had come around by the time it arrived, he was ordered by officialdom to the hospital for observation. He protested, and his pals protested, but it was all to no avail. He was dispatched to hospital, the large crowd dispersed to the match, calm was restored and the young constable, feeling very pleased with himself, was brought down to earth with a bang as his Sergeant castigated him for blowing his whistle for a non-urgent domestic problem.

*

In the ambulance, Ned protested all the way to the hospital. He became violent and had to be strapped to the stretcher to restrain him. He struggled yet more and passed out again.

*

At the football ground, the six friends filed through the turnstile and found their pre-reserved seats. Immediately, Fat Harry, who had demolished his bags of food, went for a walk and returned with six pork pies and six bottles of beer.

*

At the hospital, Ned had come round again. His violent actions and foul language were giving cause for concern and it was decided to shunt him into a side ward until he calmed down.

*

At the football ground it was half time. The home team was two up and Harry had gone in search of yet more food. Willie went to the toilet, Dick and Lewis went to talk to some friends they had spotted, whilst Eustace and Arthur were standing up, stamping their feet and flapping their arms trying to get warm again.

*

At the hospital, Ned had dozed with his eyes shut, still restrained. A nurse, who had just come on duty, had looked closely at him, decided he was asleep and removed his straps. Imagine her surprise when he'd quickly sat up, jumped off the stretcher, grabbed her, picked her up, kissed her and put her down again, then bolted out of the door as fast as he could. Being an outwardly puritanical, man hating, highly religious, spinster, she secretly looked back on that moment with a smile on her face for many a long year to come.

*

At the football ground the match was over, the final result being a disappointing draw. The gang of six was wending its way back to the station when they came across Ned running towards the ground.

'Where yer all going?'

'Home.'

'Why?'

'Because it's time to go home.'

'Why?'

'Because it's full time, the match's over.'

'Gosh! Have I been at the hospital for the entire match? I can't believe it, I never looked at the clock and I just ran out and down here as fast as I could to see the match. What was the final score?'

'It was a draw, two all,' said Arthur. 'Anyway, what have they done to you at the hospital? What happened?'

'Nowt.'

'Nowt?'

'Aye, nowt. Nowt at all. They strapped me to a bed and left me alone in a little room when I kept struggling. Then a nurse, what were a half-wit, thought I were asleep so she undid the straps, I jumped up, grabbed her, kissed her and fled down here.'

'Oh.'

'Oh what?'

'Oh nowt, there's no more to be said about it.'

Eustace came back from the dead. 'Do you think the tripe shop will be open, Willie? Arthur? Do you? Do you think the tripe shop might be open?'

'What do you want tripe for? It is Boxing Day, you know. I doubt it very much.'

'I could just eat a wasil,' said Harry.

'You are revolting,' said Dick.

'Yes I know, but its nice isn't it, nothing like a plate of tripe for putting lead in your pencil.'

'Since when did you need any lead in your pencil, from what I hear?' asked Arthur.

'And what pray do you hear?' asked Harry beginning to redden.

'Nothing that Sarah Anne Green would like to hear broadcast.'

'You wouldn't!'

'Wouldn't I?'

'No you bloody well wouldn't, or certain other people might just hear about someone's discretion with a certain lady out of Murgatroyd's mending room.'

'We are only passing acquaintances.'

'Pull the other one; it's got bells on it. Anyway I think we are quits now.'

They walked on towards the station, the others having gone on ahead leaving the two arguing. Eustace was still mumbling about the tripe he wanted to take home to his newly found, friendly wife Joan.

*

12

The train pulled out of the station dead on time, the thick, black smoke belching forth as the train passed up the narrow valley. Soon they were back at Grolsby and the seven pals alighted. Ned dashed away home, Harry went to the club to open up, Dick and Lewis slowly walked back to Dick's house for tea and the other three walked along the platform to the back end of the train to find Evans the Station Master, Porter, Ticket Collector, Lavatory Attendant, Sweeper Up, Cleaner, Buffet Manager, Parcels manager and proud owner of another hundred or so titles.

'Noswaith dda.'

'Up yours also,' retorted Willie.

'Ignorant it is that you are, William Arkenthwaite, very plainly ignorant. The word has you beaten. You cannot pronounce it, say it or understand it.'

'Of course I can, it means Merry Christmas in best Welsh with a Yorkshire accent.'

'No such luck boyo. Wrong again. However I won't enlighten you as to the refinements of the Welsh language. Go in and sit down won't you, and as soon as this one's chugged away, I'll come in and brew up.'

Willie, Arthur and Eustace walked into the Station Master's office and sat down in front of a huge roaring fire. Soon they heard the whistle blow, the train get away and Evans' footsteps approaching. He entered the office stamping his feet and flapping his arms.

'Cold enough to freeze a brass monkey's out there.'

'A brass monkey's what?' asked Willie who then belched out loud for amusement.

'Your manners not improved then for Christmas, Arkenthwaite?' Evans enquired.

Willie's hackles were rising, but he farted nice and loudly, again just for amusement.

'Calm down,' said Arthur who was picking up the signals of Willies annoyance, 'it's only a bit of fun.'

'Aye, that's right, fun it is and only fun. Sorry Willie, no offence meant.'

'None taken.'

Eustace was staring into the fire, taking no notice of the proceedings, in a trance, half dead, quiet as a mouse.

'Good match?' enquired Evans.

'Not bad, it ended in a draw.'

'You going to Arthur's for tea Willie?' asked Evans.

'Yes, they came to ours for Christmas dinner yesterday.'

'Oh, did they now?'

'Yes and Eustace came as well.'

'Did you take the dr... the wife as well Eustace?' Evans enquired

'Yes, I most certainly did. I did. I did.' Then he re-entered his trance.

'You'll be in for something good, big and hot then Willie, wish I were coming. Are you going Eustace?'

Eustace returned from the dead with a start. 'What Evans? What?'

'Are you going to Arthur's for your tea?'

'No, no, I'm not, No I'm not. Wish I was, yes, yes, wish I was. No, we're going to Joan's sisters for half past six for our tea, but then we've to come straight home after, because she's going out somewhere then. It'll be a poor tea. It's always a poor tea at her house. Still, it's not bad at home now, not bad. Thanks to Willie and Arthur. Yes, thanks to them it's much better, yes thanks.'

'Why is it thanks to you two?'

'No, it's not us, it's Jess and Thelma. At the Christmas club party, Joan was knocking seven bells out of Eustace for getting blind drunk, and who could blame him living with her, when Thelma and Jess intervened, played holy war with Joan and pointed out the error of her ways, since when she's been as good as gold with him.'

'Anyway Evans, are you going to brew up or not?' asked Willie.

'Aye, aye, bide your time, it'll be ready in a couple of shakes of a Welsh lamb's tail.'

Soon they were supping tea, sitting around the fire as warm as toast and telling the tale, which could have gone on all night if Willie hadn't said, 'I think we'd best get going before we're all dead men.'

'Not so soon,' said Evans.

'Aye, so soon,' said Arthur. 'You coming, Eustace? Come on we'll drop you off on the way.'

As a parting gesture, Willie snooked up a large ball of phlegm and spat it into the fire.

'So, you're going to Arthur's for your tea then as usual Willie?' observed Evans, who was hovering for an invitation.

'Oh yes, always enjoy my Boxing Day treat at Arthur's, particularly after the match.'

'To Arthur's, for your tea? Your tea? Are you Willie? Are you? Willie? To Arthur's? Wish I was. We're going to Joan's sister for ours. Wish we were going to Arthur's. We went to Willie's yesterday for our Christmas dinner. We did. It was good, it was, it was our Christmas Dinner.'

After this outburst he quieted down and retreated into the land of the semi-dead again.

'Come on,' said Willie, 'we don't want to be late, not today of all days.'

They took their leave of Evans, who had to wait until the six o'clock evening train from Manchester had passed through before he could lock up and go home to his cottage on the hillside where a huge log fire would be waiting to welcome him along with his wife, his relations and his tea.

*

15

For the first time in living memory, when they got to Eustace's house, he invited them in.

'Well as much as we'd like to, we're late already, but we'll just pop in and pay our respects to Joan,' said Arthur.

Joan came to the door when she heard the knocker and welcomed them with a smile. 'Come in, won't you, it's nice to see you again. Have you had a good match?'

'Aye it's been a right good afternoon, especially the bit about Ned Bennet,' said Willie.

'What about Ned Bennet?' asked Joan.

'Eustace can tell you later. We'll have to go, we're late already. So, we'll see you both soon.'

*

They opened the front door of Arthur's house and were met by a rush of warmish air coming out. Inside, the scene that met them was of a table partly ladened with food, a fairly well lit and half cosy warm room. Thelma and the three children were sitting in front of the fire talking with Arthur's wife, Jess.

Willie's first thoughts were as always on Boxing Day, gosh I'm glad I don't live here, it's not as cosy, warm and homely as ours.

Arthur's first thoughts were voiced out loud, 'What's for tea?'

'Same as always on Boxing Day.'

'Is it ready then?'

'Of course it is,' said Jess laughing. 'Have you been at the club drinking?'

'No, we've been at the station buffet drinking tea.'

Jess and Thelma looked at them disbelievingly. 'You've what?' asked Jess.

'We've been sitting in front of Evans's warm fire in the Station Master's office, drinking a mug of tea.'

'Well if you have.'

'Of course we have and then we've taken Eustace home and the dragon invited us in for a drink, but we declined as we knew we were late.'

'Don't call her the dragon again,' said Thelma. 'You know we reformed her at the Christmas club party.'

'Aye, that's alright. But old habits die hard and you must realise that it might be a short lived affair,' retorted Arthur. 'She can go back to her old ways at any moment.'

'After what we gave her, I don't think she'll go back to her old ways ever again. Do you Jess?'

'No. But if she does, we'll give her another going over, in her own home this time.'

'Tell you what,' said Jess, 'why don't we invite them round after tea, for the evening, and let's get to know her a bit better. We enjoyed their company yesterday, I just think she's a lot disappointed with her husband.'

'He can't help it,' said Willie.

'We all know that,' said Jess, 'but I still think we ought to get to know her better and we shall be doing our usual nothing after we've eaten.'

'We were going to go to…' he was stopped short.

'No you're not, not tonight. Has anyone any objections?'

'Yes I have, we always go to the club.'

'I didn't mean that. Has anyone got any objections about Eustace and Joan coming around here for supper?'

'I think it's a good idea,' said Thelma.

Willie and Arthur muttered something unintelligible.

'Arthur,' Jess demanded, 'go round there and invite them to come to our house for supper at half past eight, then call at the club and get three bottles of beer and a bottle of sweet sherry.'

'But Willie wants his tea, and anyway they're going to Joan's sisters for their tea for half past six.'

'So that's just right. Go now and come straight back. Don't stop at the club drinking.'

'I'll go with him,' said Willie.

'Not on your Nellie,' said Thelma. 'You can stop here and play with the children.'

'Eh?'

'Children. You know, these two young people here that you helped bring into the world, and Josie as well, although I expect she's a little bit too old for children's games.'

Josie smiled one of her usual welcoming smiles and said, 'Don't worry dad, I'm sure we'll find something to do.'

'But what about my tea?' said Arthur who was hungry.

'No tea until you go on the errand.'

'But…'

'No.'

Arthur, mumbling, grumbling, cogitating and generally at odds with the world, put his coat, cap, scarf and gloves on again and went out from the cosyish warmth of his front room into the cold, frosty, dark night air.

*

The house where Eustace and Joan lived was in darkness when Arthur arrived. *Good they're not in*, he thought, but then he thought again, *well he said they weren't going out until half past six*, so he walked up the front steps and knocked on the door. There was no response. He hammered the door knocker extra hard, because if he didn't get a reply, they wouldn't believe him back at home. He was just about to leave when a light came on in the hall shining through the patterned window above the door.

Joan's voice came through the door, 'Is anyone there?'

Flipping heck, thought Arthur. 'Yes it's me.'

The door didn't open. 'Who's me? Who is it again, I didn't quite catch it?' the door asked.

'It's me, Arthur.'

'Arthur?'

'Arthur Baxter.'

'Arthur Baxter?' the door shouted. 'What do you want?'

Arthur didn't know whether to answer the door or not, but he was saved from either as the door opened and Joan stared at him.

'Hello Arthur, this is a nice surprise.'

'Are you and Eustace doing anything tonight?'

'No. Why?'

'Well Jess, that is we, wondered if you wanted to come round after tea. For the evening like, you know. Willie and Thelma and the children'll be there and there'll be a bit of supper. Eustace said you were going round to your sister's for tea but you'd be back home early because she is going out afterwards.'

This question posed a dilemma for Joan, because she didn't know what to do now. She could appear to be in her old dragon mood and tell him, 'No. Go away,' or she could readily accept as she wanted to. In the end she boxed clever and invited Arthur in whilst she went to ask Eustace. Something she would never have done a few days earlier.

Eustace was in the back room, listening to the radio, sitting in front of a meagre fire.

Arthur looked around the room he had never been invited into before, at the stark décor, the hard chairs, the small fire, the poor lighting, the lack of ornaments and thought, *thank god for Jess.*

Eustace looked up as they entered the room. 'Hello Arthur. Hello. This is a nice surprise. It is, isn't it Joan? A nice surprise. Won't you sit down Arthur? Here I'll clear a place for you. I will. Here sit down.'

'No thanks, Eustace, I'm in a rush. I only called to invite you and Joan round for the evening and for a bite of supper. Will you come?'

'Yes. Yes. Yes please. We really enjoyed it yesterday, didn't we Joan.'

'Yes, we will come and thank you for inviting us,' said Joan. 'What time would you like us to arrive?

'Eh?'

'What time shall we come?'

'When you're ready.'

'What time?' She rasped, hints of the dragon beginning to resurface.

'Oh, eight o'clock.'

'Right, we'll be there, wont we Eustace. We can come straight around from my sister's place.'

'Yes, oh yes we will, yes, yes we will, yes.'

'I'd best be going. See you then, then,' said Arthur, and he went.

*

The Club was deserted when Arthur arrived. The Christmas decorations and the tree were still up, the fire in the corner of the bar was blazing away merrily, but of the club steward there was no sign whatsoever. Arthur took the opportunity, itself a rarity, of walking behind the bar and pouring himself a pint. There was still no sign of Fat Harry, so he downed the pint in one and hurriedly began to pour another.

An eerie voice broke the silence. 'This is a magic club. It is a self-service club.'

Arthur jumped out of his skin.

The voice continued. 'The self service is so good, that if the person serving himself does not pay for the one he has had, the one he is pulling now and the one he is going to pull for his friend the club steward, then the steward will descend from on high and break his bloody neck for him.'

Arthur looked up. 'What on earth are you doing up there? By gum you didn't half give me a fright.'

'I gave you a fright! What did you do to me? I wasn't expecting you or anyone else for that matter, not for a while yet.'

Harry was lying flat on his stomach on a shelf above the bar, hidden from view to all except those behind the bar.

Arthur asked again, 'What are you doing up there?'

'Well, you might think that this is a funny place to spend Boxing Day night.'

'Yes.'

'Well it's like this, I was…'

'Sleeping?'

'Certainly not! I was doing the end of year stock take.'

'Liar.'

'I was.'

'Well then, if you say so, but it looked more like sleeping to me. Anyway, get yourself down here; I want some alcoholic beverage to take out.'

Harry, with difficulty because of his enormous girth, half climbed with careful foot positioning and half slithered down to the floor, puffing, panting, blowing and going red in the face.

'Well, now that you've disturbed the extremely important task that I was performing, what do you want?'

'Three large bottles, no, you'd better make that six large bottles of York best bitter and a bottle of sherry, one pint for me and one for you.'

'Two questions: The first one is can you pay for this unusually large order? No three questions. The second is sweet, medium or dry sherry? No four questions, the third is, how are you going to carry all this lot home and the fourth, and most important is, what do you want it for?'

'The answers are, no, sweet, with difficulty and its nowt to do with you.'

'Well in that case we'd best have that pint that you're buying and can't afford.'

'Yes, why don't we?'

So Harry pulled two pints of the clubs best draught bitter.

'How's my slate?' asked Arthur.

'Same as last time you asked, same as it always is.'

'No exceptions for Boxing Day then?'

'No, you'll have to pay for it.'

The beer was by this time going down well.

'Here you are then, if I must,' Jess had given him the money to pay for it before he left home.

'Anyhow, I'd best get this lot home before I get lynched. They're waiting for me to get back so that we can have our tea.'

'This lot for your tea then?'

'No, we've invited Mr and Mrs Eustace Ollerenshaw for the evening.'

'You've done what?'

'You heard.'

'You mean the dragon?'

'The very same.'

'For the evening? By gum, that's putting service before self. Well, best of luck. Anyway how are you going to get this lot home?'

'In a box you're going to give me.'

'Oh am I?'

'Yes.'

'Oh, go on then.'

Arthur put the bottles in the box that Harry had found, fastened his coat and set off home.

'Don't forget; be nice to the dragon this evening.'

'Get stuffed.'

Arthur staggered home smiling.

Harry climbed back above the bar to continue his stocktaking, this time flat on his back.

CHAPTER 2

It was as usual, warmish, cosyish and fairly bright in the front room as Arthur opened the front door.

He'd just nicely got one foot inside whilst struggling with the box, when Jess asked, 'Well. Are they coming?'

'Nay, give me chance to get in. Yes.'

'Where have you been all this time?'

'There and back to see how far it was.'

'Whatever have you got in that box?' Thelma came over to look as well. 'What is all that beer for?'

'For me, and Willie, and Eustace.' Then he had a brainwave. 'And for you girls if you want some?' Arthur looked at Willie with a knowing smile.

'Put it in the kitchen and then we can start our tea.'

Willie took the box into the kitchen for Arthur, then came back to observe Arthur talking to Josie and playing with the two young ones. 'Right, can we get on with our teas, I'm fair starving?'

'Come on then all of you, sit at the table, it's all ready. Josie, come help your Auntie Jess dish it out.'

'We'd best put it on the plates in the kitchen I think. Arthur won't be bothered about getting involved in this part of the operation.'

Arthur, unlike Willie, was not the master in his own house when it came to carving and dishing up, so he continued to play with the children.

Josie went over to the cottage oven and brought out a large dish of hot, homemade onion stuffing, followed by a smaller dish of apple sauce and an even smaller dish of mustard sauce. Thelma was busy carrying in plates with cold turkey, roast pork and home cooked tongue. There was a mountain of mixed brown and white bread and butter and as much tea as anyone could drink.

'Well,' said Willie, 'you've done it again. A feast fit for a king. How do you manage to get all this meat? Is it black market?'

'Willie!' shouted Thelma.

'I only asked,' said Willie with a wide grin on his face.

'That's for me to know and you to find out,' said Arthur.

'Well you've certainly got it all from somewhere; it's too difficult to get hold of in these quantities without some skullduggery somewhere.'

'Some what?' enquired Arthur, somewhat bemused.

'Skullduggery, you know, underhand dealing, jumping the queue, black market trading, something like that. Mind you, I'm not complaining, just curious.'

'Any more of that and I'm taking you home, Willie Arkenthwaite!'

Arthur smiled. 'He's been asking that same question for years and years as you well know, Thelma, but don't worry about it as the question won't be answered as usual and he can keep guessing again for the next twelve months. Anyway how about us teas? Pass the stuffing and apple sauce round Josie, please.'

Jess just mentioned to them to mind her Christmas cake as she didn't want it ruined with careless passing of the stuffing. Josie passed round the sauces as requested and everyone tucked in as if they hadn't eaten for weeks.

Sitting in the middle of the table was the very large Christmas cake, home made, home iced and home decorated. It was, as every year, Jess's pride and joy, a cake to be envied by most households and she didn't want to have it damaged before Joan Ollerenshaw had seen it.

Arthur and Willie were eating well ahead of the field. 'Is there any more Jess?' Arthur enquired.

'You know there is, but as usual you'll have to wait until we've all finished. Then we'll see what there is left to share out.'

Willie looked at Arthur and shrugged his shoulders. Arthur sat motionless waiting for the next move by Willie and not daring to add to the conversation for fear of another tongue lashing from Jess.

The ladies and children finished their first round of meat so Jess said, 'Right Arthur, you can go and get the rest of it from the kitchen now.'

Arthur looked aghast. 'Nay aren't you fetching it?'

'No, it's Christmas and I'm having a bit of a rest. So if you want it, you can go and fetch it!'

Reluctantly, Arthur stood up and walked into the kitchen, picked up two plates of already carved meats and carried them back into the living room.

'Who wants some more meat?'

'Me. Me. Me. Me.'

'What about you two?' He looked at the young children.

'No thanks, Uncle Arthur.'

'Well just sit there quietly whilst the rest of us have another helping.'

Arthur served slices of cold turkey and pork, then he went back to the kitchen to fetch the tongue and sausages which he also served with his best antique carving fork. The five second rounders then piled on stuffing, apple sauce and mustard sauce. Then, armed with a fresh cup of tea each and a new pile of bread and butter, they devoured all that lay before them.

Willie decided, having given the matter a very considerable consideration, not to lick his empty plate as was his usual habit. He decided instead to mop up the remains of the sauces and stuffing with yet another piece of bread and butter, then he sat back and had a jolly good, loud, belch.

'Willie!' screamed Thelma.

Jess looked at him with her nose as high in the air as she could physically get it and sniffed several times. Arthur tried in vain not to laugh. But Willie just said, 'In some Arabic countries, it's thought to be polite to belch after a meal. Anyway, what's for pudding, or need I ask?'

'No, you don't need to ask,' said Jess. 'But after that performance you can get up, clear the plates and dishes, then bring the clean dishes and the sweet.'

Willie was about to object but decided not to. Instead he meekly got up and began to collect the plates. Arthur could contain himself no longer and began to have a serious laughing fit. Jess sniffed again another couple of times, and then said. 'Seeing that you find it so amusing, Arthur Baxter, you'd best get up and help Willie.'

Arthur immediately stopped laughing, looked at Jess, decided not to argue, then stood up and helped take away the dirty pots.

The terrible two carried their heavy loads into the back kitchen. They were stacking them by the big stone sink when Arthur Looked at Willie and said, 'Don't say it! Don't even think of saying it!'

'No, I won't Arthur. I wasn't going to. No thought was further from my mind.' Then they both burst out laughing. 'Here Arthur, you take the dishes in and I'll bring the food.'

Arthur placed the pile of dishes in front of Jess on the table and Willie followed with a large dish of trifle which he also put down by Jess.

The young children screamed with delight as they looked at the multi-coloured hundreds and thousands that lay on top of the thick layer of whipped cream topping.

They all ate their fill of the delicious, soggy mess, and then they started on the small fancy cakes, the big chocolate cake and the chocolate biscuits. The children loved it, the grown ups too.

'I'm gisened,' said Willie as he sat back, beer belly hanging in all directions.

'Yes and I'm fair pogged myself,' said Arthur

'What's gisened and what's pogged?' asked young Peter.

'Well now, young lad, how does your tummy feel right now?' Arthur enquired.

'Very, very full, Uncle Arthur. Yes, very, very full.'

'Then you're both gisened and pogged. They both mean the same except one comes from Yorkshire, that's ours, and the other comes from Lancashire. But I don't know which is which. They mean you've enjoyed it and you're completely full.'

'I am. I am.'

'I think we all are,' said Jess. 'Now we'll just have ten minutes in front of the fire then we'll wash up before the dragon comes.'

'Who's the dragon?' shouted Peter

Thelma's heart sank. 'Now listen to me. That was very naughty of Auntie Jess. Mr and Mrs Ollerenshaw are coming round later and you have got to be very polite. You have got to make them very welcome and not call her the dragon. Understand? Or we shall go straight home and then it's early to bed. But if you are very, very good you can both have an extension and stay up late.'

Margaret, who was a little older than Peter, asked, 'Is it useless Eustace that's coming?'

Thelma stifled a smile. 'Now listen good and hard young madam. That is the very last that I want to hear of that sort of talk from you ever again. Do you hear?'

'It's not my fault, everyone knows he's called useless.'

'Well maybe they do, but its not very nice is it to call people by other names now is it?'

Peter butted in, 'They call her Margaret spotty potty at school.'

'They don't.'

'They do, because you've got spots and you go to the lavatory a lot more than anybody else.'

'I don't.'

'You do.'

The inevitable fight began, to be quickly stopped by Josie, who separated the two of them and then Thelma gave them a final rebuke with the threat of immediate home and bed if there was one more naughty occurrence. Thelma stood up and announced that she was going to start the washing up. Jess followed her into the back kitchen. 'No, you go and rest Jess, you have done enough. These two fat, lazy lumps have done nothing, let them dry the pots.'

Jess protested and so did the men, but Thelma would hear none of it. The terrible two stood in the kitchen, by the sink, tea towels in hand, waiting for the first wet plate to come out of the sink.

Jess and Josie welcomed the brief period of respite, whilst Peter and Margaret played peacefully with the Christmas gifts they had brought with them.

*

The four adults were dozing in front of the fire, the youngsters were playing there also and Josie was reading the new book she had got for Christmas. It was one minute to eight and there was a knock on the door. Thelma awoke with a start at the noise, the other three slept peacefully. Josie got up and opened the door.

"Hello, Mrs Ollerenshaw, please come in, and once again a Merry Christmas, to you as well Mr Ollerenshaw."

Eustace followed his wife into the warm room. Josie closed the door and pulled the thick curtain across again to keep out the cold air. By this time the other three had come round and all were standing looking at Joan and Eustace.

Eustace was standing looking awkward, having taken off his best trilby as he entered the room, he was now nervously rolling it from hand to hand.

Jess broke the ice. 'Well now, come along over here and sit by the fire, you'd best take your coats off first though because it's getting a bit hot sitting here. Mind you, half of the heat's been generated by those two talking rubbish.'

Joan put her hand into her coat pocket and pulled out three chocolate bars which she gave to Josie and the two youngsters.

'You shouldn't have brought them,' said Thelma.

'Well, I think it's very nice of you. Thank you,' said Josie with her radiant smile. 'I'm going to keep mine for a few days before I eat it, if that's alright Mrs Ollerenshaw?'

'Oh yes, please do.'

The two young ones had by this time almost devoured theirs and they shouted their thanks with full mouths.

Joan and Eustace sat down, as did the others. Joan said, 'It's very nice of you to have invited us here tonight.'

'You're very welcome. Please make yourselves at home, we don't stand on ceremony here. But I warn you, you'll have to put up with Willie's rude noises, like it or not.'

'I think we can live with that,' said Joan. 'I think the men enjoyed the match this afternoon and wasn't that funny about Ned Bennet. I know it's serious, but it's funny as well.'

'What's that about Ned Bennet? Nobody's told us anything about him,' queried Jess as she turned to look at Arthur.

So Arthur told the tale and there was a lot of laughter, followed by even more serious discussion about his condition. The conversation then turned to holidays and the annual week at the end of July.

'Are you going to Scarborough again, Jess?' Thelma asked.

'I don't know. We haven't discussed it yet, only we've assumed we will. We shall have to let Mrs Saltly know soon though, to keep our room. We usually let her know in January.'

'I fancy somewhere different for a change,' said Arthur.

'You do?'

'Yes I do. I'm fed up with going to Scarborough. It's not that I've owt against Scarborough, it's just that we never go anywhere else and I'd like a change.'

'Like where?' demanded Jess.

'I don't know, maybe Blackpool, or perhaps Southport, that would be nice. But I want a change.'

It wasn't often that Arthur was quite so definite about anything but Jess realised he meant it and it was no use arguing any more. However, she shoved her two pennyworth in with, 'Well it'll be difficult finding somewhere to stay that we know's reliable.'

'We'll put the effort in to find it, perhaps one Saturday on the train.'

'Yes but…' She got no further as she was suddenly crippled with the most excruciating pain in the lower regions of her body and she belched out loud. She excused herself, but Joan wasn't sure what for, because Jess was moving as fast as she could to the bottom of the stairs to head for the bathroom and instant relief if she actually made it without having an accident.

Willie looked on pleasurably and belched himself.

Thelma was beginning to bend forward and was crossing her legs, hoping that Jess would not be long in the bathroom.

About the same time, Arthur began to feel the need of a handy toilet. Willie was chattering with Eustace and taking note of events that were unfolding when he suddenly felt the call from afar. At least it wasn't very far, but it was surely going to get very crowded any time now.

They heard the lavatory flush upstairs and three bodies dived for the stairs. Willie was the first to realise that there was going to be a bit of a problem and whilst his motto was, "me first and bugger the others," he decided he'd better let Thelma go first.

Willie's face was turning three different shades of red at the same time as he realised he couldn't go there and then and at the same time there was no way that he could not go.

'What…' he began.

Arthur cut him short. 'With me, behind the garden shed. Come on. Run!'

Jess came back into the front room as Thelma used the bathroom and the two men left the kitchen to head into the garden at a fair rate of knots.

Joan and Eustace sat gob smacked, watching the events unfolding and somewhat amused at the situation. 'I wonder if it's like this every Boxing Day?' Joan asked him.

'I don't think so. No. I don't. No I don't. I don't think so. No. Not.'

'No, it certainly is not,' Jess said as she entered the room having overheard the conversation. 'It must be something we've eaten at tea time. I wonder what.'

Arthur crashed in through the back door and put his head into the front room from the kitchen. 'Here Eustace, pass us that newspaper there will you, we've forgotten to take something to wipe us…'

Joan had enough presence of mind to say. 'Come on Eustace this is an emergency situation.'

Whilst Eustace slowly got to his feet and picked up the paper, Willie told him, 'There're some bottles of beer in that box on the kitchen sink and a bottle of sherry and some glasses in the dresser behind you. Just pour a round for us all will you for when we get back.'

It wasn't long before they were all back and sitting in front of the fire.

'It must have been the stuffing,' said Willie. 'Too many onions all at once, that's what.'

'Well whatever it was, it was a very close call, I almost didn't make it. As close a call as I've ever had. I don't know how I made it down the garden. I…'

'We don't want too know Arthur, thank you,' Jess was glaring at him.

'The more important question is what have you two done? Where? And who's going to deal with it?'

'Arthur looked at Jess, 'Don't worry about it, just don't go behind the pigeon loft until I've dealt with it tomorrow. Hey,

I'll tell you what, we won't half have some good big cabbages next year.'

'You wouldn't,' said Jess.

'It's the perfect solution,' said Arthur grinning. 'Has everyone got a glass?' He looked around to observe that everyone had a full glass. 'What about the youngsters?' he asked Thelma.

'Oh, they can get their own lemonade if they want some. Don't worry about them, they can look after themselves.'

Willie started to laugh to himself.

'What's amusing you then?' asked Jess.

'Eh, I was just thinking, it's a good job we weren't around at our house and Thelma's mother wasn't still living, or we'd never have heard the last of it.'

'Now, now!' she said also laughing.

There was nothing said for a short while then Jess decided she'd better apologise. 'Well I'm sorry about that little lot; I can't think what caused it. The children seem to be alright and it must have been quick and clever because it only happened the once and I feel fine again now. So what it was, I don't know, but it must have been something we all ate at tea time.'

She spoke too soon as Josie bolted upstairs.

'Best clear the way for the two young'uns,' said Arthur, 'Can't do with them going down the garden and getting nettle rash up their...'

'That's just enough of that sort of talk. It's Christmas,' said Jess.

'Ah well, I was only thinking like.'

'Well don't. Men weren't put on this earth to think. Especially you lot.'

Willie was sitting listening, glass in hand, content with life, pleased that Arthur was on the receiving end and not him, although, as he told himself quite often, he was very lucky to have married Thelma, she left him in peace to do his own thing most of the time.

Thelma was also sitting, half listening, worrying if Josie was alright, if Margaret and Peter were going to suffer and if the supper was going to have the same effect.

Joan was also sitting listening and thinking. It had been a long, long time since anyone other than relations, had invited her and Eustace to anything, except for Christmas dinner yesterday at Willie and Thelma's. She was very happy to be there, more happy than anyone could actually know, because they had got their lives into a rut. When she looked around the cottage it was warm and cosy, theirs was cold and stark. There was a big hot fire here, they had a little fire with two or three pieces of coal, just enough to not let it go out. The cottage was full of noise, admittedly of visitors and children, but she and Eustace had no children and never ever had visitors other than relations. She could not remember the day when anyone had called. This house had pictures on the wall, OK, they were only chocolate box tops cut out and put into wood frames, but they made it homely, and they had none, their walls were bare. There were ornaments all over and a big picture mirror over the top of the range. It was obvious that they were only cheap ornaments brought back from the seaside and jumble sales at the Church, but they made the house feel homely. She sat there thinking and thinking.

Eustace was enjoying himself no end. He was sitting, listening, and watching, glass in hand, and he was very happy. Before the Christmas club party, he never had a thought in his head, except when would Joan next shout at him or hit him, but in the few short days since the party he hadn't been shouted at once, or hit, and he was beginning to relax. With the relaxing was coming thinking a little bit, and contrary to Jess' outburst about men thinking, he said, 'You know, I've been thinking.'

Five heads turned towards him, some in astonishment and some with interest.

'We should have a mill trip to Blackpool.' There was a very pregnant pause in the proceedings. 'In the summer, I mean, one Saturday, just one coach full.'

In view of the present company, Joan Checked herself from getting up and giving him either a good hiding or a good tongue lashing.

Jess laughed. 'You're scheming again, you lot are.'

'First I've heard of it,' said Willie, 'but a good idea.'

'Yes, this has come completely out of the blue, but the idea certainly appeals to me,' said Arthur.

Jess just looked at the three of them and kept her thoughts to herself except to say, 'Pour another round Arthur, all our glasses are empty.'

Eustace took up the subject again. 'I meant men only you know, no women.'

Arthur poured another round using up all the beer bottles and half the sherry. There were no refusals even from Joan Ollerenshaw who wasn't used to drinking.

Joan opened the bowling on the subject of the trip. 'Where on earth did you get that idea from? Who have you been listening to?'

'Nobody, my love, it just came to me out of nowhere. I just thought we could do with having a trip.'

'And who's going to sort it out?' A week ago she would have told him to wash his mouth out and forget it and then belted him around the head for annoying her.

'I am,' he said proudly, smiling, 'and Willie and Arthur, with your help.'

'Now hang on a minute, who says me and Willie'll help?'

'You will, Arthur, won't you? Willie? Arthur? You will help me organise the trip, you will wont you? Please?' He was almost pleading.

'Yes, of course they will,' said Thelma, 'they've got nothing else to do, have you?'

Jess was nodding her assent also.

'Of course we've got something else to do. We've got next year's Christmas club,' said Willie.

'Drinking,' said Jess.

'Then we've got the pigeons.'

'More drinking.'

'Gardening.'

'Supporting the bar at the club in more ways than one,' continued Jess.

'Bowling.'

'Heavy drinking.'

'Football.'

'Consuming liberal quantities of alcohol.'

'A thousand and one other things.'

'Not forgetting drinking.'

It seemed that the matter was settled without a vote and with all dissent quelled.

*

Jess slipped out to get supper ready and asked Josie to help her. Josie came back to ask Mr and Mrs Ollerenshaw if they wanted tea or coffee to drink.

'Tea,' said Willie.

'Thank you, Dad, we know your order, it was our two guests we didn't know about.'

'Aren't your mum and I guests?' asked Willie.

Josie smiled. 'No, you're regulars, I know what you have.'

Eustace exerted himself again. 'Joan would like tea and I would like coffee, please, if that's alright.'

'That's fine, just fine.'

Joan was anticipating trouble ahead. For years after she had married Eustace, and once she'd knocked the stuffing out of him, she'd led a life of peace. He never dare argue with her or even express an opinion or anything and she was becoming wary of what lay ahead.

Josie returned with both coffee and tea pots. Jess followed with hot and cold milk.

'Will you please come along and sit around the table, supper is served.'

It was a squash; the Baxter household was the owner of four dining chairs, one more that didn't match, one bedroom chair that Arthur was dispatched to fetch and three stools from the kitchen. Thus the entire assembled crowd sat down together.

The table was laden with food. There was a big home-made pork stand pie, several varieties of cheese, cream crackers, mince pies, chocolate cakes, fancy cakes, chocolate biscuits and sitting in the middle, Jess's Christmas cake.

Joan took her sat and stared at the table. She stared at the food; a spread she could not believe was there, she'd never experienced anything like it in recent times except at Willie's house yesterday. She looked around the table at all the others seated there, Thelma, Willie and the children, obviously very happy as a family and she thought, *Willie's nothing special, only works in the mill like Eustace, same wage every week like Eustace, Thelma cleans at the big house for Margaret Murgatroyd, but that's only part time and doesn't bring that much in, but they've got a warm, cosy, happy life, and look at ours.* She turned her attention to Arthur and Jess. *Same income situation as us, their house like ours but a lot brighter, warmer, homelier and cosier than ours. I don't work, Jess doesn't work, we've saved up a few bob and I think Arthur and Jess will have. I don't think Willie and Thelma will have much, they can't with three children but yet they're happy with their lot.* She was awakened from her thoughts by Arthur offering her a piece of Jess's home made pork pie.

'Thank you very much. My word, it is nice of you to invite us and to such a spread as this. I can't quite believe it. It was just going to be another miserable night listening to the wireless and look how it's turned out.'

Eustace in his own peculiar style said much the same thing.

36

They dined long, hard and well and by the time the table was almost bare they were well and truly stuffed.

'Right,' said Jess, 'just one thing left before we finish and what's that children?'

'To cut the Christmas cake,' they shouted.

'Yes and then what?'

'To eat it,' came the chorus.

'But there's something else?'

Both children looked blank.

'Home and bedtime then,' she said, smiling.

'Oh no!' said both children.

'Oh yes. Your mum says you've both had a very long extension tonight, and that's two nights running. Good job it's Sunday tomorrow so we can all have a lie in.'

She took the outer frill from the cake and cut into it with Arthur's best carving knife, carefully wiped following its journey through the pork pie.

'Right, who's going to try the first piece?'

'I will please,' said Josie

'Yes, I think you should. It's usually Arthur who does the honours but I think you ought to now you're getting older.'

She was handed a piece of the dark coloured, moist, fruit-ladened cake and she took a big bite. All eyes were on her awaiting her verdict which was answered with a broad grin, a sparkle in her eyes and a nod of assent. She emptied her mouth and said, 'Wonderful. Fantastic.' The cake was cut and passed around.

Joan agreed with Josie. 'I wish I could bake like this.'

'There's nothing to it Mrs Ollerenshaw, I helped Auntie Jess to mix it, and it's dead easy.'

They all finished their cake and drank their beverages, then Thelma said, 'Well I think it's time for home. It's almost eleven o'clock, we've had a good long day and it's time for bed.'

'Nay, you're not going just yet,' said Arthur. 'Stay a while and we'll sit in front of the fire. Hows about another pot of tea?'

'You go and brew it,' Jess told him.

'Yes, right, I will.' And much to everyone's surprise, he did just that. Coffee as well, although Josie helped him just a little bit.

'Shall we wash up?' asked Joan.

'No, don't worry about it. Arthur'll do it after you've gone home, but thanks for offering.'

Joan took a quiet moment in the conversation to ask, 'Will you all come round to our house for supper one Saturday night, soon?'

'Oh yes, please do. Please. Please do come for supper. Soon. Yes soon, one Saturday, yes.'

'Of course we will,' said Thelma.

'And the children as well.'

'That will be very nice, thank you.'

'Yes, that's fine by us,' said Arthur. 'Isn't it Jess?'

'Yes. Yes,' said Jess, hurriedly.

So they drank tea and coffee for some time longer. They talked about this and that and then it really was time to go home.

It took Willie and Arthur quite some time to assemble Eustace into his outdoor gear, but soon the two families were saying goodnight with thank yous by the thousand being offered, especially from Eustace.

As soon as they had all gone, Arthur helped to wash up and retired to bed, well pleased with having had Joan and Eustace as extra guests.

*

Willie, Thelma and the children walked along the street with Eustace and Joan, back towards the village, then parted company at the main road.

'Well, I wouldn't have believed it,' said Thelma

'No. Yes. I know what you mean,' said Willie, it's been one hell of a good night just like last night.'

*

Out of sight of the Baxter's, Joan slipped her arm through Eustace's, something she hadn't done in years. They walked home, arm in arm, happily together for the second night in a row, but really for the first time in a long time. 'Have you enjoyed tonight Eustace?' she asked.

'More than anything. Yes a lot more,' he replied. 'Thanks for being so nice to me and even more thanks for inviting them all for supper. That's going to be super, yes it is. Super, fantastic, yes. Yes it is.'

Joan snuggled up more closely to him. A new world was beginning to open up for her and she was going to make sure she never lost it again through her own stupidity.

CHAPTER 3

'That's it. Got it.'

Joan Ollerenshaw opened one sleep filled eye, pulled back the covers, just a little, and, peering, out of the corner observed Eustace sitting up in bed, wide awake and looking uncommonly bright and alive.

'What on earth are you doing?' she demanded.

'Planning the trip. Yes, that's it, planning the trip.' This was so unlike Eustace, that to Joan it was as if she was still in a dream world.

'What time is it?' she asked.

'Half past eight.'

'Don't you think, seeing that this is the last day of your Christmas holiday, and it's a Sunday, that you might like to have another half hours sleep or so? You never get up before half past nine on a Sunday.'

'No, no that's right, but today's different. It is, it's different.'

'Why?'

'Because I've a trip to plan.' Then in a very firm style he said, 'Yes that's right; I have a trip to plan.'

'Yes, but you normally do nothing at all, nothing, not anything, nowt. You listen to the radio, you go to the club, you eat, drink and sleep, but never anything else. That's your entire Sunday lot.'

'Yes, but now things between us are different. You've given over shouting at me and hitting me, I've got time to think about other things and I'm going to plan this trip. And what's more, I'm going to give over repeating myself. I am, I'm going to give over repeating myself. Now you go back to sleep, I'm going to get up.' With which he got out of bed and made his way to the bathroom.

Joan lay on her back unable to sleep anymore, contemplating the bright new and exciting future that was about to dawn for the two of them, wondering whether or not she should make a swift return to knocking the living daylights out of Eustace at every opportunity, or whether she should let things develop and find out what sort of a brave new world awaited her.

*

At about the same time in the Baxter household, two people were snoring in harmony, a process that was to continue for some time to come.

*

At a similar time in the Arkenthwaite property, the two young children were up playing, Josie was still well asleep, as was Thelma, but Willie was awake, planning his day pottering around the outside of the house and in particular, attending to the new pigeons that had not been there long.

*

Eustace shaved, washed, abluted and went back to the bedroom where he quietly got dressed, whilst Joan, pretending to be asleep, watched him when his eyes were not turned in her direction. She had not taken much notice of him for years and she was very pleased with what she saw.

Once dressed and hair combed smartly, Eustace went downstairs and stood in the living room wondering what to do next. Realising that it was precisely this inactivity and indecisiveness that had contributed to him being in regular trouble with Joan for all these past years, he decided to be positive and make a decision, even if it was the wrong decision. So he filled the kettle and put it on the gas stove in the kitchen, then he went back to the living room where he cleaned out the fire, took the ash tray to the bin, then proceeded to light the fire with some of the wood sticks he had chopped ready for

Christmas. Then with a firelighter he got from the cellar head and a couple of carefully plaited newspapers, he lit the coal fire, only, instead of putting on just two or three pieces of coal, he put on a couple of shovels full making them a big roaring fire.

He next turned his attention to breakfast. Usually he had a couple of slices of bread and jam with a pot of tea, as did Joan, but today was going to be different. He opened the meat safe and discovered, much to his delight, that they had some bacon. He knew they had some eggs, so he found a frying pan, put the bacon in it and began to fry it on the stove. Eustace had never cooked in his life, but through years of being forced to sit and watch Joan cook whilst she remonstrated with him about anything she could think of and nothing in particular, he had picked up a fair working knowledge of the culinary art. So he coped quite well and prepared the food as Joan would have done.

He could hear Joan moving about upstairs and by the time she came into the living room, the table was laid, the tea was brewed and toast was in the middle of the table.

'Sit down,' he commanded as soon as she was through the door, 'yes, sit down.'

She was a little bit taken back and couldn't decide whether to obey his command or to refuse and lay into him or what. She decided to sit then lay into him.

'What on earth are you doing?' she started and, was going to continue but Eustace answered, much to her surprise, and he put her off her guard.

'We are having a bacon and egg breakfast. I am fed up of having bread and jam, bread and jam, and yet more bread and jam, day after day after day.' He checked himself to stop his verbal ramblings getting out of control and in so doing let Joan in again.

'Yes but you've never cooked before, ever!'

'No, that is correct, but I have now and here you are.'

He went into the back scullery and came back with two warm plates, each containing two very nice portions of bacon and egg which he put down in front of Joan and himself.

Joan was looking forward to it no end, not because she was fed up with bread and jam, but because they had got themselves into such a rut that it had taken the last few days events to begin to shake them both out of it.

'Well thank you,' she said, 'it looks good.' She tasted it, 'In fact it is very good.'

'Yes it is, better than I thought it would be. Now I don't want you to get the idea that I'm going to do this every morning, but I might do it every Sunday if you will buy the bacon, I might, yes I might. And anyway it'll have to be bread and jam during the week when I go to work. Now what are we going to do today?'

'Pardon?' She was somewhat astounded.

'What are we going to do today?' He was having the utmost difficulty not to repeat himself and not to talk rubbish, but he was determined to persevere and succeed.

'Well, what do we always do on a Sunday?'

'Nothing. Nothing at all, that's it, nothing.' He checked himself again. 'But there's more to life than doing nothing, so what would you like to do?'

'Why don't we go to Church? I haven't been in ages and you haven't been since Thelma's mother's funeral last year. No, it'll be this year yet but a long while since and before that you hadn't been since I don't know the day when.'

Much to Joan's surprise he agreed. 'Then we'll come home and cook Sunday dinner, I like my Yorkshire pudding and beef, then after dinner we'll…'

'Hang on a minute, events are moving a bit too fast for me, let's get as far as dinner time to start with.'

'If we are going to Church, I'll have to put the trip planning on hold for a little while, but I'll not have to forget about it.'

The Reverend Clifford Tunstall MA, Vicar of St Cuthbert's on the Hill, was not an incumbent who believed in standing in the church porch to welcome his flock to the service. Instead he sent his new curate the soon to be Reverend Percival Haslam, whilst he enjoyed a pre-service coffee and biscuits in the rectory with his dear wife, who herself, was always impatient to be in church in good time for the service to start. So the Curate, standing his lonely vigil in the Church porch, observed two strangers approaching and prepared to receive them.

'Good morning, Mithter and Mithith…?'

Joan was about to answer 'Yes' and walk straight past him when much to her annoyance, Eustace, who was on the opposite side of her to the Curate, walked around the front of her, held his hand out and said, 'Ollerenshaw.' Whilst at the same time almost shaking the poor man's arm off and squeezing his hand very hard.

'I haven't theen you before. Do you live in thith locality?'

Joan didn't answer and Eustace studied for a while, trying to determine what he meant.

'Yes. Yes we do. We do. We live in the locality. Yes.' He stopped temporarily. 'Sorry Vicar, I am trying to give over repeating everything I say. I've only been trying to do it today and it's bloody hard work.'

'Eustace!' exclaimed Joan. 'In God's house you do not swear!'

Eustace smiled, 'Sorry my dear. I temporarily lost control; I'll see to it that it doesn't happen again. Sorry Vicar.'

'Thath's all right Mithter Ollerenthaw, I quite underthtand. Now I'd better tell you that I'm not the Vicar, I am the Curate. I'm thtudying to be a Vicar. Can I call you Euthtath, ith thuch a nithe name?'

Joan got a small but growing feeling of unease about this curate. Nothing that she could exactly put her hand on, just a

44

feeling, so she quickly said, 'Come on Eustace; let's go find a seat before it gets too busy.' She grabbed his arm and pulled him into the Church.

'What'd you gone done that for?' he demanded.

'I don't like that new curate.'

'What's wrong with him? I thought he was very *nithe*.'

'A bit too nice somehow or other, if you ask me. Not something I can just put my finger on, but something.'

They were met inside the church by Albert Dyson, a work colleague of Eustace, and acting churchwarden.

'By gum. Hello Eustace and Mrs Ollerenshaw.'

'Good morning, Albert,' replied Eustace, brightly. 'Are these our hymn books and prayer books?'

'Yes,' said Albert as he handed them over, a bit taken back at Eustace's forthrightness because, like everyone else who knew Eustace, he wasn't used to getting an answer to a question from him. Not immediately anyway.

'Nice to see you both. Now you haven't a regular pew, have you, so where do you want to sit?'

'Not too near the front,' said Joan.

'Same as most folk then. Tell you what, about half way down on the right hand side, you'll be fine there, just fine. Come on I'll show you.'

So, much to the surprise of many already seated in the congregation, Mr and Mrs Eustace Ollerenshaw were escorted to a seat half way down the main aisle.

Eustace enjoyed the service, as did Joan. The hymns were all carols, and as a special treat, the vicar allowed his curate to deliver the sermon. It was a treat for the vicar as well. Eustace sat entranced listening to the story of the birth of Jesus with accompanying speech impediments. Joan listened but was not entranced.

The Vicar then read the parish notices. Eustace pricked his ears up at the men's fellowship meeting on Tuesday evening and whispered to Joan that he might go to that.

After the service the Vicar then stood in the Church porch to say a few words of goodbye to his parishioners. It was more to get them off the premises quickly so that he could get home for a well earned whisky.

'Now then Mr and Mrs Ollerenshaw, how nice to have seen you in church this morning. I do hope you will be coming again.'

'Well, we may come occasionally vicar, thank you,' said Joan. 'I don't somehow think that we are going to become your most regular attendees.'

Back at home, Joan began to get Sunday dinner ready. Eustace was hovering, making a nuisance of himself, watching Joan and she blew her top, being unable to control herself any longer. 'For heaven's sake. What are you doing?'

'What?'

'You'd best get a hobby if you're going to act like this.'

'Like what?'

'I don't know, you'll have to find something.'

'But you just said if I was going to act like this.'

'I wasn't talking about that.'

'What?'

'Oh, flipping heck. Go to the club out of my way for a bit and be back here by one sharp. I'm not having my Sunday dinner ruined by you being late.'

Eustace was just about to say, 'Can I? Can I? Can I go to the club? The Club? Can I?' When he thought 'No. Hang on a minute, stop.' So instead he said, 'Yes. I will.' So he did. He couldn't believe it, he'd never been allowed to go to the club on Sunday lunchtime, ever, and here he was being ordered to go.

He walked to the club, whistling, with a spring in his stride and a happy smile on his face, of which he normally never did any of the three. Those who knew him and witnessed this event could not believe their own eyes.

*

The Baxter's had risen at about ten o'clock, they had eaten their usual meagre breakfast and then Arthur had continued, until approaching midday, doing his jobs about the house, oiling a lock here, freeing a window catch there and seriously avoiding preparing to decorate the back bedroom which was featuring high on Jess' list of jobs to be done, but not getting done.

At half past eleven he downed tools and got changed ready to go to the club for his usual Sunday pre-lunch drink. He left the house with the familiar warning in his ears, 'Be back at one, I don't want my Sunday lunch ruined by you being late.'

*

At Cutside cottages, Willie Arkenthwaite had enjoyed a good morning. He had breakfasted well on a good, big, fry up, then outside he had tended the pigeons, tidied one of the vegetable beds and played with young Peter at football.

Thelma had been outside for a while to spend some time with him and at half past eleven he really wasn't ready to get ready to go to the club, so he stayed in the garden a while longer, then skimped on his preparations for going out. He didn't need a lecture on what time to be back, for he gave one. 'Now don't forget to have my dinner ready for one o'clock.' Then he left for the club.

The club room door swung open with a bang as a determined Eustace pushed it sideways and strode up to the bar.

Fat Harry, startled from his daydreaming, looked up to observe Eustace approaching at a fearsome speed and looking in a fearsome mood as well. He was just about to come forth with one of his witticisms when he looked at Eustace again and thought better of it.

'Good morning, Harry. A pint of your very best, please, and one for yourself.' Eustace took out his new wallet that Father

Christmas had brought him and produced a ten-shilling note. He had already decided to change his image from his battered old purse that he had carried for years.

Harry decided to risk all and so he walked from the back of the bar, to do a full circuit of Eustace, looking him up and down then returned to the back of the bar. "What the bloody hell's the matter with you? The last time I saw you, which was yesterday, you were stammering and faltering at every word. The time before that you were a wimp and your dragon was knocking you about, then you come in here a different person, I've never seen a transformation like it.'

'To begin with, if you ever address my Joan as the dragon again, I'll come round there and shove your false teeth straight down your gullet and to somewhere where they will hurt, they will, they will hurt, they really will.'

Harry was completely taken off-guard, confused and worried. He'd never come across anything like this before, 'Err sorry,' he said. 'Hey, you've given over stammering.'

'Yes, I've decided not to stammer anymore. It's going to be very difficult, but I'm managing so far, it's my new Christmas present to myself. Are you going to pour our beers?'

'Yes, yes, coming up right now. Anyway what are you doing here on a Sunday dinner time? You never come here on a Sunday.'

'Part of my new lifestyle. I shall be here most Sundays hereafter.'

'Why?'

'Why! Why! Because with me having changed my image, I have ordered Joan to have dinner ready at one o'clock, whilst I come down here for a drink, a drink, a…' He checked himself then continued. 'You see we've been to Church this morning, then I took Joan home, then came down here whilst she gets the dinner ready.'

'You've done what?'

'We've been to church, it was a very enjoyable service, it was, it...' again he took a deep breath, 'yes, an excellent service.'

'Was the new cruet there?'

'You mean the curate, Mithter Perthival Hathlem?'

'Aye, that's him. Him with a crack in his clack.'

'Very well described, but yet a very nice man.'

'Oh yes, he's that alright, by all accounts. Is this going to be a regular occurrence then?'

'What?'

'This going to church?'

'Oh yes, it might be, although Joan's not madly keen, but I might. We'll have to see. Yes we'll have to see, yes we will, yes...' he stopped and collected his thoughts. 'I'll have to go for a pee.' Eustace went to the gents where he gave himself a stern lecture on not repeating himself and was talking to himself when the door swung open and Willie hurtled in.

This startled Eustace, especially when Willie roared, 'Come out of the way of the pot, I'm bursting for a piss.'

'Sorry Willie. Mind you, I think I'd better have one myself before I go back into the bar.'

'What do you mean, before you go back into the bar? Have you been there already?'

'Yes, just for five minutes.'

'But you never come here on a Sunday! So what are you doing here and skulking in the bog as well?'

So Eustace explained how and why and what for and the two friends went back to the bar together, where Arthur had already bought a pint for Willie and heard all about Eustace from Fat Harry.

'Turned religious have you Eustace?' Arthur asked him.

'Not exactly Arthur, although I have enjoyed the service this morning, especially as it was the Christmas service.'

Arthur looked at him again. 'Are you familiar with the Cruet?'

'You mean Mithter Perthival Hathlem, Curate of Thaint Cuthberth on the Hill?'

'The very same.'

'Yeth, a very nithe man. Have you met him Arthur?'

'No, just heard about him. His reputation goes before him, or possibly behind him, but I also understand he is a very nithe man.'

The others in the bar burst out laughing, but Eustace didn't see the funny side of things.

'Let's go and sit down,' said Willie. 'I'm tired.'

'You can't be, you haven't been up long and you haven't done anything yet, so you can't be,' said Fat Harry.

'That's more than you know. I've done a million and one jobs this morning, but anyway come on, let's sit down.'

Fat Harry made a profound statement directed at Eustace. 'Before you all sit down, I would like you to know that these are not false teeth but my own, my very own. Looked after by me and kept in immaculate condition by me. This has been since I was a baby and they are still in first class working order.'

Willie looked at Arthur. 'What was all that about?'

'Buggered if I know. Come on, let's sit down.'

The three pals sat near the fire and got out the dominoes.

Arthur then asked the same question. 'Will someone tell me what that was all about?'

Eustace replied, 'I know, it was for me, but don't worry about it.'

'Tell me Eustace, why are you here on a Sunday lunch time?'

'Joan ordered me out until dinner was ready, because I was hovering and supervising the cooking.'

'You were?'

'Yes, I was. I've taken over in our house as from first thing this morning and there's going to be war on when I get back if my dinner isn't ready and if it isn't cooked to perfection.'

Both Willie and Arthur looked at him in astonishment. Eustace continued, 'Now then, there's two things I'd like to know, there is, two things, yes two Arthur, Willie, two. Oh hell. I'll have to give over this repeating myself, it just will not do. It's very hard not to, but I've not got to do. Anyway, two things. What are we doing on New Year's Eve and what about the trip?'

'What are we what?' Arthur asked.

Willie had a good old fashioned loud belch.

Harry offered to put him out on the street.

'What are we doing on New Year's Eve and what about the trip?'

'I thought that was what you said. Now let's take this one step at a time. First of all, New Year's Eve. Now Eustace, what do you normally do on New Year's Eve?'

'Nothing. Nothing at all. No nothing, absolutely nothing. But that was last year and this is this year and well, it's different now. Yes different.'

Willie snooked up a nice ball of phlegm, walked around to the fire and spat into the flames.

'What has my fire done to upset you?' asked Fat Harry, but they all ignored him because they were more interested in the conversation with Eustace.

'So what do you want to do this year then?'

'Don't know. What is there to do?'

'You could always come here,' said Harry.

Arthur looked at him, 'With all due respect, my good man, we have all visited your establishment on New Year's Eve in years gone by, with our wives, but it's always been a miserable do. Nothing doing is there? No band, no dancing, no supper, no nothing.'

'What about the band room?' asked Willie. 'They have a right good do; we could all go up there.'

'We'd never get tickets this late,' said Arthur

51

'It'd be very expensive,' said Eustace. 'Still we never spend anything. Tell you what; I'll see if I can get six tickets. I'll go after dinner, and talking about dinner, its time to sup up.'

'You've managed on one round nicely all morning, sir,' said Harry to the wall or the room, 'Anyway, what about which trip?'

'Another time, we must dash.'

They left a very bemused Fat Harry staring after them.

CHAPTER 4

Arthur returned home from the club for his Sunday lunch. It was, as usual, served in semi-silence and he was presented with a couple of slices of roast lamb with carrots, boiled potatoes and gravy. He thought about what Willie might be having, but he didn't dare complain.

'Eustace seems to think we ought to go to the Band room to let the New Year in on Wednesday night, with Willie and Thelma as well.'

'Oh, does he now? How long has he been thinking about anything and how does he think we are going to afford to go to that do and anyway…'

'And anyway what?'

'And anyway we never do nothing on New Year's Eve and anyway how's he going to get some tickets?'

'Well if Eustace gets some, we're going.'

They finished their meal in silence.

*

At Cutside cottages, Willie's return home had been somewhat different to Arthur's. He had walked into a warm house, with a blazing fire in the range, to find his joint of beef sitting on the table and his carving knife and fork at the ready, the children seated and Thelma in the kitchen just putting the vegetables out.

'The roast potatoes and Yorkshires are just ready love,' she called out.

Willie took off his coat and cap, picked up the carving knife, went into the kitchen with it, gave Thelma a kiss and got out the steel to hone the blade.

Their first course was Yorkshire pudding and onion gravy. Two big squares of the golden brown pudding were taken out of the range and cut into smaller squares. One each for the two young ones and two each for the rest.

Then Willie carved the beef, it was pink and rare, just as he liked it. There were plenty of roast potatoes, carrots and gravy. Then they had apple pie and custard washed down with a pint of tea.

'Magnificent!' said Willie following one of his usual displays of animal like manners.

'Thanks a million love, that was superb. Josie, what are you doing on New Year's Eve?'

'Nothing Dad, either going to Carol's or she's coming here, but nothing really.'

'Will you invite her here and look after these two please? I'm going to take your mum out.'

'Where to?' asked Thelma.

'Don't worry about where. Somewhere nice. Will you Josie?'

'Of course I will. You two go ahead and have a good time.'

'Thanks love. That's settled then.'

'We can't afford,' said Thelma.

'How do you know when you don't know where we are going? Anyway you just leave that to me.' He got up from the table, sat in his favourite armchair by the fire, lifted his feet up onto the mantelpiece and fell asleep, with the fire roasting the back of his legs.

Thelma and Josie quietly collected the pots and washed up.

*

Eustace returned home and purposely banged the front door shut as he entered. He marched smartly into the back room where he was greeted by a better than usual smell of cooking.

'My word that does smell good.'

Joan turned and smiled at him. Eustace could not remember the day when she had smiled at him when he came home. He gave her a second look and decided that she was still quite attractive.

'It's just about ready,' she said. 'Yorkshire pudding to start with, roast beef, roast potatoes and boiled onions, followed by your favourite treacle sponge and custard. Do you want to carve?'

'Er, well now, err.' The question caught him off guard and brought on an attack of stuttering. Joan never let him carve. 'Well now, there's a question, there is, isn't it? A question. Yes I will, yes, yes.' He stopped and calmed his thoughts. 'Yes, most certainly I will.'

'Good. I'm fed up of doing it.'

They sat down and enjoyed an excellent meal in an atmosphere that could not have been contemplated a week earlier.

'I'm taking you for a walk after dinner,' said Eustace.

'What? Where to? It's very cold out there.'

'Yes, it's very cold as you say, but a brisk walk won't do us any harm and I've decided that for us and Willie's and Arthur's that we'll all go to the band room on New Year's Eve to the dance.'

'We can't afford, it'll be too late to get tickets, it's...we never... I haven' got a dress to wear and we definitely can't afford.'

'We can afford, we never spend anything, we've a bob or two in the building society, it's time we started to enjoy it.'

'Yes, but I haven't a dress to wear.'

'You have. You had one on at the Christmas club party.'

'Yes, but I can't wear that!'

'Why not?'

'Because.'

'Because what?' Eustace was by this time becoming perplexed.

'Because I can't. They've all seen it.'

'Who has?'

'All them what'll be at the band room?'

'Nay, they can't have.'

'What?'

'They can't have seen your dress.'

'Why not?'

'Because none of them that'll be at the band room were at the Christmas club do!"

She calmed down and thought for a minute. 'Yes you're right, except for Thelma and Jess.'

'So only those two will have seen it and they wont mind. So it's no problem.'

'If you say so.'

'I do. Come on get your coat.'

'You are forgetting, we haven't finished our dinner yet and it's about time we did before it gets completely ruined.'

They finished their meal in peace, and afterwards they washed up together, Eustace abnormally insisting on drying the pots, something he never did. Then they had ten minutes in front of the fire, at Joan's insistence, before she reluctantly agreed to walk to the band room. So, having kitted themselves out in coats, hats, gloves and scarves they departed for their walk.

*

It was a long pull up the hill to the band room, especially straight after a big meal, but they made it to the top and went in. Neither of them had been there in years and they were both a little bit surprised at the size of the place.

'I'd forgotten how big it is,' said Joan. 'I remember it being big, but not this big. Now where do we go, do you think?'

'I don't know. I don't. I don't know where we go. I don't, no I don't...' He stopped, composed himself, counted to ten, breathed in, pulled himself up to his full height, took command of the situation and said, 'In here.' He opened a promising looking door, waved Joan in first and followed her into the practice room.

'Oh, um, well, yes.'

Joan was about to lay into him both verbally and physically when she had a change of heart and said, 'My turn next.'

'What is?' He was somewhat relieved at not having been hit or shouted at.

'My turn to guess where we go. Follow me.' Joan was just beginning to enjoy herself and she chose a room on the opposite side of the long corridor. Fortunately, she picked the right door and she entered the room with Eustace close on her heels.

Stan and his wife Molly, the Steward and Stewardess of the Band Club stared at Mr and Mrs Eustace Ollerenshaw for quite some time before anyone said anything. Then Stan spoke first, 'Eustace. How are you? Nice to see you, haven't seen you in years, how's it going?'

'We are very well thank you, Stan. How are you both?'

'Super, absolutely super, thank you. Now what brings you all the way up here and by the way, are you and your good lady members of the club?'

'No, no, you know full well we aren't,' said Joan. 'It was Eustace's idea to come up here.'

'Well in that case, what for?'

Eustace took over. 'Have you got six tickets for the New Year's Eve dance?'

'Have we got six tickets for the New Year's Eve dance? It's a supper and dance you know. Grand Gala Buffet, an extra special gourmand's delight. To a specialist gourmandiser like yourself it's a treat, a real treat. It's pies and crisps.' He stopped and looked around for Molly who had moved to the other end of the long bar. 'Hoy,' he shouted, 'have we got six tickets for the New Year's Eve gourmet supper and dance?'

'Don't hoy me. It's not a gourmet supper and yes we do have a few tickets left. I'll be there with them in a minute.'

'In the meantime, you'll be wanting a drink now that you've come all the way up here.'

'But we aren't members,' said Eustace quickly.

'Rules is meant to be broken. What will it be?'

'A glass of dry sherry please,' said Joan. 'That hill does take it out of you in this cold weather.'

'And a pint of best bitter for me,' said Eustace.

'It's Sid Sidebottom, you know,' said Stan.

'What is?'

'The band is.'

'What band?' Eustace was by now acting thick on purpose.

'The bloody New Year's Eve band.'

'Oh, that band. You mean Sid Sidebottom's Sextipating Sinctet.'

'Sid Sidebottom's what?'

'You heard.'

'Come on, let's sit down and enjoy our drinks,' said Joan. She'd heard men talking rubbish before, but not her Eustace, he would never talk like that, he wasn't capable. But he'd changed, rapidly, very rapidly in fact. In actual fact far too rapidly and when she came to think about it, why had he changed so much so quickly? From a lifelong simpering idiot to a strong willed leader that could talk to anyone on his own terms, even if it was rubbish. Had she held him down so much that he had entered the first stages of lunacy and had it taken her new found friends Thelma and Jess to bring her round to seeing the errors of her ways.

'Eustace, will you get me another sherry please.'

'Already my dear? You're drinking quickly for a non-drinker.' He took her glass to the bar.

Or was she really the dragon. She knew they called her the dragon in the village, but she'd never believed she was so bad. Or was it him, had he been acting it out on purpose all these years, showing her up in public, acting the idiot when it suited him, which was all the time.

Eustace returned with the sherry and another pint. 'Molly says it's going to be a good do on New Year's Eve, about two hundred coming. All of them got to walk up this hill.'

Now it wasn't like Eustace to converse and it wasn't like Joan to listen to him, so she didn't. Instead she gulped her sherry and gave him the glass back, 'Here go and get me another.'

'This will have to be the last, I've no money left. You're drinking a bit quick aren't you? It'll be going to your head. Don't you think you ought to give it a rest?' It was just beginning to go to her head and the bravado was returning.

'No certainly not, I'm enjoying it. Go and get that glass filled up.'

So Eustace trotted off to the bar, wondering just what was going to happen. Joan returned to her thoughts. *It can't be him though, we've always been so miserable, it must be me that brought it on. I'm the one. I've held him down all our married life. He could perhaps have made something of himself, he could have been...*

Eustace returned with one glass of sherry, he still hadn't finished his second pint. Joan was becoming depressed with her own thoughts, so she gulped down the third glass of sherry, gave him the glass back and demanded another.

'Sorry love, I cant, I've nowt left to get it with.' He was delighted he'd nothing left because he was becoming distinctly worried about her.

Joan fumbled in her handbag, found her purse, opened it and somehow managed to tip the contents onto the floor.

Eustace bent down to pick up the coins, he collected them together, put them back into her purse, put the purse into her bag, picked her up, put her coat on, finished his pint, put his own coat on and grabbing hold of Joan, marched her smartly, or as smartly as he could, to the door, bidding Stan and Molly 'Good afternoon! See you on New Year's Eve.'

As Joan hit the cold air, she giggled, belched and leaned heavily on Eustace, who had the utmost difficulty in getting Joan home. She leaned on him, she leaned off him, she insisted on trying to run downhill, she belched occasionally, she giggled a lot and he was very pleased when he got her home, without hopefully too many people having seen them.

Eustace helped her off with her coat, relieved her of her handbag, sat her down at the side of the fire switched the radio on and finally took her hat off. She belched, giggled and finally fell fast asleep.

Eustace sat down at the opposite side of the hearth, leaned back and closed his eyes. Joan was snoring and he began to contemplate his next move. It wasn't long before two open mouths were snoring in sympathy.

About an hour later, Eustace opened his eyes to observe Joan sobbing quietly to herself.

'What on earth's the matter? Why are you crying? What is it? Why are you crying? What is it? What...' He checked himself yet again.

'That is, that's what's the matter, it's you and it's me, no it's not you, it's me, I've ruined our marriage. I've ruined our life. We've done nothing. We are nothing. I've turned you into a gibbering idiot.' By now she was wailing. 'I've ruined everything for everybody.' She stopped talking and went on sobbing.

Eustace didn't know quite how to handle the situation, but he decided that indecision was not the answer. He had never been a romantic type of man, but he walked over to Joan, stooped over her, put his arms around her, gave her a big hug and kissed her very tenderly. 'Now listen. Give over crying, give over feeling sorry for yourself and brighten up. Today is the start of a new beginning in our lives. We've already done more today than we did in the previous year of Sundays and we've more to do yet. I've a trip to sort out with Willie and Arthur, we're going to the New Year's Eve do at the band room and we're going to start going to church regularly. I think you should find yourself something to do, like a little part time job or something.' Joan said nothing, she just half smiled and half sobbed. 'Anyway, we'd best go round to let Arthur's and Willie's know that we've got the tickets for the New Year's Eve do, so get on your coat and let's get going.'

'Just give me half an hour, there's no rush, let me tidy myself up a bit and have a wash.'

So Eustace read the paper whilst Joan prepared herself for going out.

They took a circuitous route arriving first at Arthur's house where they found him in a foul temper. Jess having finally got her way and made him start on decorating the back bedroom. Eustace and Joan were a welcome distraction to him and he immediately stopped work when he heard them downstairs.

'Hello you two, sit yourselves down.'

'It looks as though we might have disturbed you,' said Joan. 'We shan't stop above a few minutes.'

'Why ever not, make yourselves at home, I'll just nip out and put the kettle on.' Jess frowned at him internally but didn't let her face slip at all. 'Wasn't it a nice evening last night?'

'Yes it was,' replied Joan. 'I really did enjoy it, best night I've had in years and wasn't the supper good.'

'Just the same as always. I do try to maintain a standard on Boxing Day. Josie's a good help, but that's only recently. Thelma's a very hard working help and very kind as well.'

Arthur returned with a tea tray. 'Well this is a nice surprise. What brings you to our shores?'

'Have you washed your hands before you touch those cups?' Jess barked.

He was just about to tell them he'd just wiped his arse and not bothered to wash, when he thought better of it and instead said, 'It goes without saying, my dear.'

'Not with you it doesn't.'

'Funny how they're all the same,' said Joan.

'We've brought the tickets for the New Year's Eve dance,' said Eustace.

'By gum, that's been quick.'

'Well he's not sat down since he got up this morning, and that was early.'

'I have, I have, I sat down for my breakfast. I sat down at church. I…'

He was interrupted by Arthur. 'In where?'

'In church.'

'Since when have you been going to church?'

'Since this morning.'

'Why?'

'Because I decided we should. It was nice. We were met by the Cruet, Mithter Perthival Hathlem.'

'Oh, I've heard all about the Curate,' said Arthur.

'A very nice man,' said Eustace.

'And the rest,' Joan chipped in.

By this time Jess had poured the tea and it was soon drunk.

'You know, Eustace, you told us all about this visit to church at the club before dinner.'

'Yes, I know, but Jess hadn't heard about it, had she?'

Arthur didn't bother enlightening Eustace about the fact that he had told her about it. Joan decided that Arthur was giving up his valuable decorating time and that they had better go.

Jess sat politely conversing and drinking tea whilst at the same time maintaining her serene expression, wishing that they would go so that Arthur could get back to his decorating.

'Well, we'd better not hold you good people up any longer. Give them the tickets Eustace.'

Eustace put the two tickets on the mantelpiece and Arthur scraped together the necessary monies to pay for them.

The Ollerenshaws took their leave of the Baxters and set off towards Cutside Cottages along the canal towpath, which was full of puddles that had to be sidestepped.

'Well their home is nothing to crow about. I couldn't see it properly last night,' Joan smirked, 'It's very plain.'

'So is ours,' observed Eustace.

A period of pregnant silence followed.

'We'll have to give over meeting like this,' said Willie as he opened the door of number six to Joan and Eustace, 'Come in, come in and sit down. What brings you to our house again so soon? Put the kettle on Josie!'

'Not for us thank you,' said Eustace. 'We've only called to bring you the tickets for the New Year's Eve dance and gourmandisers experience at the band room.'

'Gourmandisers what?' asked Thelma who by this time had joined them.

'Gourmandisers experience.'

'What's that? Sandwiches?'

'No, pies and crisps.'

'Oh.'

'You've been quick getting them,' said Willie.

'He can't rest, he was up early this morning, cooked the breakfast, then off to church.'

'Aye we heard all about that at the club.'

'What did you hear?' asked Joan.

'How you'd met the new cruet with the crack in his clack.'

'Oh aye, he's got that and some more,' said Joan.

'Some more what?' asked Eustace.

'Use your imagination,' said Joan, 'but always stand facing him.'

'Why?'

'Thelma came to the rescue, or tried to. 'I think what they're trying to tell you Eustace is that he's of the other persuasion.'

'No, he can't be, he's Church of England.'

'I think I'd best pay you for the tickets,' said Willie laughing and trying to stop the conversation sliding down the slippery slope.

Willie went upstairs to get some money from his well known secret horde in a tin box in the bottom of the wardrobe.

'We did enjoy it on Christmas Day. Thank you, Thelma, again for a lovely evening and an excellent supper,' said Joan.

'Yes so did I. I did. I did. I did enjoy it. We both did. We both…' He stopped. 'Sorry. I will have to control this problem.'

Willie came back with the money and belched loudly as he got to the bottom of the stairs.

Three pairs of eyes stared at him. All to no avail.

'Well, we'd best get going again, we don't want to take up any more of your valuable time,' said Joan.

'Nay, stop for a while won't you?' said Thelma. 'We aren't doing anything, are we Willie?'

'No. No, nothing at all. What about the mill trip then Eustace?'

'Well nothing yet. I did promise myself that I'd get to it today, but I haven't had time yet. So I'm sorry, but so far nothing. I will however get to it as soon as possible.'

'There'll be nothing but trouble if you lot are organising a trip,' said Joan.

'You're dead right. I wouldn't go with them if they asked me,' agreed Thelma.

'Well we're not asking you,' said Willie. 'And anyway what are you complaining about; we sorted out the Christmas club alright, didn't we?'

'Yes love, you did.'

'So where's the problem?'

'I don't know, but there'll be one,' said Joan. 'Anyway, come on Eustace, it's almost four o'clock, it's nearly dark and it's time for home.'

So Joan and Eustace went home happily together to have tea and listen to the wireless.

Thelma and Willie sat in front of the fire with the light out, dozing. The children were upstairs playing.

Arthur went on decorating whilst Jess played at being foreman.

CHAPTER 5

Back at work on Monday morning after the Christmas holiday it had reached mid-morning break time at Murgatroyd's Mill, when the machines carried on running and the operators took a ten minute rest whilst still keeping their eye on their machines.

In the blending department where Eustace worked, his two workmates, Percy Cox and Ned Bamforth, had observed that a remarkable change had come about their colleague.

Neither of them could understand it and were a little perplexed. In fact, they were having difficulty coping with it.

'He's talking nearly proper like,' said Percy.

'Yes, he's changed so much it's not true.'

'I wonder what's happened to him?'

'Nay, don't ask me. But it's a vast improvement.'

Eustace, because of his apparent slow mental state, had always been in charge of brewing up at break times. He would collect the mashings from his mates in a morning, get them nicely mixed up, put the wrong mashing in the wrong pot and break times in the blending department were a bit like a faith supper, everyone took something, but didn't always get what they had taken to eat or drink.

This morning however, it was different. Instead of the usual slow meander from the geyser to the table where they took their break; he marched smartly up with his tray of three pots.

'There Percy, that's your tea without sugar, without, yes, and Ned, your tea with sugar and my coffee, yes, coffee.'

Percy tested his tea, 'Just right.'

'And mine too,' said Ned.

'And why not?' enquired Eustace.

'Well it never has been before,' said Ned.

'No, no, but that was then and, and, and this is now.'

They both stared at him as he smiled pleasantly at them.

'But you've not repeated yourself a lot either,' said Ned.

'No, that is true. I have to say however that it is, it is taking me all my time not to, but I must try and try.'

'So just exactly what has happened to you over this Christmas holiday?'

'Well you know what happened at the Christmas club party, when Joan laid into me for being drunk? Well who could blame her, blame her. Then Thelma and Jess got hold of her and gave her a good telling off...'

'Yes I saw it all,' said Percy

'I wasn't there but I heard about it,' said Ned.

'Well, I've had a right good Christmas, best I can ever remember, remember, and Joan has been super. So I decided it was time I altered and I've decided to organise, to organise a trip, for the mill. I've never done anything before, except do as I was told, but now I'm going to pay some peoples' kindness back and organise a trip, I am, a trip. It's difficult not to keep on repeating myself, but I'm managing, just, just, almost.'

'So what's this trip about then?' asked Ned.

'It's Murgatroyd's mill trip, sometime in early June, June, when the nights are light.'

'Where are we going to?' asked Percy.

'You're coming along then are you?' asked Eustace being much quicker on the uptake than he had known to have been.

'You bet I'm coming.'

'So am I,' said Ned. 'Where are we going?'

'Blackpool, yes Blackpool.'

'A good choice,' said Ned.

'Anyway, who says you're in charge?' asked Percy.

'I do. Why? Do you want to give it a go?'

'No. No. Not me, nothing like. You know better than that. You carry on.'

Work resumed after the break and Ned said to Percy, out of earshot of Eustace, 'We're going to have to watch him.'

'Not half.'

'What's for dinner?' Willie belched loudly as he asked Greasy Martha. He was, as always, first in the queue at Murgatroyd's canteen, a position he had held for as many years as anyone could remember. There he was, first every dinner time, always first. He had occasionally to run to be there, but he never missed.

'Cold meat, boiled potatoes and carrots, same as it is every Monday, you know full well what it is and you can give over making those ridiculous noises in my canteen or I shan't serve you.' Martha served Willie then picked up the hem of her apron and blew her nose into it, shouting, 'Next,' as the apron fell back into place.

Willie picked up his dinner and scurried off to the corner table where he, Arthur, Lewis and Dick played cards every dinnertime except Fridays when they collected the Christmas club contributions.

Eustace sat with them and watched them play cards. Unfortunately he had never been able to understand the mathematical niceties of a card game that even those who played it only guessed at certain aspects of its rules. The five friends were eating their dinner, Willie making enough noise for all five of them, when Eustace said, 'Right now, can we settle on a date for the trip to Blackpool? Yes to Blackpool.'

Dick and Lewis looked agog at him.

'You still talking normal then?' asked Willie.

'I most certainly am and I'm never going back to my old ways again, never, ever. Furthermore, just so that you will all know, I'm master in my own house from now on!'

Dick and Lewis looked at Eustace again then back at one another. 'What's going on?' asked Dick.

'Oh, it's since that skirmish at the Christmas club party with him and Joan and Jess and Thelma, he's suddenly, for no reason, reformed and there's no stopping him. He's going mad;

I don't know which is worst, him as he was or him as he is. Neither of them paints a right pleasant picture.'

'So has anyone got a particular date that suits?' asked Eustace again.

'What gives you the right to sort out this trip?' asked Dick.

'Nothing, I just decided to. Are you all coming? It's Saturday, I don't know which, of June.'

'Who's doing all the organisation for it?' asked Lewis.

'I am and you are.'

'Me?'

'All my friends around here.'

By this time Willie had returned to the servery to get his spotted dick and custard from Greasy Martha, not to mention his pint of tea. 'Now, Martha my love,' he said when he had got his dish of pudding.

'I am not your love and you are not getting any extra pudding.'

'Go on.'

'No.'

'Go on. Spirit of goodwill and all that at Christmas time.'

'No definitely not. Never. Bugger good will, and anyway Christmas has gone along with its spirit.' All this time she was spooning out another lump of pudding and quietly putting it on Willie's dish.

'Is that your last word then?' shouted Willie.

'Yes.'

'Then that's it. I'm off to eat what bit of pudding you've given me.'

The whole of the canteen was listening and pointing to Willie's overladened dish. Anyone else who tried for more got the same answer but not the same response, for Willie had a very special place in Greasy Martha's heart.

Back at the corner table they were all looking at Eustace. 'Do you mean to say that you are organising this trip regardless of what we might think?' asked Dick.

'No, no, I'm not, I'm not, am I Arthur? I'm not, I'm...' He stopped, checked himself then said, proceeding slowly, 'Sorry about that. No, but I decided that it was time I did something on my own and this trip idea will give me all the opportunity I need. But I will have to have all your cooperation, cooperation, ideas and help to get anywhere with it. So which Saturday, Saturday in June?'

'Now listen Eustace, we've a game of cards to play now and us dinners to finish. No, let's settle it in the club tomorrow night.'

'What's wrong with tonight?' Dick enquired.

Willie stared at him. 'You know full well it's Monday. We don't go to the club on Mondays; instead we stay at home like good little boys and do as our better halves tell us.'

'I could make an exception.'

'Well you'll be on your own. I for one am going fire watching.'

'You're going what?'

'Fire watching. You know, sitting in front of the fire and watching it burn.'

The others, by now having finished their dinner and having exhausted the conversation, resumed play of the card school. Eustace watched as usual. He had never been allowed to play, but decided that he would be going to before very long.

*

Tuesday evening, about eight o'clock, the bar room door of the Grolsby Working Mens Club (Affiliated) opened and three thoroughly wet, drenched, drowned and flooded bodies walked in to stand by the fire. They said nothing; they just dripped onto the parquet floor.

The silence was broken by their genial host. 'Get the hell out of here and hang your coats up in the corridor and give over ruining the polish on my highly polished floor.'

'Sod off,' said Willie, 'the last time this floor was polished was for Queen Victoria's Diamond Jubilee.'

The earth tremored as the full weight of the club steward was brought to bear in every footfall as he stamped his way from behind the bar towards Willie. He stopped with one thousandth of an inch between their two noses. 'I'll have you know,' he roared, 'that we polish this floor, once a week, every week, without fail and without missing, ever!'

Anyone else would have run by now, but not Willie. His long johns might have changed colour but they didn't because Fat Harry had given him the lead he needed.

'Who's we?' he asked.

'Eh? What?'

'Who's we? You know, you said we polish, so who's we? You and who?'

Harry moved back a little and began to redden.

'It's Alice Clarke,' said Eustace.

They all turned to look at him then all began to talk at once, all asking him the same question only different ways around.

'How do you know?'

Now Fat Harry had yet to meet the new Eustace, because the three friends had walked in together as forlorn as each other and therefore he hadn't stuck out in the crowd.

'Well it's quite simple really. Alice Clarke is long distantly related to Joan, to Joan, and I know her husband is a little bit worried about her coming down here to clean, Arthur, he is, he is, and being left alone with the big fat lecherous one.'

'Not so much of the big and fat, if you please.'

'Sorry. Anyway, he's worried stiff because she's landed home with a smile on her face, on her face, every day that she's worked here and she never normally comes home with a smile, except when she's been working here.'

Harry didn't know what to do next, whether to thump Eustace, thump Willie or to quietly go back behind the bar and secrete himself in the storeroom until things quieted down and the subject ran out of steam. Instead he turned his attention to Eustace.

'What's up with you then?'

'Me? Why, Harry old friend?'

'You're not stuttering and stammering like what you always used to.'

'No. I've given it up as my New Year's resolution.'

'You can't have. Anyway, it's not New Year yet.'

'Well I have, and to prove it, here I am as large as life. By the way, go and draw three pints please, my friends and I, friends and I, have an ongoing thirst.'

'The amount of water you lot have waded through tonight, I'm amazed you ever want to see a drink again.'

'Yes, it is rather inclement out there, and somewhat uncharacteristic for just exactly this time of year. I think we normally would have frosty nights and fairly mild days.' It was only with the utmost difficulty that Eustace had managed to deliver that sentence. Harry looked at him twice and then decided he'd best fetch the ale.

They went out to hang their wet coats then came back into the bar. Arthur, as the great thinker and member of the club management committee asked, 'I wasn't aware that we had taken on an extra member of staff, so where's the money coming from and how much are we paying the said lady?'

'It will all become apparent at the Annual General Meeting, when I present the stewards report and claim for expenses.'

'So she's an expense, is she? Not an employee then? So how long has this expense been polishing the floor?'

'About twelve months.'

'So you've been getting a bit of morning comfort for twelve months at the expense of the club, once a week?'

'Yes.'

'So where's the money to actually pay her come from?'

'Partly from the till and partly out of my pocket and I was going to make it right at the AGM.'

'Well the only comment I have to make is...' Harry was dreading what was coming next '...you lucky sod. You've picked the best looking lass in the village, with a peach of a figure and so far, got away with it. I don't know how you do it.'

Harry's face changed from red and dread to a broad grin.

'Now about the trip,' said Eustace.

'Let's establish a date to start with,' said Arthur.

Willie chipped in quickly, 'First Saturday in June.'

'Where's Whitsuntide?' asked Arthur.

'Where's Easter? Then its seven weeks after that,' said Eustace.

The club steward answered, 'We haven't a next year's calendar yet.'

'Then the second Saturday in June to make sure.'

'Can I come?' the fat one enquired.

'No,' came a loud chorus of three voices.

'Nay, go on, I assume you'll be starting here.'

'Well, we'll think about it. We shall be limited to a coach load and it's for the mill, but we will give your application due consideration,' said Arthur.

'I as good as work at that mill.'

'No you don't,' came the reply.

'Well I work on behalf of it, I keep its workers happy by dispensing ale to them all the year round and I could probably arrange a few crates of ale at a good discount to go on the coach, if I was allowed to come along.'

Arthur, whilst making a mental note to ensure that Harry's name got on the list, said, 'Yes, well, as stated previously, we will give your application serious consideration.'

'Now then, it's going to be Blackpool,' said Eustace, 'although I don't know where we shall have us dinner.'

'Let's start with breakfast,' said Willie, 'that'll have to be at The Grapes; they do a real trip breakfast at a reasonable price.'

'Yes, that's alright, that is. Yes it is, it's alright it is, it's...' he stopped, took a deep breath then started again, 'I'll go and see John George about it sometime soon. What about a coach? I suppose it will have to be Bewdlay's best.'

'Their best is anyone else's worst, but it will have to do,' said Willie. 'But as Eustace has said, the biggest problem is where to have our dinner.'

'I know,' said Eustace, 'why don't we go to Blackpool and find somewhere.'

They all looked at him astounded and speechless.

'Well?' he asked eventually.

'Well what?' asked Willie.

'Well, what about going to Blackpool to find somewhere for us dinners?'

Arthur took the matter in hand, 'What exactly do you mean by going to Blackpool to find somewhere for our midday meal?'

'Let's go. Let's me and Joan, you and Jess, Willie and Thelma, all go.'

'When?'

'Next Week.'

'We can't. We haven't got holiday, we can't just go, not just like that.' Arthur was warming to the idea. 'However, we could possibly go one day at the weekend, Saturday or Sunday.'

'What with? And what'll we do with the kids?' Willie was beginning to warm even more to the idea.

'Tell you what, why don't we go for the weekend?' said Arthur.

'Eh?' grunted Willie.

'You know, straight after work, get the train on Friday teatime, stay at Miss Shorrocks' boarding house for two nights. She has enough rooms, we'd have to take us own food, back Sunday teatime. How about it Eustace?'

Eustace had by now lost the lead in this debate, but he took a deep breath, told himself to concentrate and entered the fray once again. 'Yes, yes, that sounds just right to me. I'm sure Joan will be pleased. How about you, Willie?'

'Well I don't know. It's alright for you two, no children, no money problems, I don't just know. I'd best go and talk to Thelma about it. Anyway, who's Miss Shorrocks?'

Arthur answered, 'By Uncle Tom's Cabin, a proper boarding house. Me and Jess've stayed there loads of times. You have to take your own food and she cooks it for you. It's very clean, she's a first rate cook and it's alright. She gives you your own key so that you can come and go as you like, it's a jolly good place and I'm going to write to her to see if she's any rooms for next weekend.'

'I think we'd all better go and consult our wives,' said Eustace. 'Although I am now master in my own home, I'd best enquire from the mistress if she wants to go.'

So, following much more conversation about nothing and several pints of ale, the three friends returned home like drowned rats through the rain again, ready to prepare their wives for a weekend trip to Blackpool.

Eustace had no trouble whatsoever in persuading Joan to join the trip to Blackpool. They had a bit of money saved up, because they had never spent much, and she immediately began to look forward to the visit.

'Where are we staying?' she asked him

'Well, I'm not exactly sure, somewhere that Arthur and Jess stay near Uncle Tom's Cabin, where we've to take our own food and she cooks it.'

'That sounds alright, when are we going?'

'At the weekend.'

'Which weekend?'

'I really don't know, this next one if Arthur can get us rooms.'

'That sounds a bit close. When does he want to know?'

'I don't know.'

'Tell you what; tell him we'll sort it out at the New Year's Eve do on Friday.'

Arthur had a similar conversation. They were not short of a bob or two and Jess was more concerned that Arthur had got to get to know about the feelings of the others before he contacted Miss Shorrocks. However, she was very pleased to be asked and readily accepted.

Willie had a different problem; he had two young children and a teenage daughter, Josie. He asked Thelma if she wanted to go on the weekend away and she was a bit worried about things, wanting to say yes, but thinking of a thousand reasons to say no. 'We can't afford. What will we do with the children? Where will we stay? How will we get there When will we go? We haven't got time to go. But it's the children what'll be the problem.'

Willie laughed, having expected all of this and more. 'I've been thinking about it,' he said. 'No problem. To start with, Josie's now old enough to look after the two young ones for a couple of nights and if she gets her friend Margaret here to stay and help, they'll be alright. As regards can't afford, well you're right, but we'll have to find it from somewhere because I'd like to go and both the others will be able to. We're staying by Uncle Tom's Cabin, where Arthur and Jess stay, it's take your own food and they cook it for you. We're going weekend after next on the train from Grolsby.'

Thelma gave the matter one and a half split seconds consideration then readily agreed but adding, 'I'll probably see if I can get some extra hours up at the house to help pay for it. Still there is that money that you got from the shops through the Christmas club'

*

Wednesday lunch time at Murgatroyd's mill in the canteen arrived and after Willie had given a particularly amazing display of how to destroy his dinner, with table manners that were despicable if not laughable, the three friends all agreed that their wives had been exceptionally amenable about the visit to Blackpool.

'We'd better call at the station tonight to check the train times and prices,' said Arthur.

'Yes, let's see if we can't get a cheap weekend return,' said Willie.

Dick and Lewis jealously listened to the conversation but knew they were not well enough into the inner sanctum to volunteer to go with the other three.

'Never mind Dick,' said Lewis afterwards. 'We'll go later on, when the weather improves and check out just what they've booked.'

*

Willie, having eaten his tea, fed his hens, then shaved, washed and put his better clothes on, went round to collect Arthur and then Eustace for them to go to the station to check out the trains to Blackpool.

They called for Eustace, which had become a pleasure in the last few days, and they got a first class reception from Joan, who appeared genuinely pleased to see them.

'I am looking forward to our trip to our weekend away,' she said. 'You know, I have been an old fool, isolating us from all you nice people all these years. Anyway, you're going to see a new me from now on, I've decided.'

Willie looked at her and frowned. 'Now look here missus, one new one is bad enough, but two of you! Well it doesn't bear thinking about.' He smiled and so did Joan.

*

'Christmas hasn't improved your condition I see.' Arthur was observing Willie puffing and panting after they had climbed the short but steep hill to Grolsby station.

Willie having recovered, opened the station front door, stuck his head in and in his rich baritone voice sang out as loud as he could. 'There'll be a welcome in the station; there'll be a welcome on the trains.'

'Not for you there won't. Piss off. Anyway, is it annual wakes week again already?'

The official door of the office of Station Master, Ticket Clerk, Ticket Collector, Porter, Refreshment Manager, Cleaner, Gardener, Information Officer and General Factotum, all rolled into one in the shape of Evans the train, opened and out he came with a broad grin just ahead of the rest of him.

'Come along in won't you and sit by the fire. Don't stand out there in the freezing cold, kettle's just on the boil and I was just going to have one, so hurry along.' He turned and went back into his office and they duly followed. 'Well this is a pleasant surprise,' he said as he brewed a pot of tea. 'What brings you all the way up here? Not, I imagine, to enquire as to the state of my health, although, to put you out of your misery on that subject, I can tell you that I am on top form.'

'No, we've not come to enquire about your health,' said Eustace. 'We've come to ask about trains to Blackpool and prices.'

Evans stared at Eustace then turned to Willie. 'What's the matter with him?'

'What do you mean?'

'Well last time he was up here, he was a gibbering idiot and now he talks much better than what you two do. Has he had the operation?'

'Oh, that's my new image. Anyway, what we want to know is, is there a train to Blackpool about six o'clock on a Friday night? Is there a return on Sunday about tea time and what's the cheapest we can travel this journey?'

'I think I'll just go out and come back in again,' said Evans.

'What for?' asked Arthur.

'Because I must be dreaming.'

'Why?'

'Because…because…what's the matter with him? It's not him; it's someone else that looks like him. He can't talk proper, not like this high foluting bloke.'

'I can assure you old friend, that it is me and that I am talking in what will be my normal voice from now on, so what about these trains to Blackpool?'

Evans looked at him again, shook his head, shuffled over to his desk opened the timetable, became engrossed in it and began to whisper incantations into it. After an indeterminable time, whilst Willie and Arthur had muttered disparaging remarks about Evans, he suddenly lifted his head and said, 'Got it boyo, got it.'

'Have you now?' said Arthur. 'Is it contagious?'

'Do you know, I've got all the world and its mother comes through this station, but never a set like you lot, you must be unique. Have you drunk your tea yet?'

'You haven't poured it yet and I'm fair gagging,' said Willie.

'Yes, that's right,' said Evans not listening to him. 'Now about these Blackpool trains. Slow to Manchester, five to six here, five to seven Manchester Exchange, walk the long platform to Victoria, quarter past seven to Blackpool, Express, calls at Preston and St Annes, to Blackpool Central eight promptish or thereabouts. Sunday, reverse operation; leave Blackpool quarter past four, back here twenty past six. Fare six shillings single, nine shillings return. How's that for superb information? I assume you will want returns? Can't persuade you to take one way trips only can I?'

'Is that first class, or have we bought a share in the train for that?' asked Willie.

'Daft bugger. You'll be wanting a restaurant car with silver service next. Tell you what, as a special gesture to you I'll put my top hat on to wave you off.'

'We'll accept that.'

'Right, up and on your way now. I've a couple of parcels to get onto the Leeds train that's almost here.'

'What do you mean up and on your way, you haven't poured the tea yet,' said Willie.

'Yes,' said Evans, not listening again, as he tried to find the paper work for the parcels.

The three friends decided they may as well leave the nice warm fire and replace it with the one at the club.

*

'Good evening, oh big fat and ugly one,' said Willie as they walked into the bar at the club.

'Not so much of the ugly. I'll have you know that I won the bonny baby competition in the Grolsby Trumpet one year when I was a baby.'

'Were they using blind judges?' asked Eustace.

They all turned and looked at him

'If I hadn't seen it with my own eyes I wouldn't have believed this change at all, not at all,' said Harry. 'I have seen it with my own eyes, but it's unbelievable, it's not right, it's wrong, well it's just not Eustace.'

'Pour three pints for heaven's sake,' said Willie, 'I'm gasping for a quick one.'

'And would you care for a drink as well sir?' the steward enquired.

'Just get on with it and stick your nose out of it, we've some very important business to discuss.'

'Oh aye, like what?'

'Like our weekend in Blackpool,' said Arthur.

'Can I come?' asked Harry.

Three voices combined in blunt refusal

'It's not fair; no one ever invites me anywhere. Not ever.'

'Shut up moaning and pour us drinks,' said Willie, 'I'm dying of thirst.'

'I'll send for the undertaker, sir.'

The conversation ceased as three pints were presented and were taken to a table by the fire.

'How much is it to stay at this place in Blackpool Arthur?' asked Willie.

'It's not bad, it was thirteen and six each a night last time we went and all we have to do is to take our own food. She provides bedding and the like except we have to take our own towels.'

'So, if we go for two nights it'll be four times thirteen and six each plus how much did Evans say it was on the train?'

'Nine shillings return.'

'So that'll be, lets see now, two times nine bob is, err, err,' He took out two hands eight fingers, two thumbs and counted. 'Eighteen bob, then its fifty four bob for the boarding house.'

'How did you know that so quick?' asked Arthur.

'It's like playing cards. Four thirteens is fifty two and four tanners is two bob so that makes fifty four plus eighteen'll be now then seventy six bob.'

'Seventy two,' said Arthur.

'Yes, seventy two. Yes, that's right. Seventy two bob, that's each, so that'll be three pounds twelve shillings plus your food,' said Eustace. 'Not bad for a weekend away in Blackpool.'

'In a freezing January?' asked Arthur

'Aye in a freezing January.'

'Well I'd best write to Miss Shorrocks when I get home, if we're all in agreement. Of course come to think of it she might not be open in January.'

'You've got a point there,' said Willie

'Anyway, I can but try.'

*

Arthur, having conferred with Jess, sat at his living room table, took out his writing pad and wrote his address and date on the right hand side. He then continued "Dear Miss Shorrocks" on the left side and then he put his pen down and stared into space. For all his outward apparent masterly command of all matters commercial, he was in actual fact, much the opposite, almost useless. Over the years he had fostered, nurtured and proffered the idea that he was Gods gift to his fellow men in the world of the club secretary, treasurer, organiser and the like, when in reality, like tonight he was stuck before he started. He had always been lucky that in public he had got away with whatever it was he was trying to get away with.

'Do you want some help?' asked Jess.

'Well, err, no, not exactly, I was just thinking what to put in this letter.'

'Give it here. It's easy.' So she wrote "We were thinking of having a weekend in Blackpool next Friday 6th January with some friends, the Arkenthwaites and the Ollerenshaws. Can you fit us in? We need three bedrooms for Friday and Saturday night. We will arrive about a quarter past eight or half past." 'Here you sign it Arthur. Have you got a stamp, you'd best seal it so she will get it first post Friday, then we might get a reply on Saturday.'

So Arthur finished it off, sealed it ready to post in the box on his way to work on Thursday morning.

*

New Year's Eve had arrived before they knew it and it really was a last minute effort to prepare themselves for the function at the band room. With it being on a Friday evening, the men folk had had to dash home from the mill at 5 o'clock to have their teas and get into their best suits ready to congregate at Arthur's at seven thirty.

Willie had gobbled his tea, then he had retrieved the tin bath from its hook behind the back door and put it on the floor in front of the living room fire. He dispatched the children to their bedroom and proceeded to have his second bath in a fortnight. An unheard of practice. Thelma, who was almost ready when he decided to have his bath, came along to scrub his back, but she had to be very cross with him for blowing bubbles which erupted noisily from between his legs on the surface of the water, causing small fountains at times. When he finally stood up to ask Thelma to pass him the towel, she took one look at his rotund, bald form and burst out laughing.

'What's amusing you?' he enquired

'Nothing, dear. Nothing,' she began to have fits of hysterics. 'But do get dressed quickly, you might frighten someone.' She went upstairs to complete her own dressing, convulsed with laughter.

*

Arthur was very upset because Jess made him have a bath as soon as he had finished his tea. She told him, 'You smell of decorating.'

'But I had a bath at Christmas!'

'You've decorated since. Anyway, you can have one.'

So under duress he had a bath. He didn't enjoy it and he wasn't any cleaner when he had finished than he was before he started. Or so he said.

*

Eustace walked in home and announced that he was having a bath. Joan told him to put the emersion heater on. Then she said. 'You had a bath for Christmas and you only have two or three a year.'

'Well I'm having one tonight and you can give over arguing about it.'

*

So three smartly dressed, very clean gentlemen met at Arthur's accompanied by three very eloquent ladies.

Willie announced, 'We can call at the club on the way to the band room and have one. It's cheaper there.'

Thelma glared at him. 'No such thing! We're not going to the club. We'll go straight to the band room.'

'You didn't object to going to the club last week.'

'No, but that was a special party night. We are not going on an ordinary night.'

'It's not an ordinary night, it's New Year's Eve.'

'Yes but there's nothing on special.'

They walked up the long steep hill to the band room. When they got nearer to it they could see that it was bright and welcoming. Willie was out of breath and puffing like a little tank engine. The others were there long before Willie arrived.

Inside there was an organised cloakroom at which they deposited their outer garments and got tickets in return. They all went into the long bar on the ground floor where they were greeted by a huge log fire burning in the hearth at one end of the room. They all migrated towards the fire and congregated with many more other revelers having their first drink of the evening and getting warm again.

After the second round, when Joan was beginning to get a little bit squiffy and they were all boiling over with the heat Thelma suggested that they should get another round in then climb the steps up to the concert room.

Eustace went to the bar and ordered another round from Molly who was dressed to impress because it was New Year's Eve.

'So you all made it then, Eustace. You didn't tell us you were bringing the terrible two. I hope Willie is going to exhibit some good manners this evening. See, there you are, what was I saying?' she moaned as Willie belched out loud.

Eustace carried the drinks back to his party and they stood up ready to slowly amble out of the bar, up the steps and into the concert room. Or they would all have stood up if Joan hadn't found the move to be somewhat difficult. She did sort of half way stand up, then abruptly sat down again, grinned at everyone and tried to stand up again. The she sat down again. Finally Eustace walked to her side, put his arm through hers, took her drink lifted her onto her feet and with Willies help managed to drag her upstairs into the concert room.

Eustace confided in the rest of them that he was very worried about Joan as she appeared not to be able to consume the least amount of alcohol without getting squiffy.

'She wasn't like that before the Christmas club do,' said Thelma.

'I know. I think that the do had a very profound effect on her. But I am going to have to watch her liquor intake in future."

They went into the concert room and were astounded at the sight before their eyes. The room was decorated with balloons, streamers and paper chains. It was colorful, lively and a treat to behold. At one end on the concert platform, Sid Sidebottom and his Syncopating Sextet were playing dance music and tables were situated around the outside of the dance floor.

They picked an empty table at the opposite end of the room to the band, where they might be able to hear themselves talk. They danced, they talked, they drank, even Joan, although she was only allowed lemonade under protestation. Soon it was time for the gourmet supper, which was served in one of the downstairs committee rooms. They were not sure what to expect as pies and crisps had been mentioned on several occasions and so what they saw when they entered the room took their breath away. It was a gourmet supper and no mistake. There was everything and more. None of them had ever witnessed anything like it before.

<u>CHAPTER 6</u>

The Baxter's letter box flapped early on Saturday morning and Jess could contain herself no longer. She got out of bed, put on her dressing gown and slippers then rushed downstairs to find an envelope with a Blackpool postmark on it of which she tore open and read the contents. She took the letter upstairs to read it to Arthur.

"Dear Mr & Mrs Baxter,

Thank you for you letter. I am sorry to have to tell you that Miss Amelia Shorrocks passed away last September. My husband and I bought the business from her executors and we are now open for business every day of the year. The business will continue just as it did under Miss Shorrocks and we look forward to seeing you on Friday 6th. If you want a warm supper when you arrive, I will cook it for you, or there is a very good fish and chip shop just along the road, where they fry fresh Fleetwood cod.

Yours Faithfully

Cynthia Dobbs."

P.S. Sorry but we have had to increase the charges to 14/6 a night a person.

'Well,' said Jess, 'I never would have thought.'
'No but she was getting on a bit and let's face it, it is three years next summer since we were there and anything can happen in that time.'
'I wonder what it'll be like now?'
'She's gone and put it up you know, to 14/6.'

'Yes, but like you just said, it is two and a half years since we were there so a shilling increase in that time isn't bad.'

'Willie isn't going to like it.'

'Well he'll just have to put up with it or not come!'

*

Arthur didn't bother to break the news to Eustace and Willie until Monday dinnertime in the canteen when they were playing cards.

'Got in at Blackpool, no problem, changed landlady, she's put it up by a bob a night.'

'Each?' asked an incredulous Willie.

'Aye, each.'

'I don't know if I can…'

'Of course you can and are going to do. So that's settled. Alright with you Eustace?'

'Yes, fine Arthur, no problem at all, it's not Arthur, it's not, not at all Arthur, not, no problem.' He stopped, took a deep breath, took control of himself, muttered, 'Oh bugger,' to himself, then smiled and said, 'Yes, absolutely no problem old boy.'

*

In the meantime, Jess had called on Joan Ollerenshaw to say that the three ladies should have a meeting to decide what food to take, probably at her house this afternoon. She caught Thelma at dinner time, on her way home from her job at the big house belonging to the mill. So at about two o'clock the other two ladies descended on the Baxter household.

Jess had the best cups and saucers out, some plain home baked sponge with home made raspberry jam in the middle and the kettle on the hob, simmering merrily away when they sat down in the living room. After the usual small talk, when, unusually, husbands were not pulled to pieces, Jess asked Thelma, 'Have you sorted out Josie and the young'uns yet?'

'Yes, it's no problem. Margaret, Josie's friend, is coming to stay. The boys have been given a talking to and with a bit of luck they'll behave for the weekend. Margaret Murgatroyd said that her and Mr Anthony would have a walk around on Saturday and just pop their heads through the door to make sure that everything is alright.'

'So what about the food?' asked Joan, who was enjoying getting involved in something other than her usual nothing. 'The fish and chip supper sounds good to me for Friday night.'

'Yes me too,' said Thelma. 'Then a hot drink and a bun before we go to bed. Now what about the rest? Do we want a big breakfast, a snack dinner and a big tea, or the other way around, or what? But we should pool our money and our coupons, although, Willie'll get us some home cured bacon and fresh eggs to take if we want.'

'If we want! Of course we want,' said Jess, 'then we can have a good fry up both mornings.'

Joan said, 'That would be very nice. We don't usually have a big fry up for breakfast. Tell me, where does Willie get these eggs and bacon from?' she asked in a casual manner, but was none too pleased with the reply she got.

'It's for him to know and for you to wonder about.'

So the afternoon rolled along, the whole matter was settled and Joan was put in charge of food purchases, a job she relished because she felt important for once in her life.

*

Work finished at five o'clock on Friday, and the three friends were home quicker than usual, washed and changed, packed and they met at the station to catch the six o'clock train to Manchester Victoria.

'Well well, this is a great honour for a humble man of the valleys, like myself, observed Evans as he watched six people struggle into his booking hall with their heavy suitcases and the three children who had come to see them off.

Evans the Ticket Clerk moved behind his ticket window.

'Two for Blackpool,' said Arthur

'Single or return?'

'Return please.'

'Shame. Change at Manchester Victoria,' as he presented Arthur with two tickets and his change.

'Two returns to Blackpool.'

'Shame. Change at Manchester Victoria.'

'Two returns for Blackpool please,' said Eustace.

'Shame. Change at Manchester Victoria, and three platform tickets. Who's paying?'

Willie rounded on him. 'Don't be such a miserable Taffy, Taffy.'

'William Arkenthwaite, if you address me as Taffy again, I will come around that side of the partition and prove, in my capacity as er, er, er, er, Ticket Inspector, that you cannot possibly travel to Blackpool.'

'Come on, it's only the kids wanting to see us off, they're only going to wave us away.'

A wide grin crossed Evans face. 'Of course they can, I was only joking.' With which he slammed down the hatch over the ticket window and retired towards the hot coal fire where he stood for several minutes with his back to it, getting nicely roasted.

Suddenly his thoughts turned to his traveling passengers, not all of them, just six in particular and placing his official coat over his official suit, then putting his best official station master's bowler hat on, he walked onto the platform and made a bee-line for Willie and friends.

'Excuse me, Mr Arkenthwaite sir, will you require any assistance with your luggage when the train arrives, and here it comes now, or do you need anything else?'

Willie looked at Evans, leaned over to him out of earshot of the others and whispered in his ear, 'Bugger off.' At which they both laughed.

The train pulled into the station; they found an empty compartment with eight seats, put their cases on the other two, waved to the children and they were on their way.

Evans the Station Master walked the three children back to the entrance hall. As they were going, Evans the Cleaner picked up a discarded cigarette packet and deposited in a bin.

The train puffed its way along the shallow incline up the steep valley and into the long tunnel that joins Lancashire and Yorkshire. The traveling party sat back to enjoy the journey and to make plans as to what they would do in Blackpool this weekend, knowing full well that the object of the exercise was to try to find a restaurant for the trip lunch in June. They were aware that it would be quiet and that most places would be closed for the Winter season, so it might be difficult filling in their time until the return journey on Sunday evening.

They had just begun to roll along through the villages of eastern Lancashire when Eustace became visibly agitated.

'What's the matter Eustace?' Willie enquired.

'Nothing. No nothing. Yes, I want to go to the toilet.'

'Well there's nowt you can do about that until we get to Manchester and we've about a quarter of an hour to go yet,' said Arthur.

So for the next fifteen minutes, Eustace fidgeted and groaned. When the train pulled into Manchester Victoria, Eustace jumped up and began to open the door before the train stopped.

'Where do you think you're going?' asked Joan.

'To find the gents.'

'And what about us?'

'Eh?'

'There's the suitcases, then we've only got not long to catch the Blackpool connection, so we'd best make a few arrangements before you disappear.'

In the end, the ladies stood in a heap around their suitcases on the platform whilst all three men went in search of the gents with the excuse that it was better if they all went together then they would be back quicker.

'Some logic,' said Jess.

It didn't take them long and they were soon on the platform waiting for the Blackpool train to come in. When it arrived, it was an express with corridors and toilets, much to Eustace's and the others relief.

The train pulled into Blackpool North station dead on time at five minutes to eight. They all dismounted and carried their cases through the ticket barrier and out into the front of the station, where they took a tram to Gynn Square, then walked the remaining few hundred yards to the boarding house of Mrs Cynthia Dobbs.

'I wonder what she'll be like?' said Arthur. 'Probably she'll stand on the front doorstep, arms folded, No fighting, no spitting, no belching and no farting after ten o'clock.'

'Arthur,' screamed Jess.

'Sorry dear, just soliloquizing.'

They knocked on the big, highly polished, brass knocker.

'It still looks the same,' said Jess.

'Yes, it hasn't outwardly changed,' replied Arthur.

The door was opened by a plump, middle aged, attractive lady, who had a most welcoming smile. 'Do come in. I assume you are the party from Grolsby for the weekend. It's nice to have visitors at this time of year. It's not every weekend and only rarely mid-week that we get anyone to stay. Anyway that's enough from me. Have you had a good journey?'

Arthur took charge. 'Yes thank you, we've had an excellent journey. Pity it wasn't daylight so that we could have seen where we were, but even so everything went off very well. So you're Mrs. Dobbs?'

'Yes, and this is Fred my husband.'

A well rounded friendly sort of man appeared.

'How do lads and lasses, welcome to our humble home. Shall I show you to your rooms?' He led the way upstairs. 'Have you had owt to eat?' He asked.

'No not yet and I could eat an elephant,' said Willie.

'No problem. There's a café not far from here where the contents of the home made steak and kidney pie is reputed to be elephant. I'll take you there if you want after you've unpacked.' He convulsed with laughter.

'I think we're going to be alright here,' Arthur said to Jess.

'Yes, it looks like they're a good pair.'

They all unpacked, abluted and congregated in the lounge on the ground floor which was next to the dining room.

Cynthia Dobbs was knitting in front of a big coal fire. 'Are you going out for something to eat?'

'Yes, for a fish and chip supper,' said Joan. 'You said you could recommend somewhere?'

'Well there's not that many open at this time of year, but you could try Bertie's Plaice. It's the one that I told you about in my letter. It's about half a mile walk straight along here towards Bispham, but usually well worth the walk. And anyway, the walk back'll do you good after a big plate of fish and chips.'

Willie was about to argue that he didn't need the exercise when Cynthia Dobbs got her second wind and began to talk again. 'Come to think of it, I fancy a fish. How about you Fred?'

'Yes, yes. I could just eat a fish. Mind if we tag along?'

'Err, no,' mumbled each and every one of them not sure whether they wanted strangers with them or not. But it was too late as Cynthia and Fred were already putting their outdoor gear on and getting ready to lock up.

As they strolled along the back streets of the North Shore, Fred and Cynthia talked and questioned the others about Grolsby and what they did and why they'd come to Blackpool just after Christmas and did they fancy a drink at The Seagull.

'Well it is a well known fact that Willie never refuses a drink,' said Arthur, 'but I'm hungry just now and so are the girls, so let's go and eat first.'

They had a first class cod, chips, mushy peas, bread and butter and tea sitting in the dining room behind the shop and were all well gisened afterwards. On the way back they succumbed to Fred's wishes and called in at The Seagull for a quick half, which became a long session and only ended when the landlord finally managed to tip them out. They all sat down in the lounge in front of the big fire when they got back to the digs.

'Now then, how about a cup of tea or coffee before we go to bed?' asked Cynthia.

'That would be very nice, thank you,' said Joan. 'I'll just nip upstairs and get our tea and coffee and I'd best bring down the breakfast things at the same time.'

'It would be handy if you would bring down all your food, then I can sort out what I am going to cook for you tomorrow and Sunday lunch.'

All three ladies went upstairs to unpack the food. Their cases were more or less empty then as they'd brought only a few items of clothing each.

Fred asked the men, 'Where are you thinking of going to organise your trip lunch then?'

'Well that's the problem,' said Arthur, 'we don't know. We were half hoping that you would be able to help us with that one.'

'Well there're a lot of places you could go. Mind you, I wouldn't send the wife's mother to most of them, so that doesn't leave a right lot to go at. I'm sure you'll want a good meal at a sensible price and that narrows it down a lot further to just one or two. I'll have a think before morning and tell you at breakfast. What time do you want breakfast by the way?'

'Half past eight,' said Thelma and then she looked at the others.

'Yes, half past eight'll be good for me,' said Joan and Jess nodded her consent. The men folk weren't even consulted.

*

At half past eight on Saturday morning, Willie and Thelma walked downstairs to the fantastic smell of freshly cooked bacon amongst other things.

'Ee that smells right good, right good,' said Willie.

Thelma agreed with him. She was enjoying her time without the children for the first time in years. She was thinking about them, and worrying about them, but she was enjoying herself nevertheless.

There was only one table laid in the dining room and that was for six people. So Willie sat down at it.

'Don't you think we'd better wait for the others Willie?'

'Nay, if they can't be here…'

Joan walked in.

'Good morning, Joan. Where's Eustace?' asked Willie.

'Gone for a walk to see if he can get a newspaper, but that was ages ago and I told him to be back by half past.'

'Morning, morning,' said Arthur and Jess as they breezed in.

The front door banged and Eustace arrived all muffled up.

'Morning all. Bloody cold out there.'

'Language Eustace, please,' commanded Joan.

Strangely he ignored her. 'I've just seen the balls fall off the brass monkey.' He took off his coat and hat, then carefully hung them in an armchair before sitting down at the remaining seat at the table. 'I'm that hungry I could eat a rancid pig.'

Joan was too upset with him to speak and Thelma said to him, 'I think you're going to be disappointed, it all smells too good to be rancid.'

Cynthia and Fred Dobbs arrived carrying six plates of a most excellent fry up, a mountain of toast and a huge pot of tea.

'Now get set in whilst it's hot,' said Fred. 'Now, I've been giving your problem a bit of thought. You've not got a lot of choice at this time of year, but half way down the Golden Mile, between two amusement arcades, not far from central pier, you'll find up a narrow alley, the Golden Cockerel restaurant. This is open all the year around and I am given to understand it serves amazingly good lunches, teas and dinners for big gatherings, parties and the like, and that's about the only one I can think of.'

'Well thanks,' said Arthur, 'we'll certainly give it a good coat of looking at.'

So after they had finished eating their delicious breakfast, they got well wrapped up against the biting wind. Eustace got a ticking off for use of foul language and they walked onto the promenade by Uncle Tom's Cabin.

'Let's walk,' said Jess, 'we'll just about get to the Golden Cockerel in time for dinner and we'll see all the sites on the way there.'

So they set off at a brisk pace with the wind coming off the sea making their faces icy cold.

By mid morning, they were at Blackpool Tower. They had examined in minute detail every square inch of the hotels, boarding houses, pubs, clubs and shops that lined the promenade. They'd been inside Derby Baths and the Metropole Hotel. They'd been on a deserted North Pier and now they were inside the tower itself, watching the ballroom dancing to the Wurlitzer organ in the famous Tower Ballroom.

'Come on Joan, let's have a dance.'

She looked at Eustace. 'Nay, nay, I couldn't, not in front of all these people that are good dancers. Look at them, they're all dressed for the occasion and they're all professionals. Nay lad, I couldn't. Sorry. No.'

'Jess, how about you?'

Jess colored slightly and politely refused.

'Come on Eustace, I'll give you a twirl. Willie rarely dances as you know and I'd love to have a dance in the Tower Ballroom.' So they walked downstairs hand in hand and were soon to be seen by all and sundry dancing with the rest of the best and thoroughly enjoying it. They had a couple of waltzes and a foxtrot before they came back upstairs to rejoin their party.

'Well that was absolutely marvelous, thank you Thelma.' He turned to Joan. 'You should have come down you would have enjoyed it.'

Joan began to dread the future yet again.

Arthur began to move. 'Well it's getting on towards dinner time, and we've a bit to go yet, so I say we make a move.'

'But it's nice and warm in here and I'm enjoying listening to Reginald Dixon playing the organ. Do we have to go just yet?'

'Alright, ten minutes more but we must go then.'

Fifteen minutes passed by and Arthur began to fidget. 'Come on, we'll never get there at this rate.'

'Go on then,' said Willie begrudgingly. 'Come on all of you, let's go get us dinners.'

They walked out onto the promenade, across the tram lines and over to the railings to look at the sea. They turned around, leaned on the railings and looked up at the tower.

'Why didn't we go up to the top?' asked Eustace.

'Because it's closed for winter,' said Joan.

'Yes, but I've never been up there, I haven't, never, no I haven't,' he decided to shut up.

'Well you will have to make a point of going up when you come on the trip. Now are we going for lunch? I'm beginning to get hungry.'

It took a while to get as far as the Golden Cockerel Restaurant. In fact, it took even longer because it was as Fred Dobbs had said, tucked away between two amusement arcades and took quite some finding. The lure of the slot machines, the Grand National, the Ski Roll and all the other attractions had split the party into factions and it eventually took Jess to go around, drag them all out of the arcade and assemble them at the bottom of the steps leading up to the restaurant.

The narrow entrance soon widened into a long staircase leading to a large foyer, which opened into a big, well appointed bar, which then opened into the restaurant which had large picture windows looking towards the sea.

'I think it calls for a pint first,' said Willie.

'Why not,' agreed Thelma. 'We girls will have halves.'

'Not me. I'll just have a sweet sherry,' said Joan.

A bright young girl served them and asked them if they wanted a table for lunch.

'Yes please, for six, by the window if you have one.'

The young lady brought them some menus to study whilst they sat around a table and enjoyed their drinks.

Arthur was the first to speak. 'Not bad, not bad at all so far.'

Eustace followed, 'I think it's good. It's not a bad menu for the price. I'm going to have the set lunch, it should be good value.'

Thelma raised her hand. 'Now hang on a minute. We should all try something different to get the true feel of what the quality of the food is like, across the board, so to speak. Then if we've all had a good meal, we know it's alright.'

The young lady returned. 'Your table is prepared, in the window, when you are ready.'

'Well I'm ready now,' said Joan.

'Me too,' agreed Willie.

So they emptied their glasses and went into the light, spacious restaurant, where a smartly attired, middle aged waitress took them to their table and sat them down.

'Nice cutlery and table cloths, a jug of water. Very nice, spotlessly clean, first impressions very favorable,' said Jess.

The waitress returned to take their order. 'Now, for starters?' She went around the table then when she had finished she said, 'Now let me just check it again. That's three chicken soups, one tomato soup and one egg mayonnaise. Then for main course, one rissoles and chips, one sausage and mash, one cod and chips, one grilled ham and chips, one chop and chips and one steak and kidney pie with chips. Thank you.' She departed to the kitchen.

The starters arrived, they didn't have long to wait. It was good and wholesome. When they had finished, the plates were quickly cleared away and the main course served. Once again they all had a good, hot, well cooked, well presented, large portion.

'That fish was delicious,' said Joan, 'it tasted like it had come fresh from the sea and the chips were superb.'

'Yes,' agreed Arthur, my steak and kidney pie was just right. The meat was tender, super pastry, very tasty. Yes I think we'll be alright here.'

The other four had no hesitation in agreeing.

'What's for pudding?' enquired Willie.

'Wait until the waitress comes,' Thelma scolded him.

The young lady returned to their table, cleared up the dirty pots and came back with desert menus. The choice was limited to treacle sponge pudding and custard or rice pudding. Both were tested and both enjoyed. Tea and coffee were taken to round off an excellent lunch.

Eustace had enjoyed his lunch just as much as any of the others and had decided that it was excellent value, warm, clean, well served and just right for the trip lunch. So he ventured to mention the subject, first taking a deep breath and composing himself. 'Now then. I've enjoyed my dinner so much that I think we should investigate holding the trip dinner here. The place is very nice, it's spotlessly clean, the food has been excellent, the service first class and it's nice and warm in here. But more than that it's in a good central position here on the Golden Mile, with excellent sea views and I think just right.'

The other five stared at him in disbelief. None of them had ever heard him put more than a few words of sense together without faltering and Joan was secretly becoming very proud of him.

Eustace also secretly was very proud of himself and heaved a sigh of relief when he had finished.

There followed a long pause before anyone spoke, giving Willie the opportunity to have a jolly good loud belch, followed up by one of his famous farts.

Thelma shouted, 'Willie,' and then gave her opinion. 'Yes, I agree with all you have said, Eustace, but there's one more thing; it will save you the trouble of looking anywhere else.'

'Thank you, Thelma. That's very kind of you to agree with me.'

Willie entered the debate. 'Another thing that you haven't mentioned is that it's licensed as well, which is very important.'

'What about the menu?' asked Arthur.

Eustace came into his own again. 'Perhaps we'd better ask the management. Let's get the bill and take it from there.'

So the waitress was summoned and Eustace explained the reason for their visit and asked to see someone in authority.

'That's my mum and dad. Tell you what, my mum's at the cash desk now, she's the money grabber. I'll go tell her you want a chat, then when you get there to pay she'll be prepared.'

'What's her name?'

'Elsie Proops. I'm Susan and my dad's Ken.'

They made their way to the cash desk. They had already sorted out the money and Eustace had left a tip on the table.

'Hello, Mrs Proops,' said Eustace.

She looked up. 'Hello there. Are you the party that wants to discuss an organised luncheon?' She spoke affectedly posh with her being the proprietress of an up market café and with it being situated on the front at Blackpool.

'Yes, we want to organise a dinner. Sorry, lunch for our mill trip.'

'Let me just take your money, then I'll get Ken, my husband, and we can sit in the bar and have a nice talk.'

She gave Eustace his change then left the cash deck to walk into the kitchen to get her husband, Ken, who was the chef.

A large, red faced, rotund, jolly sort of man appeared wearing the chefs standard blue checked trousers, white smock top and white chefs hat. He walked over to the six friends who were seated in the bar.

'Now then everyone, my name's Ken Proops. They tell me you want to talk about an organised lunch.'

'Yes, that's right.' Eustace took command, much to Arthur's annoyance.

Ken Proops then played his ace card. 'Before we start talking, can I get you all a drink, I find that a lot of talking dries out ones throat.'

'That's very civil of you indeed,' Arthur got his spoke in quickly. 'I think we need three pints and possibly three halves. He looked at the ladies, two of which nodded in assent, but Joan asked for her favourite sweet sherry.

'Right then. Elsie,' he shouted, 'four pints, two halves and a sweet sherry.'

He looked around and could not see her. 'Where the hell is the woman,' he said. 'Oh, you're there. Where have you been?'

'To the ladies.'

'Oh. You're forgiven then. Go and get four pints and two halves of South Shore best bitter, a sweet sherry and whatever you're having.'

'That the local brew?' asked Willie.

'Yes. Good stuff. Brewed by a mate of mine, but it's only available in Blackpool, it's especially for us locals. So now then, what can we do for you good people?'

Eustace took a deep breath. The other five were waiting in eager anticipation of what he would say. He collected his thoughts and began. 'We have come for lunch to try out your food and facilities because we are looking for a restaurant to have our mill trip lunch this summer.'

'Good, good. So how have you enjoyed your lunch?'

'Absolutely fine. First class.'

'Good, excellent, well even better. I'm pleased you have all enjoyed it and let me assure you that the same standard of food and service will be available for you for an organised meal. So let's start with the proposed date.'

'Well, we're looking at Saturday fourth of June.'

Ken consulted the diary that he just conveniently happened to be carrying. 'That date is free, so that's the first hurdle jumped, now what about the timing?'

Ken was beginning to ask questions they hadn't thought of and they all looked at one another in blank amazement.

Thelma came to the rescue. 'Half past twelve.'

'A nice time. Just right. Helps me a lot if I can get all prepared before the rush in the restaurant. Perhaps it would be prudent at this stage of the proceedings to nip upstairs and examine the facilities.'

'What facilities?' asked Willie.

'The function room and bar where we serve organised meals.'

They all traipsed upstairs into a big room with a bar at one side and dining tables overlooking the sea through another set of large picture windows.

'Now, you can have the whole function in here. The bar will be open, the toilets are there and we can either give you an informal layout, with individual tables for eight or you can have a formal wedding type layout.'

They had a wander around, gave the room and facilities a good inspection and finally retired to the bar on the floor below to complete their discussion.

Eventually, without too much difficulty, it was all agreed. Forty eight people, plus one driver, informal layout and the meal to be served about one o'clock. The menu to consist of chicken soup with bread rolls and butter, roast lamb with accompanying vegetables, treacle sponge pudding with custard and tea or coffee.

They thanked Elsie, Susan and Ken then went back downstairs onto the Golden Mile.

The Proops family looked at each other, smiled and agreed that they were nice folk that would be no trouble on the day.

*

'Who's that that Willie's talking to over there?' Thelma asked the others. They were still on the Golden Mile sauntering through the amusement arcades.

Willie had wandered away from the others and was talking to what appeared to be a tramp with torn clothing, unshaven appearance and definitely unwashed.

'He's got a placard around his neck and Willie's buying something from him. It looks like a newspaper. Still, we haven't bought a paper this morning.'

Willie returned to the fold, newspaper in hand.

'Daily Herald?' asked Arthur.

'Danny's Monthly Liar,' replied Willie.

'Don't talk so daft.'

'I'm not. It is.'

'Never heard of it.'

'Well here it is. Only available on the Golden Mile. I always buy one when I come to Blackpool.'

Arthur grabbed it and began to read. 'So it is.' He read a few paragraphs. 'It's disgusting and it's rubbish.'

'Yes, that's right, but it's good fun to read.'

'Come on,' said Eustace, 'let's go onto Central Pier and try the humpty cycles.'

'It's winter, they won't be open,' said Joan.

'Well come on, let's go and look.'

So they crossed the road, crossed the tram lines and walked onto the pier where, as predicted, everything was closed.

The three men were leaning on the fence that surrounded the humpty cycle track.

'It's a bloody great, crying shame that this lot isn't working,' mused Willie.

'Hang on a minute…' said Arthur. He'd just seen a man emerge through a small door at the side of a shed near the track. 'Hoy, come here a minute lad.'

He came over to them. 'Hoy! To me? It's sir around here, I'll have you know.'

'Aye, but we're from Yorkshire.'

'And that makes a difference, does it?'

'It does to us. How about letting us have a ride on the humpty cycles?'

'For nowt,' added Willie.

'Can't you see we're shut?'

'Aye we know that, but like I said, we come from Yorkshire.'

'And like I said, that makes a difference does it?'

The three ladies meandered along and joined their men folk.

The proprietor of the humpty cycles was enjoying the cross banter as he missed the crowds during the closed season, many of whom were from Yorkshire. He nodded to the ladies, smiled at them and said, 'Tell you what. I've been doing a bit of maintenance on the bikes this morning, it might be a good idea if you came in and tried one, just to make sure that they are in good fettle.'

Willie and Thelma jumped at the opportunity and went in. Arthur, despite him having started the conversation in the first place, hung back along with Jess. Eustace went in, but Joan stayed back with Jess and Arthur.

It had been a long time since Willie and Thelma had ridden a humpty cycle, but they both called upon their experience and it didn't take them long to get going. Riding first high up and then pushing down on the saddle for all they were worth to get the saddle to the bottom with enough inertia to get it to come back to the top again and over top dead centre again. This way the bike went forward, the momentum increased and the rhythm built up. If they failed to go fast enough on the upstroke, then the bike went into reverse and they fell off, or if they were clever enough, they could ride it in reverse.

Eustace had never tried to ride one before and to begin with was making a serious attempt to find the non existent pedals, however after a while he studied the other two and attempted to follow suit.

'You'll never do it,' Joan muttered to herself and was more than annoyed to see him start bobbing up and down like Willie and Thelma and having a jolly good time.

'Well, you've got to admit they look good at it. Ridiculous but good,' Arthur said to Joan.

'Yes. I didn't think Eustace had it in him.'

'Come on you lot, come in here and try one,' Thelma was shouting as she precariously balanced her cycle.

'No, no, we think not,' said Joan. They turned away to go and look at other stalls and amusements that were shut.

Over at the humpty cycles, the riders were thanking the proprietor. 'Well that were fair grand,' said Willie.

'It was my pleasure. I love to do a favour for a fellow Yorkshire man,' he said laughing.

'You're from Yorkshire?'

'Scarborough.'

'Scarborough, that's East Riding.'

'Yes I know. But by the sound of your accents, you're from the West Riding.'

'Heavy Woolen District. Grolsby in fact.'

'Ah well, we all have our cross to bear.'

They thanked him again and left in good, high spirits.

'Where next?' Willie demanded of the reassembled party.

'Let's walk up the prom towards the Pleasure Beach.'

'It won't be open.'

'Like the humpty cycles weren't.'

'Come on then, let's go and find out.'

They hadn't gone far, still within the confines of the Golden Mile, when Eustace stopped at the open door of the Emporium of Madam Zsa Zsa. Fortunes told, tarot card readings, crystal ball predictions and palmistry.

'Hey you lot, let's go in here and get us fortunes told.'

Joan gave him a withering look. 'We are having none of that nonsense. If you want to spend some money, you can buy me a new dress.'

'Yes, but I just thought it might be fun.'

Willie intervened. 'Why don't we all go inside and watch Eustace have his fortune told?'

Madam Zsa Zsa came outside. She was mid thirties, small, dark skinned, big earrings, scarf over her head and a touch of Romany in her. 'Are you coming in or not?'

'Nay, you're the person what can see into the future. Don't you know?' asked Arthur.

Madam Zsa Zsa took a good, long, slow look at them all and decided there and then to double her charges, if she could get them inside.

Eustace had been studying the bill of fare that was plastered all over the front of the shop front. Well it couldn't exactly be described as a shop front. More a hovel between two broken down amusement arcades, that was keeping them apart.

Eustace said, 'I think I'll just have five bobs worth of palm reading.'

'Ten.'

'It says five.'

'That's last season's notices. I've not had them changed yet for the new season, but it's going to be ten.'

'Daylight robbery,' said Willie. 'Come on, we might find another, cheaper one along the prom, there's plenty of 'em.'

They moved slowly away and Madam Zsa Zsa let them get a few paces on their way before shouting. 'Hey you. Yes you, the five bob man.'

They turned around to look at her.

'You know the tall, old, ugly woman that I was going to tell you you were going to meet. Well I was wrong. I think you've already met her.'

She turned around, went indoors and slammed the door hard behind her.

'Well, well,' said Joan in tears, 'that was very nasty. What a horrible woman.'

Eustace put his arm around her. 'Come on love; forget about it, I think you're alright.'

They crossed the road again, over the tram tracks, onto the promenade and headed for the South Shore.

After half an hour of brisk walking, with the north wind on their backs, they were just about at the Pleasure Beach which had a few signs of life. It was beginning to come dark and Thelma fancied a pot of tea.

'There's not a lot of spots open,' she observed. 'But I could just fancy a right good cuppa.'

They searched their surroundings but the possibilities were just about zero. The hotels and boarding houses were closed for winter. They looked cold, lonely and abandoned. The fish and chip shops, gift and souvenir shops and the side shows were all begging for the better weather, the new season and the return of their owners.

Arthur suggested they should cross the road and go into the Pleasure Beach as they might get a cuppa in the café in the bottom of the Trocadero entertainment complex.

'Let's go and see if the Big Dipper's working,' said Willie.

'No. I want a cup of tea. I'm gagging for one.'

So they did as Arthur had suggested and found a very meagrely stocked, self service café on the promenade, not quite at the Pleasure Beach, with no one else in it. They went in for a cuppa, which along with some lemonade and a few biscuits was all that was on offer.

'You've not got much to eat,' said Willie to the more than disinterested lass sitting at the till, filing her nails.

'Yes.'

'How much is tea?'

'What?'

'Six teas please.'

'Hurry up, we're shutting in a couple of minutes.'

'Six teas please,' he bellowed.

'Alright, alright, keep yer long Johns on.'

'Young lady, if I was your father…'

She stopped pouring and stared at him. 'Well you're not, thank goodness, and you wouldn't anyway because I wouldn't stand there long enough to let you and anyway you're not big enough.'

'You might just be surprised.'

She leisurely finished pouring their teas, put the cups and saucers on a tray, charged them for them and then said, 'Don't take all day over it. Some of us have got homes to go to.'

They sat in silence, unable to talk.

Thelma eventually ventured to open her mouth, 'Not a bad cup of tea.'

'No, quite good really,' agreed Jess. 'Well spoiled by a mannerless, young lady. I think you'll find that with the relatively few people that there are here, she's bored out of her trolley. And anyway, she looks like a regularly bored person.'

'I would like a ride on the big dipper,' said Willie.

'Why don't you three men go to the pleasure beach and meet us ladies back here in an hour. It'll be dark by then and time to go back to the digs,' suggested Thelma.

The Big Dipper was ready for closing, but they got onto the last train of the day and had a very enjoyable ride around the circuit. All the lights of the promenade were visible from the top of the incline.

'Ee that were grand, its years since I were on there,' said Willie as the train pulled back into its station.

'Yes,' agreed Arthur, 'a good ride. Just like it used to be. How was it for you Eustace?'

There being no reply, they both turned to observe a very green, old man.

'I think I'm going to be, be...' he got no further as his lunch arrived back onto mother earth, much faster than it had disappeared the first time, right down the side of the train.

'We'd best get you back to your Joan.'

'No, no, not just yet. Let's just take a walk around, can we? Can we, Willie? Arthur? A walk? Oh bugger. Never mind. Let's just walk.'

So for ten minutes they walked and Eustace regained his usual pallor. He felt much better and so they returned to the café where the ladies were sitting chatting, awaiting their return and being visibly growled at by the serving wench.

'That was real,' Willie shouted. 'Could have gone again if they hadn't been closing.'

'Same here,' agreed Arthur.

Eustace managed to keep a straight face and lie, 'Yes. Where are we going now?'

Joan looked at him. 'I should think we're going back to the digs. She's making tea for six o'clock. So we'd better get a move on and catch a tram. You look ill, are you alright? You never could stomach these fairground rides.'

Eustace, who by then was back on good form again, told her that he was fine and that he was ready to go for the tram.

They got a double-decker outside the pleasure beach, which was going to Thornton Cleveleys, so they travelled all the way on the one tram and after a short walk from the stop at Uncle

Tom's Cabin. They arrived at where a delicious smell greeted them.

'Now then, tea's just about ready. As soon as you've freshened up, I'll serve it.'

They were greeted with a warm smile and an even warmer house, which was cheerfully decorated. In fact they all felt right at home.

They all had a quick wash. The rooms all had wash basins with hot and cold running water. At least, the ladies enjoyed their wash; the men were forced into it.

They took their places in the dining room and were served up a giant plate of cold boiled ham, scrambled eggs and chips. There was plenty of tea to drink and lashings of bread and butter.

'This really does look good,' said Joan.

'It doesn't taste too bad either,' Willie mumbled through a full mouth. He had been warned several times by Thelma that he had to be on his best behavior and that his table manners had to be impeccable. So as the meal progressed, and despite an ever increasing build up of pressure within, he retained his composure and did not release one rude noise of any sort.

Thelma was carefully trying to count the slices of boiled ham, without arousing suspicion as she was of the opinion that Cynthia and Fred Dobbs were also dining on cold ham, scrambled egg and chips that they hadn't paid for. But despite her best endeavors, she could not sort it out properly so she gave up trying. Anyway they had a good plateful each, so why worry.

'Special treats for afters,' said Cynthia as she cleared away the dirty pots and Fred walked in carrying a dish that looked suspiciously like trifle.

'I didn't bring a trifle,' said Thelma.

'Well actually you did. You brought a sponge cake, a tin of fruit, some custard powder and some milk. So I made a trifle and there's enough cake left for your supper. Sorry I've no cream, you just can't get it in Blackpool.'

They enjoyed the trifle, they completely drained the teapot, and then all but Willie went to sit in the lounge. Willie, in order not to engage Thelma's wrath, went out through the front door and let forth from every orifice in every direction. He felt much better for it, but a little old lady who just happened to have been passing at the time didn't.

'What are we doing for the rest of the day?' Jess enquired of the assembled throng.

'Let's go up to Uncle Tom's Cabin for a drink and take it from there. It's half past seven. By the time we get there it'll be eight and by the time we've had a couple of drinks it'll be bedtime.'

So they paraded up the road to Uncle Tom's Cabin, where they sampled a couple of rounds of the local brew, then sauntered back to supper and bed.

*

They were all down early for Sunday breakfast, the cooking aroma of which had reached the bedrooms. It was served by the smiling pair of Cynthia and Fred.

'Sunday lunch at one sharp,' she told them.

'Super,' said Thelma. 'Train's at four, so we'll be in nice time. Where are we going this morning folks?'

'Why don't we set off in the other direction toward Bispham and then we can get a tram back when we've had enough.'

There being no objection that is just what they did. They set off walking towards Uncle Tom's Cabin, then away along the cliff tops towards Bispham where they found a nice little café open to partake of a cup of coffee. They then set off further along the cliff towards Cleveleys, but took the tram back to their lodgings from Norbreck to arrive just in time for lunch.

Stephen Bailey

After they had eaten, came a doze in the lounge, then the tram back to North Station for the train back home.

They struggled with their luggage up the street, onto the tram, off the tram, into the station and onto the train, where they sat back in the comfortable seats as it pulled out dead on time.

'A right good weekend,' said Thelma and those that were still awake mumbled their agreement.

They alighted at Grolsby and put their suitcases in a heap on the platform. 'Where's the porter?' asked Willie.

'Not in evidence,' replied Arthur, 'we'd best carry our own bags. We'd have had to anyway, the porter wouldn't.'

They struggled up and over the footbridge and were walking out through the booking hall when a voice without a body stopped them.

'Let you back from Lancashire have they now? Didn't keep you then? Wouldn't want to if I know anything.' The station master's office door opened and the smiling face of Evans appeared accompanied by the rest of his body. 'Sorry I couldn't carry your bags but I was just too busy.'

'Doing what?' enquired Willie.

'None of your business, boyo. Station Master's things. But just for the record, this and that. Had a good weekend?'

'Super thanks,' said Eustace.

Evans stared at him. 'Good, good. Well now, don't let me keep you. Last train that was and I'm for my home now.'

The Baxters and Ollerenshaws returned to their cold empty houses and the Arkenthwaites to there warm cottage to tell the children all about the weekend, to ask the youngsters about theirs and to give them the sticks of Blackpool rock that they had bought for them.

111

CHAPTER 7

The big, roaring fire made the terrible three feel good and warm as they arrived at the club on Tuesday evening.

'You didn't stop then?'

'No.'

'Pity. Mind, you'll be ready for a decent pint I expect?'

'The beer wasn't that bad. In fact the South Shore bitter was better than anything that you've got to offer.'

'South Shore bitter? Never heard of it.'

'It's a local brew, served only to those of us with a discerning palette.'

'And that'll be you three then, I expect.'

'Oh yes, very much so. When you're well in with the locals it's no problem.'

Harry pulled three pints and another for himself. Then he carried them over to the corner table by the fire which was their usual perch. There being no other customers in the club, Harry sat down with them. He sat there in eager anticipation until his inquisitiveness could hold him no longer.

The other three, on the other hand, being aware of why Harry was sitting there, just sat in silence.

'Well come on then, tell us all about it.'

'Eustace was sick on the Big Dipper,' said Willie.

'Am I surprised? Is that all?'

'No. We've had a very good weekend. It was very cold, the digs were alright, we've found a good, posh restaurant for the trip luncheon and we've had a right good do,' replied Eustace. 'If it had been a lot warmer we might have stayed a while, but as it was, we came home.'

'What's all this posh bit about restaurant and luncheon?'

'The proprietors of the Golden Cockerel restaurant, Mr and Mrs Ken Proops and their more than delightful daughter, Susan, are going to organise our trip luncheon on Saturday the fourth of June at one precisely."

'Bit up market is it? Posh?'

'No, just very nice. In fact just right for a trip dinner.'

'Luncheon,' said Harry laughing.

'Anyway, down to business,' continued Eustace producing a scruffy pad and pencil from his jacket pocket. He put the pad on the table, took the pencil in hand, licked it with a flourish then looked around. 'Excuse me, Harry, but haven't you something else to be doing?'

'No. No. You're alright. There's nothing that won't wait. I'll just sit here and mind my own business.'

Arthur looked at Harry. 'May I just remind you that the trip is for employees of Murgatroyd's Mill only and not for interlopers, hangers on and those that'll make one when one's required.'

'But you might have a spare place.'

'Not a chance.'

'Well bugger it then.' He stormed off towards the bar, then stopped and turned. 'And you don't need to ask my advice when you're stuck. A trip expert, I am, a trip expert.'

Eustace carefully wrote the date at the top of the first piece of semi dirty paper. 'Now I've been thinking. We should write down the important parts of the trip to start with so that we know exactly what we have to talk about.'

'Breakfast,' said Willie.

'Oh yes. Breakfast. I had forgotten about breakfast.' So he put down:

1. BREAKFAST.

'Coach,' said Arthur.

'Yes we need a coach.' So he wrote:

2. COACH

Then he added:

3. LUNCH.

'I've put number three, lunch. But that's all arranged except I'll have to confirm it in writing. So what else?'

Arthur brought his superior knowledge of such matters into play. 'There's not a lot more. Just who's going? And how much will it cost? And oh yes, how do we collect the money.'

So Eustace added to his list:

4. WHO'S GOING?

5. HOW MUCH WILL IT COST?

6. HOW TO COLLECT THE MONEY?

'Right. So, let's get back to number one. Breakfast.'

'Fox and Grapes,' said Willie. 'Best trip breakfast this side Watford Gap. Sensible prices, big portions, full house every time. You just can't beat it.'

'Yes, I have to agree, although it's a long time since I sampled it. Its reputation goes before it; most certainly it goes on hearsay as excellent value. You get your fruit juice, porridge, a full fry up that they pass around on big plates so that you can help yourself, toast, jam, marmalade, tea and coffee. Bar's not open, but you don't want it for breakfast. Yes, it gets my vote. Mind you, there is a downside to it though, the landlady does not always conduct herself in a ladylike manner and that we can do without. However, weighing one against the other, the food wins every time.'

Arthur sat back and took a long swallow of ale.

'What is the unladylike manner of her conduct?' enquired Eustace.

'She's permanently pissed out of her mind,' shouted Harry who had been ear wigging from behind the bar. 'She gets up like that and goes back to bed in the same state.'

'Yes, well, I knew that. I thought that maybe there was something else.'

Arthur turned in his chair to look at the bar. 'Excuse me steward, if we have any more interference from outside sources, I shall have to recommend an adjournment of this meeting to other, more suitable licensed premises.'

Harry stared at him for a while. 'See if I care,' he said and turned away.

Arthur turned back to the table and was about to suggest a move when he was beaten to it by Willie. 'Come on, let's go to the Fox and Grapes.'

'Yes, I agree,' said Arthur.

'Me too,' said Eustace. 'Its years since I was in the Fox.'

So, to the background noise of Fat Harry, bleating, pleading and threatening for them to stay, they quietly left with the information that the beer was always warm at the Fox and Grapes ringing in their ears.

*

They were greeted by a totally different scene to the empty and desolate club they had just left. The pub was warm, it was full, it was bustling, there was nowhere to sit and there were five people serving. The interior was bright, there was a darts match in progress in one corner, a one armed bandit in another, a juke box and the whole place had a right good atmosphere.

'So she's let you out then has she, Eustace Ollerenshaw?'

Eustace spun around to observe a short, thin lady of undeterminable years, sitting on a bar stool leaning on the bar, a glass of gin in one hand and a smouldering cigarette in the other. Her faded, grey twin set and red skirt were fitted awkwardly to her body, she was wearing worn out slippers, her hair looked as if it had been dragged through a hedge backwards and her teeth were yellow, broken, missing or just fangs.

Eustace stared at this ugly apparition before asking, 'Do I know you?'

Arthur and Willie were crowded up behind him, nudging and winking at each other.

'He hasn't recognised her yet,' said Arthur.

'He'll not need to, she's recognised him.'

'Don't you know me? Don't you? I thought you might have married me once over, but that was years ago. Have you forgotten how you used to carry my school books for me? Mind you, from the look of how things have turned out, I've had a lucky escape.'

Eustace was dumbstruck. He stared at the lady, although he was sure she was no lady in the literal sense. Finally he spoke quietly to himself, telling himself to hold firm and deal with the situation in a proper manner. Then he said. 'The feeling is mutual. Is it Rosie? Rosie May Smithson?' He looked at her again. 'It is, isn't it? My word you've…'

'What?'

'Err, certainly changed. You were always plump, now you're thin. So anyway, what are you doing here?'

'I'm the landlady. Rosie May Whiteside. I live here. Wife of Freddy Whiteside.' With a smile on her face, she uncrossed her legs, loudly let one go and crossed them again. She then slurped a drink, belched and took a long, long drag on her cigarette.

'I think I'm the one that's had the lucky escape.' Eustace turned to Willie and Arthur who were in stitches of laughter behind him. He had sensed their amusement at his embarrassment and he began to scold them, but this only made them laugh more than ever. Finally, Eustace, who was not blessed with the best sense of humour, cottoned on and began to laugh with them.

Rosie May, as she was known to all and sundry, was not amused by the outburst of laughter at her expense by the terrible three, but even she eventually began to see the funny side of things and joined in with the laughter.

When it had all calmed down again, Willie said, 'Well are we having a pint or not?'

'Three pints is it then?' she asked them.

'Aye. Three pints of your cheapest, we're used to club prices.'

'Yes, that fact had not passed unnoticed,' said Freddy Whiteside who had quietly crept up behind them.

'Hello Freddy,' chorused all three of them together.

'Hello Willie. Hello Arthur. Hello Eustace. How's it going? Long time no see. What brings you around here and may I say whatever it is you've come to the right place. There's nothing in the line of victuallary that we can't do here. So what will it be? Or have you just come for the benefit of your health? A change of scenery? Or, is it as it is rumoured, that the club is becoming a right miserable dump to visit of an evening, almost empty most of the time, the ale flat and warm and the steward being a right fat, horrible slob, who's only words are to insult his regulars, resulting in no regulars.'

During this homily he had been pulling three pints which he presented to his three customers in exchange for their money, as their reputation for not paying, if possible, preceded them.

Much to Freddy's amazement, Eustace took up the reins. 'Well yes, and there again no, don't know and pass.'

Rosie May's thoughts were that she really had had a lucky escape.

Eustace continued, 'We have come specifically to enquire about a trip breakfast.'

'When?' He was quick off the mark.

'Fourth of June.'

'Don't think it's a problem. In fact, I'm sure its not, but we'd better ask the social secretary.' He turned and bellowed to Rosie May who was now sitting at the other end of the long bar. 'Rosie, can we do a trip breakfast on the fourth of June?'

She half fell, half slithered from the stool she was occupying, and tottered away into the back. She was not long in returning, nor in adding to Eustace's embarrassment, as she stood at the side of him put her arm around his waist, squeezed him and then fondled his bottom.

'It's no problem, my love,' she said, looking into Eustace's eyes. 'We've no bookings that day, so we can book you in.' She continued to play with his bottom.

Eustace became a gibbering wreck and couldn't answer her.

Arthur, observing the unfolding situation decided that he had better take over. 'Yes, err, provisionally. What's the exact form?'

'Where's the trip to?' asked Freddy

'Blackpool.'

'You got a dinner booked?'

'Yes.'

'What time and where?'

'Half past twelve. Golden Cockerel Restaurant.'

'Very nice. Yes, very nice. Good café that is, you'll get a good meal. So if it's half past twelve, you'll need to be here at eight sharp. Rosie, put Eustace down, there's a good girl, you don't know where he's been. Now then, you'll be wanting the full works, how many for?'

'Forty eight.'

'Plus driver?' Rosie May enquired.

'Yes.'

'Are you having Bewdlay's coaches?'

'Not decided yet. We've not got so far.'

'Well, if you are, insist on not having Norris Oakes to drive.'

'Why?'

'He has the manners of a pig, gets drunk, and gets lost, just to mention a few points, and they always send him.'

Eustace, having been released by Rosie May having on her husband's insistence, began to take an interest in the proceedings again. 'Where have we got to, Willie?'

Willie laughed at him. 'Well, we've just booked the breakfast.'

'Here, I thought I was doing all the booking and organising.'

'Yes, you are, but you were playing with an old flame at the time, your childhood sweetheart if I remember rightly, a right dashing young thing.'

'Shut up.'

'Yes I will, I'll just sit here quietly and enjoy my pint. You get on with your trip organising.' He went over to chat with Rosie May in the hope that she might play with him.

Eustace returned his attention to the conversation between Arthur and Freddy at which Freddy was still berating Norris Oakes.

'Eustace,' said Freddy. 'No playing with Rosie May on the fourth of June, the early morning thereof, she'll be too busy and won't have time to attend to your every little personal requirement.'

'Right oh, Freddy. Yes. Thank you. Now where have we got to?'

'Well, we're just about finished. We've booked the breakfast, we've been warned off Norris Oakes driving the coach, there's no playing with Rosie May and that's it.'

'Have you finished the menu?' asked Eustace.

'Menu!' shouted Freddy. 'Menu! You're having one of our internationally recognised trip breakfasts. There's no menu. You'll have what you're given and like it. I don't discuss menus for trip breakfasts. They're good, wholesome and market fresh meals that will set you up for the rest of the day, or if you're a bad traveler, not, as the case may be. However you can be assured of a first rate do at a very economical figure.'

'What might that figure be If I may be so bold as to enquire?' asked Eustace.

Freddy tapped the side of his nose. 'Don't worry about a thing. Mr Baxter and I have sorted it out already.'

'Yes, but...'

'There is no yes but. The matter is resolved, completed, booked, done and dealt with. You should have paid attention instead of attending to your extramarital activities.'

Eustace was embarrassed, annoyed, upset and getting into a state again. Fortunately Arthur recognised the signs and took him to sit down, leaving Willie leaning heavily on Rosie May.

'Now listen. There's absolutely no problem. To start with there's no menu, they only do one trip breakfast and it's always the same. Fruit Juice and porridge. Then bacon, tomato, mushrooms, fried eggs, fried bread, black pudding, beans and potatoes. To finish jam, marmalade, toast, tea and coffee. It's always the same, a right good do. Now as far as charges go, they charge half a crown a head and throw one in for the driver. So that's all arranged. So now, with half a crown here and four bob for the lunch, we've got up to six and sixpence a head, so all we need to do is to get a coach organised and we're on our way. I think you should sort out the coach. We'll leave you to it, there'll be no Rosie May to distract you at Bewdlay's.'

'Time for another pint, I think. We're not going back to the club again tonight are we?' asked Eustace.

'No. I think that Fat Harry can keep his own company this once; he's a waste of space at the best of times. Apart from that he can't keep a civil tongue in his head and anyway it looks like we might have problems getting Willie away from here.'

But they had no problem at all, for as it happened three or four times every night, Freddy toddled along and separated Rosie May from whichever man she might have her hands into at that particular time.

They sat around the table and played a few hands of dominoes before retiring home at a sensible hour, well satisfied with having booked the trip breakfast.

*

On Saturday morning, Eustace was up and about early as he had made up his mind that today was the day to organise the coach. One thing in his favour was that he knew Joseph Bewdlay quite well as he was a very distant relation of Joan.

He prepared breakfast, lit the living room fire and was ready to eat when Joan appeared, a vision of loveliness in her curlers, hair net and dressing gown.

'Now don't forget to send our best wishes to Joseph and the family will you?' she asked Eustace.

'Certainly not, my dear. Your every wish is my command.'

She gave him a withering look.

It was a bitterly cold day and Eustace was very well wrapped up when he set off on the short walk through the village to Bewdlay's Transportation Company Limited. No Journey too far. It is our pleasure to serve you.

Eustace approached the area described as a forecourt with his heart in his mouth. He observed a set of broken down buildings, three rusty petrol pumps, a forecourt constructed from well squashed rubble and the proprietor himself applying hot liquid tar to the underside of a coach with a long handled brush. It had been a long time since Eustace had been past the garage and so he took a closer look at it. The windows were either dirty, cracked or non existent, the window frames appeared to be rotten, the roof felt was flapping in the wind and the front had been painted, once, sometime before the war. Various parts of old vehicles littered the sides and back of the premises; there were cars, vans, wagons and coaches, all ready for the scrap yard.

The business supported six coaches, a similar number of vans and wagons and two taxis, well known in the village as limousines, although like the rest of the stock they were on their last legs and destined soon to join the great junk yard in the sky.

Eustace walked up to Joseph. 'Now then, Joseph.'

'Joseph jumped up, turned around, looked at Eustace and enquired, 'Who's died?'

'No. No, it's nothing like that. In fact Joan sends her best wishes to you and the family. No, I come on a far more important errand.'

'What?' enquired Joseph somewhat startled.

'I want to talk about a coach for a trip.'

'Where to? When? Come in. Hang on a minute, let me just put on a bit more weatherproofing; it'll only take a few seconds.

Anyway what are you doing organising a coach for a trip? The last time I saw you you were under the thumb and not allowed to express your own opinion. In fact a right...'

Eustace had heard enough and cut him short. 'You are now dealing with the new Eustace Ollerenshaw. Never before seen down this street, but nevertheless a much happier and far more articulate fellow than the one you were used to dealing with. So I am here as the official representative of Murgatroyd's Mill Trip Committee and I have come here to explore the possibilities of hiring a forty eight seater coach for a trip to Blackpool on Saturday the fourth of June.' He took a deep breath and watched carefully for Joseph's reaction.

Joseph, being a true Yorkshireman, did not have any reaction; he just took the new Eustace in his stride, much to Eustace's annoyance.

'Well that shouldn't be a big problem at all. We've a brand new fifty seater coach arriving in March, especially for the summer season and you'll be able to have that.'

'You're going to garage it in this, err, dump?' enquired an incredulous Eustace.

'It's weatherproof.'

'On a hot, sunny midsummer's day,' observed Eustace.

'Yes almost. Anyway, come along in and I'll put the kettle on.'

They entered the general office, or so it said on the door.

There was a desk piled high with papers of all descriptions, four very rickety chairs, a half dim with dirt light in the middle of the ceiling and a piece of wallpaper that had peeled from the ceiling downwards, and was resting on the desk ready for Joseph to add notes to the dozens that were already there.

'Sugar?' Joseph enquired.

'Is it tea?'

'Yes.'

'Please. So what is the new coach?'

'It's a Bedford. Fifty seats, all with arm rests and ash trays. Individual light above each seat, plush upholstery, heating and pull down curtains around the driver to keep out the light at night and what about this one, a pre-selector gearbox.'

'Marvelous. Absolutely fantastic.' Eustace didn't want to show his ignorance of matters mechanical, so he just applauded them. 'A good cup of tea is this, Joseph.'

'Yes I pride myself in brewing a good cup of tea. You see the secret's in boiling the water with gas. It's far hotter than electric and brings out the flavour better.'

'Eustace nodded in disbelief.'

'So you're off to Blackpool?'

'Yes. Fourth of June. We need the coach at the Fox and Grapes at nine o'clock prompt.'

'You're having breakfast to start then?'

'Yes.'

'Where's the dinner then?'

'Lunch is at the Golden Cockerel Restaurant at twelve thirty.'

'On the Golden Mile. I know it well. I think I might drive you myself; I might as well make a day of it. I know all the lads at the mill and I would much rather drive my own new coach than leave it too those morons that drive for me.'

'Well, we have been advised to refuse Norris Oakes.'

'Oh aye. Who's advised you?'

'I am not allowed to disclose my sources.'

By gum, we do have a new Eustace here, thought Joseph to himself. 'Well anyway it's of no consequence. Norris Oakes is not, and I repeat not, touching my new coach. He's unreliable and he gets lost. Mind you, he does know the way to Blackpool.'

'Bit of a problem is he?'

'Aye you could say that, more of a bloody nuisance. I only use him as a part time driver when I'm getting desperate.

Anyway, you've no need to worry on that score; he's definitely not touching my new coach.'

*

On occasional occasions, Saturday fell as the sixth day of the week, and this particular Saturday was one of those that the terrible three met at the Grolsby Working Mens club Affiliated for a pre-lunch aperitif.

'Mine's a pint.'

'So's mine.'

'I'll have half.'

Three pairs of eyes, including those of the club steward, turned to look at Eustace.

'You'll have what?' Three voices shouted in unison.

'You'll not, you'll have a pint and like it, like what you always do,' snarled the steward.

'Who's paying?' asked Eustace.

'You are,' replied Willie quickly.

'Then I'll have a half. I don't need a pint right now, not before a good hot dinner at home.'

'Your Joan cooking for you? On a Saturday dinner time? At home?' asked an incredulous steward.

'But of course. It'll be bacon, cabbage and mash, with loads of bacon dripping on the mash and loads of seasoning on the cabbage. I'm fair looking forward to it.'

'No pudding?' asked Fat Harry.

Arthur leaned over and whispered in Willie's ear. 'Bet I know what The Fat one's next question will be.'

'What?'

'Wait and listen.'

Eustace continued, 'Yes. Oh yes. Apple Charlotte and custard. Makes a very good Charlotte does my Joan, now that she's started cooking proper like again.'

Harry began again. 'Would there be, er, that is er, do you think er, well let's put it this way er, would it like be a possibility err, err…'

'Oh for heaven's sake, Eustace, ask the big fat ugly brute for his dinner and put him out of his misery,' said Arthur.

'That's what it was all about is it?' said Willie laughing.

Harry coloured up and clammed up, but then added, 'Not so much of the brute if you don't mind.'

'Sorry Harry old fruit, she'll only have cooked enough for two of us. Now if you'd ordered in advance… But apart from that, we'll not have time for visitors today, I've to take her shopping when dinner's finished.'

'Where to?'

'The big town, not that it's any of your business.'

'Not going to the match then?'

'There isn't one. They're playing down south today, away.'

'Oh yes, in the excitement I'd forgotten and there was me all ready to go with you. I was just fancying something better than my meat paste sandwiches for my dinner.'

'That's about all I'll be having,' said Arthur.

'And what will you be doing this afternoon then?' enquired Harry

'Sleeping some of the time and then no doubt my dearly beloved will find me a list of chores to do.'

Harry laughed at Arthur, but then thought that maybe it might just be better to be married and to have someone to give out a list of chores rather than live a miserable existence on your own.

'No need to tell me what you'll be doing, Arkenthwaite. Big dinner, then pigeons, then gardening, playing with the kids followed by a big cooked tea and then sit listening to the radio in front of a big roaring fire with your Thelma.'

'That's just about hit the nail on the head, Harry old fruit. Sausage, beans and chips and a pudding for dinner. I don't know what's for tea. Anyway, what about you Harry, what will you be getting up to?'

'Nothing more than the usual boring routine. When you lot have gone for your dinners, there'll be no more than a handful of bloody miserable, bloody ignorant, bloody useless, bloody no good, bloody human bloody beings who sup one pint a session and stop here till I throw them out because they've no bloody homes to go to, or so it bloody well seems. So I'll have my more than delicious sandwiches and at the same time listen to the radio. Then I'll shut up the club, go home, fall asleep, have some fish and chips, come back here, open up, and if you lot are not coming in, spend all night looking at a load of bloody miserable, bloody ignorant, bloody useless, bloody tight fisted, bloody no good, bloody apologies for bloody human bloody beings. Then at eleven o'clock, I'll shut up the club, I'll go home to no welcoming wife and a cold unwelcoming house. Life's a bugger... Can I come on the trip?'

'No,' said three voices in harmony.

'You see what I mean. Even you three are against me.'

'No we're not. It's the system.'

'What bloody system?' roared Harry.

'The trip is only for Murgatroyd's employees.'

'Well if you get short of takers, you will let me know, won't you?'

'You will be the first to be informed,' said Arthur.

'Hey up, it's nearly a quarter past twelve,' said Eustace. 'My bacon will be almost ready. It's time for home.'

'Same for me,' said two more voices.

'That's right. Leave me here to the tender mercy of the other bloody morons.'

'Aye, we will that,' said Willie.

And they did.

As they were walking towards their respective homes, Arthur put forward the idea that they should put Harry out of his misery and try to find him a lady friend. It was generally agreed that it was a good idea but none of them could find a suitable candidate there and then.

'I'll ask Thelma if she knows anyone,' volunteered Willie.

'Joan will never, ever talk about anything like that,' added Eustace.

'Jess'll kill me just for mentioning it,' said Arthur.

Nevertheless they all three did mention it over dinner.

*

Eustace took the bull by the horns and asked Joan if she knew anyone. Very unexpectedly she replied, 'Well, you know at the bottom of Moses Street, that cottage which always has the nice flowers in summer…'

'Yes I know the one. That jolly fat woman lives there.' Eustace could not believe what he was hearing.

'Yes, Mrs Peace. I sometimes meet and chat with her at the knitting circle and I know she'd love to have a man in her life again. Her husband was killed in the war, she's no children to get in the way and she'd be a right good match for Harry.'

'How well do you know her?' this was too good to be true, here they were discussing important issues where before Christmas she would have smacked him for even thinking about mentioning the subject.

'Well enough,' replied Joan with a twinkle in her eye.

Eustace was beginning to fall in love again with the girl he fell in love with once before.

'That's all very well, but if she's a nice lady, how's she going to put up with a big, fat, foul mouthed idiot like Harry?'

'That'd be for her to worry about and for us not to know once we'd made the introduction.'

Eustace was beginning to realise that there was more to his Joan than he had forgotten about and he wondered if she would actually do something about the matchmaking.

'When is the next Saturday night social at the club?' she asked. 'I'd right like us to go anyhow.'

'First Saturday in the month. That's in three weeks.'

'We'll go. Get the others to come along too.'

*

Arthur didn't take the direct route. 'We've had a nice drink at the club, Willie and Eustace and me. It wasn't very busy; in fact it was very quiet. We were talking with Fat Harry and he was moaning that he was fed up with life in general and particularly with living on his own. In fact, he said he could really like to find a wife and so after we left the club we decided we ought to help him but we don't know where to start. Have you any suggestions?'

He sat in fear and trepidation of the icy blast to come. Instead he was gobsmacked when she said.

'Yes.'

'Yes?'

'Yes. I just said so.'

'Who?'

'Your sister.'

'My sister? Amelia? For Fat Harry? Nay! Never! You can't even begin to... Well! Well, I never did. I would never have thought... Not Amelia.' He sat back in awe of the recently presented situation.

'Why not? She's not married. Never has been. Not exactly a cover model, I grant you, but she's on the shelf and a bit of rough in the form of Harry won't do her any harm at all.'

Arthur just sat dumbfounded staring at Jess, so she continued, 'When's the next social evening at the club?' She was eager now. She'd been trying to get Arthur's sister coupled to someone, anyone, for years and Fat Harry had never before entered her thought processes. But here was an opportunity that she wasn't going to miss under any circumstances.

Stephen Bailey

'In about three weeks. First Saturday in the month.'
'We'll go. Get Eustace and Willie to come as well.'

*

'Willie took a more leisurely approach. He was well into a big, round sausage when he announced to the table in general, 'The big fat one's looking for a wife.'

'Harry?' asked Thelma.

'Yes.'

'So what do you want me to do about it?'

'Find somebody to fit the bill. It doesn't matter who, how or what, but just find somebody.'

'Well I don't know who right now, but I will give it a coat of thinking about. Why don't you ask Martha on Monday?'

'Will she know?' he asked.

'Well she'll know a darned sight better than me. Anyway I'll think about it. Has he asked you to find him a wife?'

'No, but he was moaning on so much about going home to an empty house and that he was lonely, that we decided that we should help the matter along a little if we could and find him a wife…or try to.'

'Have the other two gone home to ask the same question?'

'No, they daren't. You know what a prude Jess is and I don't think that Eustace dare test the atmosphere for that just yet.'

'I know what you mean,' said Thelma.

Josie, Willie and Thelma's daughter listened, but kept her own counsel. She had ideas on the subject but she knew they would only be cross with her for getting involved in something that was for grown ups and not for young teenagers.

*

They had only just started in the dye house at Murgatroyd's Mill on Monday morning when Arthur broached the subject. 'Have you found anyone for Harry, Willie?'

'No, not yet.'

'I have.'

'You have?' asked Willie doubtfully.

'Yes. My sister Amelia. Jess suggested her. She's been on the shelf for years and it would be a right good do to get her wed off, and anyway she'd be just right for Harry even if she is a couple of years older than him. I wonder I didn't think of it myself before now.'

Add another ten years, thought Willie, a face that's just right for a Toby Jug model, the biggest arse in the western world and to cap it all a right bundle of misery.

'Anyway,' continued Arthur, 'Jess thought we should all three couples go to the next club social night, a fortnight on Saturday, and take Amelia with us to introduce her to Harry.'

'Yes. Yes a very good idea. I'll mention it to Thelma.'

Willie was as usual first in the canteen at dinner time. Greasy Martha was waiting to serve him and the rest of the workforce. She was, as usual, smoking and serving at the same time with the cigarette hidden out of sight of her customers. Instead of the usual exchange of pleasantries, Willie explained the situation to her and Martha said she'd think about it adding that there were bound to be a few likely candidates if she could just sort them out.

When Eustace arrived with his plate of dinner, Willie was almost finished. Just a couple of mouthfuls, a lick of his plate and he'd be clear.

'Guess what,' said Eustace.

'What?' asked Arthur.

'Joan says that Cybil Peace is just right for Harry. She's a war widow and available and looking for a man. Joan says we've got to take her to the next club social night and you two with your wives have to come as well.'

'Great minds think alike,' said Arthur. 'We've just come to the same conclusion about my sister Amelia and Jess thought we should all go to the club social.'

'This is going to be good,' said Willie. 'It only needs my Thelma to come up with a candidate and it'll be four in a bed. So are we going or what?'

'Wouldn't miss this for the world.'

'Me neither.'

'Ok. We'll get the tickets at the club tonight.'

*

When Willie arrived home, Thelma said, 'Our Josie was listening to yesterday's conversation and she thinks that Mrs Bryce, her maths teacher, and a middle aged widow would fit the bill for a companion for Harry.'

'How the hell does she know? She's only a young lass.'

'Don't underestimate your own daughter. She's got her head screwed on.'

Willie looked at Thelma. 'Who's going to ask her and how can we broach the subject? We don't even know the woman.'

'Don't worry, Josie's already done it for you. Her and her friend Margaret are coming to the social and bringing Mrs Bryce with them.'

'They can't. They're too young.'

'Not to go to the social, and anyway it's all arranged. So you just get the tickets.'

*

They arrived at the club at half past eight to go finely over the trip details.

'Usual is it?' the fat one enquired in his well known miserable tones.

'No. One pint and three tickets for the social evening, please.'

'What's with the please? You expecting company?' asked Harry.

'Jess instructed me to ask nicely, and no, you are.'

'Eh?'

'The club is you daft halfporth.'

'Oh aye. Who you bringing then?' he asked hopefully.

'That's for me to know and for you to wonder about.'

Harry dispensed the ale, presented the tickets and took the money. 'Eustace?'

'Same as Arthur please.'

'Is there some sort of conspiracy here? First, you are all polite, then it's very rare any of you lot come to a social, but even rarer for you to have guests.'

'It's just circumstantial, Harry. Joan has invited a friend.'

'I hope these are free, loose, good looking women,' said Harry. 'I could certainly do with one.'

'You will find out on the night.'

Finally it came to Willie's turn. 'One pint of your most magnificent ale and…'

'Yes. Yes. Go on,' cried Harry, by now in a euphoric state in view of the prospect of a club full of available women.

'Five tickets for the social.'

'Five?' asked Arthur.

'You said there was only you and Thelma coming,' said Eustace.

'Yes five and don't ask.'

Harry was by this time over the moon. 'Just confirm that some of these will be ladies.'

'Yes. Thelma, our Josie, and her two school friends. So you can keep your great big mauling claws off.'

'I only asked,' said a once again despondent Harry.

132

The three friends sat at a table away from the bar and put their heads together so that Harry could not hear the conversation.

'Where's the five tickets come from then?' They enquired.

'It's like I said, it's our Josie. She heard me asking Thelma about finding a suitable lass, so she does no more than go and invite her maths teacher who's a widow and she says is very nice. Thelma and me have never met the woman so we don't know what we're dealing with.'

'Has your Josie told her what it's all about?'

'Haven't got the foggiest. We'll find out on the night.'

Harry watched the three friends with their heads together in deep conversation and told himself, 'They're up to something those three are. Yes definitely up to no good.'

'Another round?' asked Eustace.

'Yes,' said Willie, 'I'm ready. Summon the steward.'

Eustace gave Harry a sign which in one movement summoned him to their table and at the same time told him to go away.

Harry ambled over.

'Three pints please, Harry.'

'There was no need to give me a sign like that.'

'I was ordering three pints. Pity you couldn't understand it.'

'Bloody funny way of counting,' he ambled his way back to the bar.

'Now about the trip,' said Eustace.

'We are all ears, my dear boy.'

Eustace continued, 'We've got the coach, the breakfast and the lunch sorted out and confirmed. Now all we need is the names and numbers of those that are going.'

'I'll put a notice on the canteen wall,' said Willie.

'They'll not let you,' said Arthur

'Oh yes they will. I've made arrangements already.'

'Who with?'

'Mr Anthony.'

'And he said yes?'

'Yes, of course he did. I'm well in there, you know. Don't forget that my Thelma cleans for Margaret Murgatroyd'

'Who's going to write the notice?' asked Arthur.

'Oh, I'll get our Josie to do it. She's got loads of coloured pencils at home and a ruler. She's very artistic. I'll tell her what to put and the she'll make it look good.'

Harry had by this time returned with the three pints and his curiosity was getting the better of him. 'Who's this that's going to make what look good?'

Three pairs of eyed stared at him.

'What the hell has it got to do with you?' Willie growled in his best growling voice.

'Nothing. Nothing at all.'

'Well keep your long nose out of our affairs in future.'

Harry shuffled back to the bar, telling himself, 'They're up to something those three. They are.'

*

'Willie.'

'Yes Martha.' It was dinner time the next day in the canteen at Murgatroyd's.

'I've got a candidate for Fat Harry.'

'Who?'

'Bessie Griggs.'

'Bessie Griggs?'

'Yes, Bessie Griggs. Hector and me'll bring her if you can get us some tickets. It's a long time since we went to a do.'

'Well you and your Hector are very welcome, but, Bessie Griggs. It's unbelievable. She's big.'

'Yes.'

'Fat.'

'Yes.'

'Ugly.'

'Yes.'

'And Dozy.'

'By gum you know your local women, Willie.'

'But she's a dead ringer for Harry, because she's big, fat ugly and dozy.'

'Yes, that's right,' agreed Martha.

'Well this is a turn up for the books. It's now going to be five in a bed. What are we going to do with all these spare women?'

Martha looked at him. 'You'll have to move on, Willie, the queue's getting restless and ugly.' But before she served them she just found time to dodge behind the partition where no one could see her and empty the contents of her nasal passages into the bottom corner of her pinafore.

Willie took his dinner over to the corner table, sat down and began to trough. It wasn't long before he was joined by Arthur and Eustace, who also began to eat their food.

'Well we've got four women for Harry now.'

'Four?' asked Arthur

'Yes, Four. Martha and Hector are bringing along Bessie Griggs.'

'Bessie Griggs?'

'Yes. You heard right first time, Bessie Griggs.'

'Well you can take me to our house. It's unbelievable. It's gross. What the hell are we going to do with a lump like her?'

'I don't know,' said Willie. 'But one thing's for sure, we are heading for a major crisis. Four loose women and only one loose man. What will we do?'

That evening at the club, Willie ordered three more tickets for the social evening. Harry again enquired as to who they might be for and again was told to keep his nose out. He was thereafter even more convinced that the terrible three were up to no good but he could not for the life in him figure out what.

Willie returned to the bar later. 'By the way Harry, we'll need a table for fourteen.'

'You haven't a hope in hell. You know the situation as well as I do.'

'Just see to it. There's a good fellow.'

For two and a half weeks, Harry made himself quite ill trying to figure out what was going on.

CHAPTER 8

Club social Saturday dawned bright, fair and moderately warm, allowing the participants to dress in a more relaxed manner than if the weather had been very cold.

The four men, for instance, still put their best suits on but managed without overcoats. The ladies all wore dresses, but just put cardigans over. The two young girls were very excited at getting dressed up to attend their first grown up social occasion. The four contenders for Fat Harry's affections were going to great lengths to look their utmost best.

Arthur and Jess were the first to arrive at the club. They had called for his sister Amelia who had done the best she could to look glamorous. Even Arthur had been somewhat surprised at her when he had first seen her, but he had to admit to himself that no man worth his salt would give her a second glance. Jess was quite pleased with the result of Amelia's efforts and confided in her that she could get off with Harry if she tried hard enough.

Harry was like a cat on hot bricks, wondering who the terrible three were bringing to the social at his club that evening. He hoped they were going to arrive with the lady of his dreams and he put extra effort into his preparations for the occasion. He even applied a few extra drops of Brylcream to his hair, and trimmed both his nose and ear whiskers. But the biggest sacrifice to his preparations was to have a bath, even though it wasn't Christmas. Harry had eventually reasoned that they were all bringing spare ladies, just for him. He did have his secret helper, Alice Clarke, but she was only there to do some of his work in return for a small amount of pay, and an occasional good time in the manager's office. She was not however a refined lady for him to settle down with and so the anticipation was mounting as seven o'clock approached.

Arthur, Jess and Amelia walked up to the bar and exchanged pleasantries with Harry, who expertly served them, then ushered them to their table. He laughed and joked politely with them and even took an interest in Amelia, whom he had known for years, but there was no spark of interest on his part, for Amelia was plain, very plain in fact. She had short grey hair and a big, pointed nose. Not Harry's ideal partner. So Amelia and Jess sat talking and looking miserable, whilst Arthur sat there wishing the others would arrive.

Martha, Hector and Bessie Griggs were next to arrive at the bar.

'Bloody hell! Bessie Griggs,' said the steward, forgetting himself for one moment.

'Hello you fat twat,' said Bessie, 'how're you going on?'

'All the better for seeing you. Haven't come across you in a while. When it's quietened down a bit, we must have a chat.'

Bessie could be, if nothing else, extremely crude, rude and horrible and very much on Harry's wavelength. He poured their drinks then, with a twinkle in his eye, he escorted them over to the large table he had specially prepared for them. After a lot of 'Hellos' and 'how dos' they all got introduced and sitting together. Harry helped Bessie to sit down then pushed her chair in and fussed around her for a while. Amelia observed this, but kept her own counsel.

Eustace and Joan appeared next with Cybil Peace. She was plump but very attractive and very neatly presented. She greeted Harry with a broad smile.

'Well I never did. Cybil Peace. How nice to see you. What are you going to have to drink?' Harry was politeness itself. He had known Cybil all his life, but not very well, and he had always admired her from a distance.

'I am very well, Harry, thank you, all the better for seeing you again. It is nice to come out to a social evening for a change. You look to be busy just now, but we must get together later.'

Once again, Harry poured the drinks, escorted them to their table and fussed over Cybil until she was settled.

Willie and Thelma along with Josie and Margaret were running late. Jenny Bryce had called at their cottage as she lived further away, but as Willie and Thelma had never met her, they stopped at home chatting before they left for the club.

Josie and Margaret had opened the door. 'Come in Mrs Bryce. This is my mum and dad.' They shook hands and invited her to sit down.

Willie observed a middle aged, very attractive, slim lady with a very nice figure, extremely well turned out and dripping in jewellery.

'Now, you'd all best call me Jenny for the social, though not at school, girls, next week, please.'

Thelma was very pleased that her daughter and friend had brought along a very presentable lady that they would be proud to take to the club.

When they did arrive at the club, Harry was gob smacked when he saw Jenny. All he could do was to keep saying, 'Gosh.' His heart was all a flutter and momentarily he was unable to get up and serve the Arkenthwaite contingent.

However, he managed to move his eyes from Jenny and got on with his official duty of pouring drinks for the members and guests. He had his usual temporary bar staff in place, as he always did for club social evenings, but he insisted on serving the terrible three and Horrible Hector himself because he knew that something was afoot.

Harry, was to say, the least a little bit dim, but even he had by now worked out that they had all four arrived with an unattached female and that could only be as a gift for him. Once again he poured the drinks then ushered them to the big table where he went to great lengths to make sure that Jenny Bryce was more than comfortable. The other three pairs of available eyes watched his every move without comment other than to themselves.

With the arrival of the Arkenthwaite family, the conversation around the table really kicked into gear. The four unattended ladies were introduced to each other and greeted one another politely but distantly. Amelia and Bessie knew each other quite well. They both had a passing acquaintance with Cybil, but none of them knew Jenny Bryce at all.

All in all, the party was going well. The two young ladies were permanently on the dance floor; dancing away none stop, with most of the other revelers sitting watching them. The other twelve around the table were talking one hundred to the dozen, finding it more than difficult to get a word in edge on.

The music was in full swing, in the form of the club record player, with the club MC who also put the records on after he had announced the next dance.

It came to the end of a waltz and the MC had a breather to have a drink and to prepare his record for the next dance. Most of the punters were now in and Harry, leaving his second in command temporary wench in charge, wandered over to the record player and whispered in the MC's ear. He then began a slow amble around the tables, having a laugh and a joke, hither and thither. He had decided that he would dance with each of the four ladies in the order that they had arrived at the club. This was just to try them all out, although he really didn't want to dance with Amelia as he found her repulsive. There again, he was not the type of chap to ignore her on purpose, and anyway, he had reasoned that if he did dance with her, the worst was out of the way first.

The MC announced, 'Ladies and Gentlemen, please take your partners for a quickstep. Harry dashed over to Amelia and asked her for a dance. She graciously accepted and with some difficulty they took their places. The tables were all around the outside of the floor, with the MC occupying a small raised podium by the bar.

Harry was an accomplished dancer, who, for his weight, was very light on his feet. Amelia on the other hand was very unaccomplished in the dance floor arts. Harry found the going almost impossible. *A bit like pushing a heavily loaded wheelbarrow across a stony building site,* he thought afterwards. Amelia was stiff, rigid, unbending and she shuffled her feet. She had no sense of rhythm or timing and, try as he might to talk to her, all he got was yes or no. In the end he gave over trying as a bad job and they were both relieved when the dance finished.

The MC, who was in on the act, realised that there was no future in this particular union having observed the difficulties that Harry was having and brought the dance to an early end by lifting the needle from the record and apologising to the dancers.

Harry escorted Amelia back to her seat, thanked her profusely and chatted to the others around the table.

Willie leaned over to Arthur who he was sitting next to and said, 'Well I think that'll be the end of that then.'

'Yes,' he replied glumly. He was wishing they hadn't brought her anyway because she was no fun to be out with.

Harry gave a pre-arranged signal to the MC, who then announced a foxtrot. Harry asked Bessie Griggs to dance. She jumped up, grabbed hold of him and virtually dragged him onto the dance floor. It took him a little while to get into her rhythm, but all in all, the dance went well. They enjoyed a good, humorous, if in parts crude, conversation as best they could for the noise of the music and they both thoroughly enjoyed the chat.

The other couples at the table all got up to dance for the first time, leaving the three ladies sitting looking at one another. Jenny Blyth asked Cybil Peace if she would like to dance. She said yes and away they went, Cybil playing the man.

Amelia sat bolt upright, stared at the dance floor, sipped her drink and looked very glum. She was fed up. She wasn't enjoying it and she really didn't know why she'd agreed to come to the social in the first place.

The dance finished, they all returned to their table and the men went to the bar for another round of drinks.

'Enjoying it Harry?' asked Eustace.

'Oh yes, by gum I am. I would like to thank you boys for bringing this bevy of beautiful maidens along. I can't wait to try out the next two.'

'How did you get along with our Amelia?' Arthur asked him.

'Do you want the polite answer or the truth?'

'The truth.'

'It was just like pushing a wheelbarrow with a rusty wheel, or trying to drive a camel across the Sahara Dessert. To add to that, she can't dance, she has absolutely no conversation and to crown all that she's very ugly.'

'I have to agree.' Arthur was more than annoyed with Amelia that she had not even tried to enter into the spirit of the evening.

'How about Bessie?' asked Horrible Hector.

'Oh, she's as right as rain, she is. No problem with her once we'd sorted out our feet. Good dance, good conversation, she can be just a little bit crude at times, but there again, aren't we all.'

They took the drinks back to the table just in time to hear the announcement for the Gay Gordons.

Harry dashed over to ask Cybil Peace, who shot straight out of her chair and went entwined with him onto the dance floor. She had been fancying him all night and she was going to ensure that she enjoyed what little time she had with him. They joined the big circle of dancers and away they went.

Harry and Cybil were both very good dancers, so they hit it off straight away and whirled around the floor. The conversation was not brilliant, for the obvious reason of not been able to communicate too well in the Gay Gordons. When they reached the table, Cybil whispered in Harry's ear that she hoped he'd come back for more, later.

Harry dashed away to the bar to make sure that his temporary staff were coping, then he walked over to the record player and asked the MC to announce the supper waltz. He then walked back over to the table and asked Jenny Bryce for the dance.

Jenny accepted graciously and they stepped out onto the floor. With Jenny, Harry had met his match. She was far more sophisticated than he was. She was prim, neat, very well turned out, bedecked with jewellery and her waltz steps were perfect. Her conversation was scintillating and left Harry stammering and grasping for answers. She soon realised that Harry was not the man for her and when the dance finished, she sat down relieved that it was over. Harry was similarly relieved that it was over. She was the most attractive lady for her age that he had seen in a long time, but he could not have coped with her prim and proper ways at all.

Harry had to go help serve the supper, the obligatory two sandwiches and two small buns each, it being pot luck who got what and who had made it. The quietness in the room with the MC having his break, allowed the punters to talk, and on the big table, talk they did.

'Now then, Mrs Bryce, are you enjoying yourself?' asked Josie.

'Oh yes, very much. I'm having a lovely evening. But not Harry, no, not him. He's not for me. But I am enjoying being here and thank you for asking me. Are you enjoying it girls?'

'Oh yes, we are thank you. We're learning to dance and most of it's not too difficult.'

'Tell you what, after supper, I'll give you both a lesson or two, shall I? I can dance the man's part as well as the lady's.'

'Oh thanks, Mrs Bryce. Dad. Mum. Mrs Bryce is going to give us both some dancing lessons after supper.'

'Very Good,' replied Thelma. 'How are you enjoying it Jenny?'

'More than you can imagine. I don't get out often and it would be nice to meet another man again, but not the one you introduced me to this evening. He is a little bit on the large side for me, but, I really do appreciate the girls asking me and for you two for bringing me.'

At the other end of the table, Arthur and Jess were having a somewhat different conversation with Amelia.

'I'm going home when I've had my supper.'

'Whatever for?' Jess asked her.

Arthur just thought, *Good. Happen we'll have a pleasant time for the rest of the evening.*

'Yes. I am. I didn't enjoy dancing with Harry. I don't know why you brought me here. I've never liked him. I'm only having my supper because it'll be easier than starting to make it when I get home.'

Eustace and Joan were faring far better with Cybil.

'Thanks for inviting me Joan. I've had a lovely evening so far. I've fair enjoyed talking and dancing with Harry, he's just the bloke for me, big, round and something to get hold of. Yes, he'll do for me.'

Eustace and Joan were pleased about this. They were glad they'd invited Cybil and they were having a good time themselves. They were dancing together and really enjoying each others company for the first time in years.

Martha and Hector were also having an enjoyable evening and so was Bessie Griggs. Bessie had a reputation for being crude and horrible and tonight was no exception as she spat out a mouthful of food onto her plate. 'This fish paste's bloody awful.' She changed over onto the ham sandwich.

'Aye, it's a bit gruesome,' agreed Hector. 'God only knows what they put in it.'

'Ground up fish and other bits. The only thing is you don't know where it's come from or how long it's taken to get here. How are you getting on with Harry?' asked Martha.

'Oh, Harry's Harry. He'll never change and I don't know that I'd want him to. I've known him all my life, same class at school, but like I say, Harry's Harry. He's a bit rough around the edges and always will be.'

The conversation melted into a general hub hub with everyone talking at the same time and everyone enjoying the occasion.

The club door opened and in walked Anthony Murgatroyd, Margaret Murgatroyd and a complete stranger who was very smartly dressed, tall, extremely handsome and was wearing a pair of cowboy boots.

Anthony Murgatroyd was the owner of Murgatroyd's Woollen Mill where many of those attending the social worked. He would often, on a club social evening, pay a short visit to the affair for he was a fully paid up member of the club and he quite enjoyed an occasional night out with the locals. Margaret, his wife, was also quite used to visiting the club, so tonight was no exception except for the tall, dark, handsome stranger that was with them. Every table was speculating who he might be and the gossip intensified when he pulled out an enormous cigar and lit it with a match that he struck on the sole of his boot.

On the big table, three of the unaccompanied ladies, were dumbstruck at the sight of the stranger, but soon got around to discussing his finer points. Only Amelia didn't join in, as she was still going home.

Anthony Murgatroyd took his party to the bar. 'Good evening, Harry.'

'Good evening Mr Anthony, Mrs Anthony and Sir.'

'Harry, I'd like you to meet my cousin, Chuck. He's a cattle rancher from Texas and is over here for a few weeks studying farming methods.'

'Well hello there, Mr Chuck, and welcome to our little club.'

'Now then, howdydoo, Mr Harry. It's a pleasure to make your acquaintance and I hope this will be the first of many visits to your superior little club.'

'What will you have to drink, Mr Chuck?' asked Harry who was already pouring Anthony's beer and Margaret's orange soda.

'Oh, just a cold can.'

'Eh?'

'A cold can of beer.'

Anthony intervened and explained to Chuck about the beer pumps, draught beer and dark British bitter beer.

'OK then, I'll have a pint of your best bitter beer.'

Harry poured it, carefully watched by Chuck and accompanied by 'Gee whizz, well isn't that quaint. Well wait until I tell the folks back home. Well, Jesus Christ.'

The record player was being prepared for the second half and the Murgatroyd party was making a slow parade around all the tables talking to everyone they knew, which was most of the people there. They arrived at the big table where Chuck realised that there were spare females. This was excellent news as he was a bachelor who had devoted his life to farming and never had the time to take a wife. But now, approaching late middle age he had been thinking that it was about time he did something to rectify the situation. Anthony was introducing everyone to Chuck and they were all getting up in turn to shake his hand.

Amelia took his hand, then grunted and reached for her coat.

Bessie Griggs shook his hand warmly, but realised there was no future for her here.

Cybil Peace also greeted him warmly, but knew she was after Harry. He was her future man.

With Jenny Bryce it was a different story. She just melted to his touch and he to hers. They did not release hands for a very long time until Anthony decided that it was time to move along to the next table.

The record player struck up with a quickstep and Jenny Bryce, being as good as her word, took Josie onto the dance floor to teach her the rudiments of the dance. Jenny was a very good dancer and Josie a quick learner so, that by the time the dance was over, Josie was confident enough to be able to do the dance the next time she was able.

146

The party goers had enjoyed the quickstep and applauded enthusiastically until the MC agreed to an encore. This time Jenny took Josie's friend Margaret onto the floor and gave her instructions. She was equally as quick a learner as Josie and was soon dancing away. Willie took his favourite daughter onto the dance floor and Thelma sat chatting to the others. She observed Chuck walk purposely across the floor to Jenny and Margaret, straight into the middle of them.

'Excuse me, ma'am,' he said to Margaret and took hold of Jenny.

Margaret somewhat nonplussed, left them.

Chuck took hold of Jenny very tightly and they began to dance with all eyes in the room on them.

Will and Jenny danced the night away together, never leaving one another's company. He dancing like a professional, she his equal.

Anthony Murgatroyd was ready for home, so was his wife, but Chuck showed no sign of leaving Jenny. Eventually, Anthony went over to them during a gap between dances and asked him if he was ready for home.

'Not yet, cousin, not yet. Say, you go home. I'll find my way there later; it's not that far to walk.' They lived quite close to the club in the big house attached to the mill. 'Say Jenny, where do you live?'

'Waterside,' she replied. 'It's not far, but don't worry about me, I can walk there with Willie and Thelma.'

'No. No, I can't have that. I will escort you,' he said, and she was delighted. 'OK cousin, you go home. I'll walk Jenny home and come along later after the dance has finished. Leave me the key under the front mat if you want to go to bed.'

So Anthony and Margaret took their leave of everyone. They said goodnight to Harry when they eventually found him, dancing with Cybil.

Amelia was by this time at home, being miserable and drinking her cocoa alone. Arthur and Jess were enjoying themselves without her as were all the others around the big table.

From time to time, Chuck and Jenny did come and sit at the big table with the others and chat a while. Josie and Margaret were firing questions at him about America. Willie tried his best to make them leave the happy couple alone but to no avail. Chuck didn't mind, nor did Jenny, as long as they were sitting together.

Cybil soon found herself in the small private office behind the bar which acted as Harry's headquarters. She was being molested in a big way and so was he. They were both enjoying it immensely.

Bessie Griggs was enjoying herself too. She hadn't found the man of her dreams, but she was having a good night out. They were all changing partners and dancing every dance.

All too soon, almost midnight arrived and it was time for the last waltz.

Harry and Cybil reappeared with smiles a mile wide and cuddled their way around the dance floor.

Chuck and Jenny did much the same thing. 'Ma'am, can I escort you to your home afterwards,' he asked her formally.

'I will be very offended if you don't. The night is yet young.'

'I beg your pardon?'

'It's only midnight and I've nothing planned for tomorrow.'

'OK. Now I understand.'

Arthur and Jess, along with Hector, Martha and Bessie got ready for home. They were all going the same way. They said goodnight and went.

Eustace and Joan, who had had a lovely evening looked for Cybil and found her helping Harry to count the bar takings. 'Are you ready Cybil?'

'No. Not yet. Thanks for bringing me. It's been an absolutely super evening. If it's alright with you two, I'm going to stop and help Harry clear up, then he's going to escort me home.'

'Are you sure?'

'Yes. Your little plot worked better than I ever could have imagined.'

'Don't know what you mean,' said Joan.

Cybil gave her a knowing look.

Eustace and Joan went home arm in arm, pleased that Cybil had stayed. Harry's bed didn't get warm that night.

'Are you ready, Mrs Bryce?' asked Josie.

'Yes. Chuck and I will come with you as far as your house then he can escort me the rest of my way home.'

They all walked into the cold night air. Chuck cuddled Jenny to him to keep her warn although, after Texas, he was feeling the cold himself.

Willie began to question Chuck. He thought it best to find out what he could about him as he felt just a little bit responsible for bringing Jenny Bryce along and he was just a tad worried about leaving her with a total stranger.

'So where is it you come from, Chuck?'

'Quite near to Austin, Texas in the U S of A. I have a twenty five thousand acre cattle ranch and at the moment run about fifteen thousand head of cattle'

'So what relation are you to Mr Anthony?'

'Cousin. Yes, he's my first cousin. My mother and Anthony's father are brother and sister.'

'That'll be Lottie Murgatroyd,' said Thelma

'Gee whiz, say how do you know that?'

'I clean for Margaret Murgatroyd and the whole village knows the family history. We've all lived here for long time.'

'You do what for Margaret? Clean? Oh I know, you're her domestic.'

'Ah yes, I suppose I am. I know Lottie went to America many years ago.'

'Yes. She sailed from Liverpool to go stay with an acquaintance of the Murgatroyd family and whilst she was there she met my father and married him.'

'Aye. The wedding was here in the local church. It was
before I was born, but it's been talked about ever since. How all
the Americans sailed here and took the village by storm. Then a
few weeks after the wedding she sailed away for ever.'

'I guess you got it in one. So I thought it's about time to pay
a visit to my relations and study your intensive farming
methods at the same time. So I arrived yesterday and today I
meet the most pretty lady I ever did ever clap eyes on.' He
squeezed Jenny and she let him.

By the time they reached Cutside cottages Willie had run out
of questions.

'Gee, is this where you live, Mr Willie?'

'Yes, this is our cottage.'

'How quaint, how super, can I be very rude and ask to come
inside just to take a look?'

About this time, Harry was saying something similar outside
Cybil's semi.

'Of course you can, come in and have a cup of tea.' Willie
cordially invited him.

Chuck was given a guided tour, upstairs, downstairs, cellar
and back garden.

'How many of you live here?'

'Five.'

'Five persons, gee whizz.' He was just about to say 'in this
little space.' When he thought better of it and asked. 'Isn't it a
little crowded?'

'It was when Thelma's mother lived here.'

Thelma brewed the tea and poured. 'I assume you live in a
much larger house than this, Chuck?'

'Just a little. Just a little. It's a ranch house with room for me
and my staff. My head cowman and his family live there and we
have stables for fifty horses for the cowhands. It is situated on
the top of a small hill, overlooking a lake with the pasture land
rolling away as far as the eye can see. Gee ma'am this tea's real
good. We don't drink tea at home. My housekeeper always

makes coffee. We don't drink a lot of tea in Texas. We just drink coffee, beer, cola and water.'

'Is it very hot?' asked Josie.

Well young lady, I can tell you that it gets up to one hundred and ten degrees in August and can be freezing at this time of the year. We get many daily variations in temperature, but we don't get snow and we have to use the air conditioning for eight months of the year.'

'What's air conditioning?' Josie continued.

'Well this is some question to answer. Let's just say it's like a big refrigerator unit that keeps the house cool in hot weather but also can be used as a heater in cold weather.'

'Don't you have a fire? This one warms our house.'

'Yes I know. We do have a big log fire some evenings, but only when it's very cold. Well Willie, Thelma, Josie and Margaret, I guess it's time we were going. It's getting late and we're keeping you from your beds. So thank you for your generous hospitality and we'll bid you goodnight. Oh, by the way Josie, keep on saving up the questions, I'd love to answer them all for you before I return home.'

'Thank you all for inviting me. It really has been a magical evening,' said Jenny standing on the doorstep. She also had been entranced listening to Chuck talking about his ranch.

Chuck and Jenny walked away arm in arm along the canal towpath towards Jenny's house. They kissed and cuddled, both at one with the world.

Anthony Murgatroyd lay in bed until late listening for Chuck returning, worrying about him and finally falling asleep.

Harry's bed wasn't the only one to remain cold that night.

*

Tuesday was the first time that the terrible three had visited the club since the social. Habitually they never went on a Monday, unless it was a special occasion, because Willie cleaned out his pigeons, Arthur got in Jess's way and Eustace tootled around doing not a lot, but looking busy and nicely filling up the evening. So on Tuesdays they always sat down to a pint with Harry in attendance.

'I just want to say that I knew that you lot were up to something. I just knew it, but I couldn't figure out what until you all turned up with a spare woman each. But, boy oh boy, has it been a good weekend? I'll say it has. Anyway, I want to thank you all from the bottom of my heart and most sincerely for what you did for me and Cybil, your Joan's fault I believe Eustace, and to show my appreciation I'd like to buy you all a drink.'

'A drink!' said Willie who was overcome with emotion. 'Harry's going to buy us a drink.'

'It will be a pleasure to drink it,' Eustace shouted as he dashed off to get rid of one lot of liquid before he could take in any more.

Arthur enquired. 'So you clicked? You and Cybil?'

'Clicked and three quarters. I don't know why I didn't ask her out years ago. I've known her all my life. I'm as happy as a pig in clover. By the way, you know how I've always worked on my rest day because I've never had anything else to do and nowhere to go? Well I'm starting to have it off as from Thursday so the committee will have to do something about a temp for one day a week.'

'Hey we had a letter at our house this morning.'

'A rare occurrence, Willie,' observed Arthur.

'Aye, it were from Jenny Bryce. It were addressed to Josie and it thanked us all for bringing her here last Saturday and saying what a super night she'd had and how good it had been to meet Chuck and of course, being with us.'

'Is she still with him?' asked Harry.

'Don't know. I'll ask the girls to get to know, mind you knowing those two they'll have found out already. Wasn't it a super night on Saturday? What started out as a bit of fun because of your continual moaning about not having a woman in your life turned out into a bloody good do and double matchmaking.'

'Yes. I think I'll start moaning about my lack of money next.'

<u>CHAPTER 9</u>

The end of winter heralded the lighter nights of spring and Willie turned much more of his attention to his kitchen garden. He was slowly getting later and later arriving at his favourite evening hostelry, The Grolsby Working Mens Club, Affiliated.

*

Jenny Bryce kept the girls informed about her ongoing romance with Chuck. She told them that she had decided to travel to Texas for the whole of the School summer holiday.

*

Harry didn't keep the terrible three informed of progress of his romance with Cybil, but they knew it was moving along because every time which was frequently, that they questioned him on the subject he turned bright red.

Eustace had an answer to the "was he or wasn't he" question. 'If we're going to the match on Saturday, let's come here early, about a quarter to one and I bet she brings his dinner in.' This was the following Wednesday night after the social and they had gathered specifically to review trip progress.

Eustace took charge. 'Everything is now arranged except for them what's going. How many have we so far Willie?'

Very luckily for Willie, he'd had a count up at lunch time in the canteen, so he knew the answer. 'Fifteen so far.'

'Have we got any money in from them yet?'

'No, but I'm expecting a down payment on Friday.' This came from Arthur, the self appointed treasurer of anything he could become treasurer of except for the Christmas Club where he had let Willie do the job.

'How much will that be?'

'Half a crown each.'

154

'We must make sure that we get all the money in before we go to Blackpool. You know what a mess it gets into if we don't.' Self-styled Chairman Eustace was beginning to show his authority.

'Don't worry,' replied Arthur, getting slowly wound up into one of his committee moods, 'I've taken the liberty to ensure the down payment on Friday and the rest before we go. Anyone who isn't fully paid up on trip morning isn't going.'

'How are you going to make sure about that?' Willie enquired.

'Because I shall tell them in no uncertain terms that if they haven't paid not to bother turning up.'

'It'll be an empty coach then.'

Eustace asked, 'How do you make that out?'

'Because the vast majority of them won't have paid by next Christmas,' said Willie

'Oh they will. They will that. I'll make sure they do. Oh yes, by jove, I will that.'

'So you're the treasurer Arthur, are you?' asked Eustace.

Arthur looked stunned for a second then said, 'well, er, well go on then seeing as you're asking.'

'I wasn't, but go on then. So your job will be to get all the money in and pay it all out again.'

'Ok,' said Arthur with a broad grin.

The club was empty and Harry sauntered over to the meeting. 'How's it going boys?'

'It's going fine, just fine, but it's you we're worried about.'

'You've no need to worry about me, I'm in fine fettle. Never felt better.'

'Oh, we thought you were looking a little tired, worn out perhaps, or even a bit flushed.'

'Pale, I thought,' said Arthur.

'You're not getting to hear about it, it's for me to know and for you lot to stick your noses out of,' Harry growled.

'But it was us what brought you together,' continued Willie.

'Yes, that's true, but that was then and this is now and that's that.' With which he sauntered away behind his bar.

Eustace asked, 'What did you mean you're going to make sure you're collecting the down payment on Friday?'

'Just watch this space on Friday dinner time.'

*

'You can stick that right back where you got it from Arthur Baxter. I'm not having an article like that on my canteen wall and that is for sure. So take the bugger down now and piss off.' This was Greasy Martha at her best.

Arthur had just begun to pin a large poster that he had made onto the wall at the side of the servery.

'You not coming on the trip then, Martha?'

'Certainly no! Yes I might. I'll see. I'll be the only lady on the coach if I do. Me and forty seven men. Gosh, but seeing that it's you lot, no! No chance at all so you can get that poster off the wall now.'

Arthur, who was being watched by a canteen full of his workmates, took the somewhat brave, adventurous and foolhardy step of reaching through the servery hatch, grabbing hold of Martha and giving her a long, full kiss on the lips, to much applause from the diners.

'Thanks, Martha. I'll take it down again in a short while.'

'It's not the only thing you can take down if you come in the back with me now.'

'Sorry. No time. I've work to do.' He picked up a spoon and banged it on the nearest table, several times, hard. 'Now then. You all know about the trip as illustrated on the poster. Those of you that have got your names down already, I want your down payment of half a crown, now, and full payment before the trip day. Anyone who hasn't paid in full on the night before the trip isn't going and the down payment will go towards my dinner,' Arthur poised for breath...

An anonymous voice from the back of the room shouted, 'Is Martha coming?'

'It's nothing to do with me if she is,' he countered.

'You could have fooled me,' said the voice.

'I did. Now to continue. We've still got a few places left on the coach, but you'd best get your names down fairly sharp as they're going fast.'

Willie turned to Eustace. 'By gum, he can't half tell a good one when he tells one.'

'He's had practice you know.'

Arthur's stretching of the truth did have some positive results as another ten people came forward, put their names on the list and paid their down payment.

*

On Saturday, the terrible three each had an early lunch and arrived at the club, well before one o'clock, on their way to the match. Sure enough, they were hardly into their first pint when Cybil walked in with a neat parcel of food for Harry's dinner.

He had for many years kicked the table leg, or just had a packet of crisps for his lunch, so this was paradise. Cybil acknowledged the three drinkers, then was hurriedly ushered into the back room, where she was given the private reception she deserved.

'Told you. Let's see if he's coming to the match.'

Willie shouted for Harry who eventually appeared, 'Are you coming to the match?'

'Better things to do, but thanks for asking.'

'Oh, come on.'

Harry pulled the door of his office closed so that Cybil could not hear him, then with a smile on his face he leaned over the bar and whispered firmly, 'It's your fault that I'm living in paradise so you can sod off.' With which he turned his back on the three of them and went back into his office.

Eustace suddenly said, 'It's time we were at the station.'
'Aye. Sup up and lets get going.'

*

'It is rumoured, Arthur Baxter, that you are having an affair
with Greasy Martha, boyo.'

They had walked into the station to catch the early train to
the town, as they did every Saturday that there was a home
match, so that they could get a good seat. As usual the place
was moderately busy and the booking office window was
closed with the board over it so that Evans could rest in peace
without being disturbed by the likes of passengers. They were
startled to hear Evans's voice without observing his features,
but then he appeared from the parcels office across the booking
hall.

Arthur reddened, huffing and puffing, 'Now, you know it's
slanderous to make unfounded accusations in public without
proof or knowledge of the events that you are talking about.'

Willie and Eustace were in stitches.

'Common knowledge, this is, boyo. Not something I've just
made up. Well known throughout the length and breadth of the
village. Your Jess thrown you out yet, has she?'

'Flaming hell Evans. There is no affair; I just made a gesture
to prove a point.'

'A gesture. A gesture was it. Not how I heard it described.
Anyway, there you are, no doubt it will be a seven day wonder
if I'm not mistaken. Can I come on your trip to Blackpool?'

'No,' shouted three voices in unison.

'Not even as my price for silence in this sordid matter?'

'No!'

'Three returns as usual, is it? Two o'clock. It's delayed by
five minutes by a highly technical problem further up the line.
Are you sure you haven't a place for me on your trip?'

'Yes. Yes, very sure. No outsiders.'

'Full is it?'

'Yes. Almost.'

Evans looked at them. 'Liars,' he said laughing.

They stood out on the platform waiting for the train. Quite a crowd was gathering as they were coming to the most interesting part of the season. They stood discussing the prospects for the match and the fact that they were still short of numbers for the trip.

'It's not been taken up as well as I thought it might be,' said Eustace. 'In fact, I am more than disappointed. I mean it's not expensive and it'll be a good day out.'

Willie was the first to reply. 'I think we might have to let Harry and Evans come along. In fact, Hubert Gormley were asking me if he could bring his brother.'

'Well I've no objection. They've had plenty of chances at the mill to put their names down, so we might as well fill it with strays as having it cost us brass or even having to cancel it.'

Just then the Reverend Clifford Tunstall walked up to the boys. 'Are you going to the match boys?'

'Yes, Vicar.'

'Mind if I come with you? It's been a long time since I went to watch them play. So I thought, why not? I've nothing ecumenical on this afternoon so here I am, all ready and raring to go. Just as an added incentive, I've left my dog collar at the vicarage.'

The three of them didn't mind in the least, the vicar was a good sort who would always pay his fair share and more at times.

They had a good chin wag on the journey to the town station and then a long walk to the football ground where they mingled and chatted with the away supporters. They had popped into the Rising Sun near the ground for a pint and once in the ground, the Vicar produced four pork pies to keep them going.

They had a very nice afternoon, it was a good clean match which ended in a draw. The vicar's language at times was not for the faint hearted which explained why his dog collar had stayed behind. It was warm in the early spring sunshine and they enjoyed a pleasant walk back to the station, talking to all and sundry on the way. On the train journey back home, the Vicar enquired, 'Can I come on the Blackpool trip?'

They looked at each other and nodded in agreement. Eustace spoke for them. 'Vicar, you can if you moderate your language. We can't do with a carry on like what we've had this afternoon. Not on Murgatroyd's mill trip.'

'Ah, yes. Sorry and all that. I got carried away with the excitement. I've already said a silent prayer of repentance on the train to confess my sins.'

'I hope you confessed ours as well,' said Willie.

The Vicar burst out laughing.

They alighted the train and walked into the booking hall, where they stopped.

'Evans!' Willie shouted at the top of his voice.

From somewhere came a muffled reply, 'Sorry. Closed.'

'Evans! Come here a minute.'

A small, thin figure clothed in British Railways black, with a British railways peak cap came shuffling out of the ticket office. 'What it is that you are wanting William Arkenthwaite, soon to be the late William Arkenthwaite if he shouts at me again that loud.'

Willie put his arm around Evans' shoulder. 'We've decided that you can come on the trip to Blackpool, as a special gesture from your favourite customers.'

'Well that's grand. Thank you. Yes indeed, that is just grand.'

'Half a crown down payment right now, please,' asked Eustace, then as an afterthought, 'and you too Vicar please.'

'No money,' said Evans.

'Plenty of money in there, in the till.' He indicated the booking office. 'Go and make a small British railways loan to yourself.'

'Not possible, all accounted for. Let's see now. I know, yes, yes, just wait there a minute I shan't be more than two shakes of a donkey's tail.'

The Vicar was fumbling in this pocket and, being a vicar, he had plenty of pockets to fumble in. He had a few coins in one hand and was searching with the other.

From the ticket office there was the sound of money being shaken then hit, then bashed and shaken again. Coins could he heard falling on the floor. Finally Evans reappeared with a fistful of pennies, halfpennies and farthings. 'There you are. Sorry it's all small stuff.'

'Raided the poor box again, have you?' enquired Willie.

'Something like that. Anyway, that's my affair, and in any case, I am poor.'

'Two and two pence three farthings,' announced the Vicar. 'I'll have to owe you three pence farthing. Come along to church in the morning and I'll give it to you.'

Willie gave him a look. 'You can come along to the club in the next half hour and give it to us there.'

'Yes I might. Are you going straight there?'

'Yes, we're going to tell Harry he can come on the trip.'

*

The club was deserted. The door was open, but the steward was conspicuous by his absence.

Willie looked around carefully. 'Well, he's not here. I think we might as well pull ourselves a pint.' He headed for the back of the bar and was well into filling the third glass when a very red faced Harry appeared out of the back office. Not the usual ranting and raving Harry, but a much calmer human being.

'Sorry boys, I was just busy. I heard you come in, are you alright? Here pour me one, Willie, whilst you're in charge.'

They all looked at him. Normally they would have been suffering verbal abuse, particularly as Willie had poured the drinks.

Arthur was the first to comment on the situation. 'Why don't you ask Cybil to come out from your office and join us?'

Harry was just about to launch a major verbal assault when he stopped, counted to ten, smiled and replied, 'OK I'll just go and get her.'

'No wonder he didn't want to go to the match with us. Did he? Willie? Arthur? Did he?' He stopped himself and took a few deep breaths. Eustace had done very well recently and was under no circumstances going to slide back into oblivion.

They all greeted Cybil, who took a gin and tonic with them.

'I think the club could see its way to forgetting about these drinks,' said Willie.

'Well, I err…Oh go on then. Who's to know?'

'Only the good Lord and I,' whispered the vicar who had crept in quietly and unseen. 'However, I could stretch a point and join you for a pint then say one for all of us tomorrow.'

'Good man,' said Arthur. 'I have always said you were a good sort, Vicar.'

'I can ask for forgiveness for all liars as well, Arthur.'

'Yes.'

'Here's the money I owe you.'

'Thanks.'

'What's that for?' asked Cybil, who wasn't backward at coming forward.

'Vicar's coming on the trip.'

'It's alright for some folk. I'm banned.'

'No you're not, Harry, you're invited, but you'd best get Cybil's permission.'

'Nothing to do with me. You lads can go on your trip. I hope you all have a right good do. What's this I hear about you and Martha, Arthur?'

The Vicar pricked up his ears. 'Have you been a naughty boy Arthur?' He sensed that his official capacity may be called on shortly.

'No I bloody well have not and I'm bloody well fed up of folk saying so and spreading vile rumours.'

'Well I only asked as it's common knowledge in the village.'

*

Both Eustace and Willie arrived at their respective houses to find their tea prepared. Arthur did not.

'We not having tea then?' he enquired.

'Not until you've told all about your affair with Martha.'

'You what?' He shouted.

'It's all over the village that you and her's been having an affair.'

'I've had the same daft tale all afternoon. It's nowt of the sort. Still I'd best tell you what it's all about.' So he did and eventually got his tea, but whether or not he was completely exonerated, he could not tell.

*

The trip was getting ever closer and the lads were very worried about the numbers that had signed up. The meals didn't matter, they just had to give final numbers at both venues and pay for those numbers, but the coach was a different matter. They were still at thirty eight, needing another twelve. They managed to persuade a few more to join in and then one morning in the mill bottom, when Mr Anthony was doing his morning round, he came over to Willie and asked.

'Can I come on the trip, Willie?'

'You Mr Anthony?'

'Yes, me Willie. Not on the coach, but to the lunch?'

'Yes, Mr Anthony. No Problem. Nice of you to show an interest.'

'How are things going for the trip?'

'Well, meals are no problem, but we've only got about forty bums on seats so far and we have to pay for the whole coach. So we either make up the difference out of our own pockets or ask them all that's going for an increase or get some more folk to go. But I really don't know where we are going to find them.'

'Don't worry about it too much, Willie, I'll help you out if you get stuck. I'd just like to come to the lunch, where are you having it?'

'The Golden Cockerel Restaurant on the Golden Mile. We've been and sampled it, it's very good food, nice people, nice room on the top floor, just right as long as everyone behaves themselves.'

'Do you think they might not?'

'Well, Mr Anthony, you know a mill trip as well as I do.'

'Indeed I do. Just book me a lunch please.'

'No problem. Thanks.'

Mr Anthony turned to continue his tour then turned back. 'I say Willie, what's this I hear about Arthur and Martha?'

Willie laughed. 'Don't believe a word of it. It was just a bit of fun and all to do with the trip. Another seven day wonder.'

'What did he want?' Arthur came over as soon as Mr Anthony had gone on his rounds.

'Oh, he only wanted to know about you and Martha.'

'Did he heck. Did he?'

'I'll let you know later. He wants to come for his dinner on the trip, but not on the coach.'

'Good job. It won't be fit for him.'

'I know that and so does he.'

'He went last time we had one, years ago, got home in a right state. His father begged him not to go but he insisted. He arrived home paralytic and his father nearly killed him. He's grown up a lot since then though.'

'Does that mean that Margaret will be coming as well?' asked Willie.

'If he didn't mention her, I doubt that she will, but just to be on the safe side you'd better ask him next time you see him.'

'He's still over there talking. I'd best go and ask him.'

Willie walked across the dyehouse to where Anthony Murgatroyd was deep in conversation with the dyehouse foreman.

The foreman looked at Willie. But he moved around until he came into Mr Anthony's field of vision.

'Yes, Willie?'

'Will your Margaret be coming with you to the trip dinner?'

'I do think, Willie, that it will not quite be the place for a lady. Fifty men and one woman. No, I'll take her with me to Blackpool and send her off shopping for a couple of hours over lunchtime.'

'Thanks, Mr Anthony.'

'No problem, Willie.'

'That doesn't solve the coach problem,' said Arthur as Willie returned to his work station. 'Do you think we could persuade old misery guts to go?' he pointed to one of their workmates.

'I doubt it, but we can have a go at him and see what he says.'

They did and after a lot of talking and the application of much verbal pressure, he succumbed and agreed.

'What about Horrible Hector, he'll come. I'll tell Martha to send him at dinner time.'

*

In the canteen, in his rightful place at the head of the queue, Willie told Martha to tell her Hector that his seat was reserved on the trip coach.

'By gum, he'll be fair suited with that information,' Martha said. 'He's been grumbling for days that you haven't asked him. I think I'll come as well.'

'Sorry, men only.'

'It's not fair.'

'It's as fair as its going to be.'

'I'll tell him tonight, it'll make his day.'

In order not to encourage further vile rumour, Arthur picked up his dinner without either looking at or speaking to Martha.

'What's up with you, Arthur Baxter?' she shouted at his rapidly disappearing back.

'Nowt,' he shouted back.

'Not a very nice way to treat your girlfriend,' said Willie when Arthur had joined him at the corner table.

'What?' asked Eustace.

'Shut up the pair of you.'

'Charming,' said Eustace and went on eating his dinner.

*

The same evening, Arthur, Eustace and Willie rolled into the club about half past eight. They had all been home, eaten, washed, part changed and were all present and correct, their usual smart selves.

The steward was not in attendance behind the bar.

'Probably attending to Cybil in his office, I'll just go and get him,' said Willie, who farted good and loud.

'Oh, leave them alone; let him have his few moments of fun and pleasure. He's had precious few of them in his lifetime.'

'How do you know that?' asked Eustace.

'Only from what he always says.'

'Yes but you know the man's a born liar, so you don't know whether to believe him or not, do you?'

'Well no, but he has made a lot of noise about it in the past.'

'Shall we just wait until he appears? I'm getting very worried about the trip numbers. I think it needs serious discussion.'

'Come on then,' said Willie, 'let's go and sit down and see if we can ease your troubled mind, Eustace.' He farted again just for good measure.

Arthur said, 'If you do that again I'm going to ban you from the trip.'

'Well carry on,' Willie replied and belched very loudly just to add fuel to the fire. But Arthur chose to ignore him.

They had just made themselves comfortable, when the door burst open and a vacuum cleaner dashed in, all on its own and came to a quiet halt in front of the bar, standing there quietly and looking at no one in particular.

'Is it a fully paid up member?' Willie enquired of the others.

'Don't know. I don't think it's on the books,' Arthur replied.

'I'll go and ask it.' Eustace stood up and walked over to the bar, looked at it, walked around it then tapped it smartly on the handle and said, 'Excuse me, Sir, but are you a fully paid up member of this club, for if not, I am afraid that you cannot drink in here.'

'How bloody daft can you buggers get?' There came a voice from the door. It was the steward.

'Ah. Mr Steward. Mr Suction Sweeper here came in all on his own for a drink and I was just ascertaining as to whether or not he was a fully paid up member of the club and therefore legally entitled to partake of alcoholic refreshment here.'

'You must be nuts, anyone knows that a vacuum cleaner is female, not a Sir. Anyway it's Cybil's.'

Arthur and Willie were in tucks of laughter.

'Is it now? Cybil and a vacuum cleaner. The mind boggles.'

'No. No, you don't understand, it's broken and I'm going to mend it.'

'You are going to repair this vacuum cleaner?' asked Arthur gravely.

Stephen Bailey

'Do you think I can't?'

'Well going on past performance, I'd say you stand a very good chance of electrocuting Cybil.'

'You do?'

'We do, don't we?' there was a chorus of three voices in harmony.

'Pour three beers, Steward, please,' ordered Willie.

In a foul mood, Harry went to get the beers.

'Now then Eustace, exactly who's going on this trip so far?' Arthur asked him.

'Well, here's the full up to date list.' He pulled a piece of paper from his pocket containing a neatly hand printed list of names.

Arthur studied the list very carefully and counted the names twice. 'Forty three. So we either need five more, or we'll have to either pay up ourselves or increase the price to the others. So we'd all best try and persuade some more people at the mill tomorrow. Any ideas who?'

'No, let's play dominoes. We'll try again tomorrow as you suggest.'

Willie wasn't going to tell them about Mr Anthony's offer to pay for the empty seats because, he thought that the other two would just accept it and give up the fight.

They got the dominoes out and were well into a game. The club was beginning to slowly fill up and Eustace suddenly said, 'There's Walker Johnson and his brother Joshua. There's neither of them with their names on this list. I'll go and have words with them.'

A long conversation with the Johnsons ensued. Joshua was all for going and had to persuade Walker to join in, but they did and that added two more to the list.

'So we only need three more now, we should be able to make it.'

'I'm sure we'll get them tomorrow,' observed Arthur.

Willie asked, 'Is there anything else then?'

Yes,' replied Arthur, 'there's the most important bit. We haven't ordered the beer for the coach. How much will we need?'

'Best ask himself. On matters such as this, he's better informed than the Encyclopedia Britannica. Hey Steward, may we have five minutes of your valuable time over here, not to mention your undisputed knowledge.'

'You can have a bunch of fives, William Arkenthwaite,' and he carried on trying to prepare Cybil for electrocution.

'No, no, Harry, please come over here a minute, will you? We have need of your advice and it's in your own financial interest.'

'Is it now?' The scowl slowly turned to a smile. 'Just hang on a second whilst I put this screw into place, please.'

He ambled over a few minutes later. Pint in hand.

'Now then, what can I do for you Gentlemen?'

'Are you determined to go ahead and try to kill Cybil with that vacuum?' asked Willie.

The smile returned to a scowl. 'If that's all you wanted you can bloody well stick...'

He was interrupted by Eustace, 'It isn't Harry. Please sit down for a minute will you. We want to know how much ale to put on the trip bus.'

'Well I always reckon a crate each and a few in reserve. It depends on the coach.'

'Why what has the coach to do with it?'

'Well some have bigger luggage space than others. Then some of them, if you load them right up, won't go up hills because there's too much weight for the engine. Then some drivers won't take a full load and anyway, which of Bewdlay's coaches and drivers are we having?'

'The new coach. Bewdlay is going to drive it himself. We told him we didn't want Norris Oakes.'

'No, you're better without him. He's always getting lost.'

'Mind you, I can't see Bewdlay coming himself or sending a new coach for a day out of vomiting etcetera,' said Harry.

'Well he is going to. In fact, I'll call tomorrow and make sure that everything is in order. It's only ten days away now, so I think we'd best get sixty crates ready for the occasion.'

'Who's paying for it?' The steward made a general enquiry.

Three faces peered at him. 'Eh?' Each face said in turn.

'Who's paying for it? It's not coming for free you know.'

'The one small matter that's escaped our attention,' said Eustace. 'We'll have to sell it by the bottle.'

'Fat lot of use that is. We'd never keep track of it. Not when we've had three or five. No, the only thing to do is to have a kitty, so that everyone pays for a crate and some surplus. We'd best collect the money at breakfast.' Willie relaxed again.

Arthur put the cat amongst the pigeons. 'They'll not have enough money with them, particularly the Vicar.'

'Of course they will. They know they've a lot of ale to buy,' said Willie. 'They'll all have enough with them and I'll get it from them.'

The subject was by this time exhausted and so they continued with their game of dominoes. By the time they had finished it had reached chucking out time, so they all went home.

*

Eustace told Joan the next morning that he would be half an hour late for his tea as he had to call in on Bewdlay's garage on the way home from work. Joan didn't make a scene, she was pleased to see him getting involved in something. It was better than having him sitting in the armchair staring into space as he had done for thirty years. Eustace was equally delighted that Joan wasn't going to crucify him as she would have done twelve months ago.

As soon as work finished for the day, Eustace walked the short distance from the mill to Bewdlay's garage and transport depot. There, sitting in one of the half ruined sheds sat a brand new Bedford fifty seater coach, which was the last word in luxury as Joseph Bewdlay had promised. Eustace found Joseph with his head under the bonnet of one of the ancient taxis in another of the sheds, both of which were accidents waiting to happen.

Eustace tapped Joseph gently on the back, causing him to jump up startled, bang his head on the bonnet, knock out the upright support and the bonnet to drop. Luckily, Eustace just caught it in time to stop Joseph receiving a square head.

'Good job I was here then, Joseph.'

'Wouldn't have happened if you hadn't called in. What do you want?'

'I only called just to make sure that everything is in order for a week on Saturday.'

'Did you see the new coach as you came through?'

'Yes. It looks good.'

'It's better than good. It's fabulous and I'm looking forward to taking it on its first long distance outing to Blackpool.'

'We need the coach at the club at seven thirty on Saturday morning.'

'Whatever for? I'm not picking you up at the Fox and Grapes until nine o'clock.'

'Well we've got to load all the crates of ale into it before breakfast.'

'You've got to do what? I'm not having crates and crates of ale in my new coach. If that's the way it's going to be, I'll bring one of the older coaches. I'm not having a brand new coach vomited up with excess drinking.'

'What do you think a mill trip is all about?' Eustace asked him.

'Well, I must admit I never gave it much thought properly until just now. But there is no way that I'm carting a load of crates of ale in the new machine. Mind you, there's not a lot wrong with the best of the older models.'

'Yes, but you said you'd bring the new coach when I booked it.'

'You didn't tell me you were taking loads of ale and like I've said, I'm not having loads of ale in my new coach. So you'll have to have the newest of the others.'

Eustace had a sudden horrible thought. 'How many seats are there in the other coach?'

'Forty five.'

'Good job we're still short of numbers. I'd best make sure we don't sell any more seats. I don't think that Willie and Arthur will sell any more before tomorrow morning.' A very disgruntled Eustace went home for his tea.

Joseph Bewdlay also went home for his tea in a foul mood.

'What on earth is the matter with you?' asked Joseph's wife as she prepared to feed him.

'They were going to put crates of ale in my new coach. Crates of ale I ask you. Crate after crate after crate.'

'Who were dear?'

'Murgatroyd's mill trip next Saturday.'

'What, when you were going to take the new coach out for its maiden voyage?'

'Yes, and they were going to fill it with crates of ale.'

'Mind you, when you think about it, it is a mill trip and what always goes on a mill trip?'

'I never thought. I was so looking forward to taking the new coach to Blackpool, I just never thought. However, I'm not having ale in my new coach. I've told them they can have the best older one and I'm not driving that ramshackle contraption to Blackpool. They can have Norris Oakes to drive it and stuff em.'

'You are mad,' said his wife.

'I am not mad. At least, not in the sense you mean. Yes, I am mad and I'm going to stay mad.' He sat at the table with a face like thunder.

'Put your other face on and get your tea eaten,' she told him.

*

Joan had not seen Eustace in such a bad temper before and whilst trying to calm him down actually became just a little apprehensive of him.

'Whatever is the matter with you, you're huffing and puffing and not fit to talk to. For heaven's sake sit down and calm down before your eyeballs shoot out of their sockets. You're not even fit to eat your tea. Whatever it is, it can't be that bad.'

'It is that bad. In fact, it's worse. Bewdlay won't take any crates of ale in the new coach as he promised us, so we have to have the best old one.'

'Is that so bad a thing? Or situation solved, go without beer.'

'What are you thinking about woman? It's a mill trip. We'll just have to have the older coach. I'll have to explain to Willie and Arthur. The rest of the punters wont know any different as they haven't been involved and the new coach was going to be a surprise on the day.'

'Well just sit there and relax for a while. Listen to the light programme for a little. Tea will be a few minutes before its ready.'

'Yes alright, and sorry love, it's not your fault, but I never thought to mention ale when I booked it. I am however really annoyed with Joseph Bewdlay. If there had been another coach firm in the vicinity, I'd have cancelled Bewdlay and got one from elsewhere, but there isn't. There's nowt we can do. First time in my life that I've organised anything like this and it has gone wrong.'

'It's not gone wrong, love. It's just a little setback. There is one thing however; you'll not get Joseph to change his mind.

He's been awkward all his life and I should know. I'll just go and see how tea's getting along.'

Eustace sat back and smiled to himself when Joan had gone into the kitchen. Six months ago he wouldn't have had any sympathy from her at all. She'd just have shouted at him for being stupid and maybe even clattered the side of his head. Now it was all love and help. *Thank goodness we ran the Christmas club last year,* he thought.

*

The next morning, Eustace was at work early in the blending room of Murgatroyd's mill. When it came to breakfast time he asked the foreman if he could go to the dyehouse at the other end of the mill to have a very quick word with Willie and Arthur.

'What for?'

So he had to explain briefly that there was trouble with the coach for the trip and as organiser he needed an urgent word with them.

The foreman was one of the trippers so he readily agreed.

'Don't be too long. I'll cover for you whilst you are away.'

The other two were eating their breakfasts when Eustace appeared.

'Hey up. Look here. What's this?' Willie mumbled through a mouthful of bread and dripping.

Arthur looked up. 'I don't know, but it smells of trouble. He looks very determined. What's up lad?'

'I called at Bewdlay's last night to check that everything was in order for Saturday. I told him we needed the coach at the club at half past seven to load the crates of ale and he refused to put the crates of ale into his new coach. He said we could have one of the older coaches instead.'

'The bastard. He knew it was a mill trip and he'd be taking ale.'

'He was adamant about it. There's no way he'll take his new coach.'

'Do you know what?' said Willie. 'He'll not drive the old coach himself; He'll send Norris Oakes, just to be awkward.'

'Well, he's the one that will miss out on a day in Blackpool.'

Anthony Murgatroyd, on his morning tour, passed through the dyehouse and came over to the three of them. 'Now what is going on here?' he enquired.

Eustace explained all.

'Bewdlay always was an awkward sod and it will be pointless me trying to change his mind because I know from experience that it is just like dealing with a lump of rock. That is why I only go to him when I am stuck. So unless I am very much mistaken, you are stuck with the old coach. If I was you, I would grin and bear it, then wait until after the trip then I will go with you to see him and we will demand a substantial reduction in his charges.'

'There is just one other thing before I go back to the blending room. The old coaches have only forty five seats so don't sell any more places, we're full.'

'So you need the refund on the number of seats less on the coach and you are in the clear as far as worrying about the financial implications are concerned. Does anyone know that you were having the new coach?' asked Mr Anthony

'Not as far as we know. It's not been mentioned to anyone.'

'So you're in the clear. Get off and have a good trip and I'll see you all in Blackpool.'

CHAPTER 10

'Will you please stop fidgeting and go back to sleep. It's only five o'clock.' Just for once, Joan dared to raise her voice to Eustace.

'Yes, but its trip day, and I'm all excited. I have to be at the club at half past seven and I can't sleep.'

'Then will you please go downstairs and brew us both a pot of tea so that I can go back to sleep. We are both going to have a late night. You, because you'll be late home, it'll be well into the early hours and you'll be in no fit state to get yourself to bed if past performance is anything to go by. I, as you know, need my beauty sleep and I will have to stay awake to get you into bed. So I'll have a drink of tea now and then go back to sleep for a long lie in once you've gone off to the club. So don't disturb me again, please.'

Eustace went downstairs, brewed the tea, took a mug of it upstairs to Joan and left his own mug downstairs. He returned to the kitchen and sat down with his tea. He got up, walked around the ground floor, sat down again, and then didn't know what to do next. He wasn't sleepy, but it was only twenty past five. It was light, the sun was rising and it had prospects of being a very nice early summer's day. He read yesterday's paper again; the radio didn't start broadcasting until six o'clock. And he couldn't take the dog for a walk because they didn't have one. So he just sat and contemplated. He dozed a while, then walked around the ground floor again, then he went to get shaved and washed and dressed, all without disturbing Joan, so that by the time he had finished his ablutions it was a quarter to seven.

Eustace popped his head around the bedroom door to see that Joan was awake. He told her he was going and in return received the statutory warnings about behaving, not drinking too much, or coming home paralytic. He went over to the bed, gave Joan a kiss, picked up his best hat and Mac, and then left the house, heading for the club.

In order to kill some time he went the long way round, slowly, but even so he arrived at the club at a quarter past seven.

At about this time, both Willie and Arthur were also receiving their good behaviour lectures before departing for the same venue.

Meeting time was seven thirty at the club. Harry was there with Cybil, whom he had promoted to deputy head steward in his absence, not that there would be much trade with most of the club regulars on the trip, but at least they could leave the club knowing that it was in safe hands.

When Harry and Cybil had arrived at the club, they had found Eustace standing on the doorstep waiting for them. He'd called in at the newsagents to say good morning to the proprietor and whilst there he had purchased a packet of cigarettes. Following on from that he had done some window shopping in the high street, and then paraded up and down in front to the club until Harry and Cybil arrived at about twenty seven minutes past seven.

'My words you're looking very smart, Eustace.'

'Thank you, Cybil. I've had time to prepare myself. I've been up since five, too excited to sleep.'

'Come on, Eustace, lend a hand.' Harry had already opened wide the front door, fastened back the inner double doors and was preparing to carry out sixty crates of beer.

'Coach isn't here yet and anyway let's wait for the other two.'

'We might as well be having one to kick off the day,' said Harry.

'You don't need one yet,' Cybil scolded Harry.

'No dear.' He pulled his tongue at her back.

Another good man henpecked for good, thought Eustace.

The other two arrived. 'Not got all those crates outside and onto the pavement, Eustace? We thought you'd be ready for loading the coach by the time we arrived.'

'The coach hasn't arrived yet.'

'A keen observer if ever I met one,' said Arthur.

'Why don't we get this lot out onto the pavement, then when the bus does come we'll be ready for a quick load up and off to the Fox and Grapes.' Willie was eager.

'There are a lot of crates in sixty,' Eustace observed once they had finished stacking them. 'Where's the coach? Bewdlay's late.'

They heard it coming before it appeared at the top of the street, as it backfired just before the corner.

Willie groaned. 'It's the bloody exploding coach, the oldest in the fleet.'

'No. No, it's like he said, the best of the rest. This one must have started exploding as well. Just listen to it chugging and, well I'll be buggered, it's Norris Oakes in the driving seat. I knew it. I just knew what would happen. I'll murder that Bewdlay next week, relative or not.'

The coach ground to a halt, the door opened and a smiling Norris Oakes alighted. 'Morning all. Is this the cargo?' he asked looking at the pile of crates. 'There's rather a lot of it. Not much room in the luggage compartments but let me get the key and we'll see what we can do.'

He climbed back into the coach, got a square key out of his locker, alighted from the coach and opened up the two doors on each side, effectively opening out the bottom of the seating area.

'Best put them on the pavement side as much as we can and seeing that I've parked the wrong way around, I'll get inside and you can pass them over to me. That way I can shove them to the far side so that they'll be instantly ready for drinking. Mind you, we'd best leave a few on this side, just to balance the coach.'

They carefully completed the loading and Norris locked the cargo doors, put the key away and invited the four passengers aboard for the very short journey to the Fox and Grapes.

Cybil gave them all the standard female lecture about sobriety and behaviour and they then all sat at the front of the coach for the short hop.

'Bewdlay only called at our house on Thursday night and asked me to do this trip. Said he should have been doing it himself as a favour to one of his relations, but something had come up and he couldn't come, so I know nowt about it and before we set off, I've two questions. The first one is what the form is for today?'

'Well, I'm the relation you mentioned,' said Eustace. 'We should have had the brand new coach, but when it arrived he wouldn't let us put the crates of ale in it. With it being new he was going to drive it himself and when we get back, I am personally going to kill him, kill him. Anyway the form for today is as jotted down on this bit of paper. It goes something like this.

1. Load coach at club at 7.30. We've done that.
2. Breakfast at The Fox and Grapes at 8.00.
3. Depart Fox and Grapes 8.45.
4. Stop for roadside drinks.
5. Stop at pub about half way.
6. Stop for roadside drinks.
7. Get to Blackpool in time to get to golden cockerel Restaurant for 12.30.
8. Free Afternoon.
9. Leave Blackpool at time to be determined by coach driver.
10. Stop for roadside drinks.
11. Stop at pub about half way.
12. Stop for roadside drinks if there's any left.
13. Unload empty crates at club and have a swift half.

14. Get home when we get home.

'That's fine, just fine, suits me down to the ground. Second question and one I always ask. Have we got a bottle opener?'

The four passengers looked at one another.

'That's a stupid question to ask four professionals like us,' said Harry with a smile. 'Have we hell as like as got a bottle opener. Here open that door and I'll go and get some.' He dashed off the coach and into the club.

'What have you forgotten?' asked Cybil who was cleaning up the remains of last nights mess.

'Just a small matter of half a dozen bottle openers.'

'Ee, even I'd forgotten about bottle openers.'

He collected what he could find and puffed his way back to the coach. 'OK Driver,' he roared, 'let's get to that breakfast.'

The Fox and Grapes, an imitation half-timbered building standing at the side of the village green and duck pond, looked good in the June sunlight as it had recently been painted.

'If the breakfast is half as good as the building looks it'll be excellent,' Willie said as the coach pulled up outside.

There were several sarcastic comments about them being chauffeured to breakfast, but all were in good humour.

The dining room at the back of the pub was half full when they arrived and was rapidly filling. Rosie May Whiteside lost no time at all in squashing Willie against the corner of the bar and playing with whatever bits of him she could get hold of.

Freddy came in from the kitchen and said, 'Rosie, my dear, do put Willie down, he's come for his breakfast, not a fright and then he's a long way to travel, so do let him get on with it.' He knocked loudly on the bar with a spoon. 'Now gentlemen, please take your seats as breakfast is about to be served.'

The young lady waitresses of the village came into the room with big steaming tureens of porridge. There was sugar, milk, honey and golden syrup on the tables plus a large glass of orange juice for each diner.

The waitresses were quite safe from the amorous intentions of the diners as said diners all had other things, namely beer, on their minds.

They were all very smartly dressed, all wearing ties, and sports jackets and all were very well behaved. There was a little bit of rowdiness and a slight excess of toilet visiting from those that had loaded the ale onto the coach. Sixty crates being fifty-nine and a half by now. This had been only to sample the quality. But otherwise the breakfast was a function that anyone could be proud of.

The porridge was demolished, the dishes cleaned, some by spoon, others, and only a few, by licking, then the dishes were cleared away and hot clean plates served to each person. Then huge plates of bacon, sausage, black pudding, fried eggs, tomatoes, beans and fried potatoes were passed around. Mountains of toast were put on the table and all assembled had a right good breakfast. They finished off with marmalade or jam for the toast and mugs of tea or coffee.

The bar of the Fox and Grapes was not open for trip breakfasts, as Freddy knew only too well, as it became impossible to move the trippers and clear up the ensuing mess. The only exception to the bar not being open was Rosie May who had her own special stock of gin elsewhere and who was well drunk, enjoying herself with forty six males, fondling and touching the customers wherever and whenever she could.

At nine o'clock, when all had eaten their fill and more, and those who habitually licked their plates clean had done so, Eustace stood up, banged his spoon on the table, called for silence and announced that about fifteen minutes after they should have done, it was about time to hit the road for Blackpool.

There was an immediate scramble for the bladder emptying suite, resulting in a few minutes further delay, but nothing too serious.

In good humour, and even better order, they boarded the coach. Eustace counted them all carefully and gave Norris Oakes the all clear. The coach coughed and spluttered its way into life and then, with a couple of minor explosions, it jolted into full life and pulled away from the village green.

Back at the Fox and Grapes, Rosie May began her long standing Saturday après trip breakfast ritual of gathering up all the left over food to give to the ducks, on the pond in the middle of the village green.

The ducks were clever, they knew when a good feed was coming their way because they had seen the coach stay a while outside the pub and they knew that soon after it left, the human would come along and feed them. They were also clever enough to realise that the human was unpredictable in her habits and that the food could be distributed anywhere on the village green or even straight into the pond. They had also learned to stand quite some way from her as she sometimes served them the tray as well. One duck in particular had hatched her new brood of ducklings since the last trip and she was busy giving them a lecture about avoiding the human.

Rosie, with a supreme alcoholically retarded effort collected the scraps, put them all onto her tray and made her way, as best she could, to the front door, banging into this and that as she went. The cigarette, stuck to her bottom lip, dropped ash hither and thither as she went on her way.

She half tottered, half fell, down the two front steps of the pub, recovered her balance, squinted, focused her eyes as best she could on the duck pond in the distance and without looking she proceeded to meander across the road.

At exactly that precise time, Alec Sykes, the local milkman, was heading in his truck at full speed with a full load of full milk crates towards the centre of the village. He was late and rushing. Rosie May stepped from the pavement right in front of him. He braked violently, and well over two hundred pint bottles of milk and their crates were, split seconds later, sitting well smashed to smithereens in the middle of the road. Alec just sat there, gobsmacked and paralysed, unable to move or speak with his fist firmly locked on the vehicle's horn.

Rosie May ignored the truck and its horn and carried on tottering towards the ducks as if nothing had happened.

Freddy and the staff hurtled outside to see what all the horn blowing was about. They discovered the scene of devastation with Alec sitting there unable to move and with force they managed to move his fist from the horn.

Eventually Alec rejoined the land of the living. 'She just. She just. Is she dead?'

'No. By look of things you didn't hit her, or if you did, it wasn't hard enough. She's over there still walking to the ducks.'

Police constables Patrick O'Donovan and Alice Wrench, who were on their beats in the vicinity of the Fox and Grapes, had taken the opportunity of a quiet Saturday morning to get to know one another a little more intimately than they had before by arranging their separate beats to cross in a quiet secluded alleyway behind the pub. They were becoming quite well acquainted when the horn began its noisy tirade.

As was always the case on trip breakfast Saturdays, a small crowd of locals had gathered once the coach had departed, to watch Rosie May feed the ducks. This was usually good entertainment, particularly for the younger members of the village.

Today, the entertainment had an added item of the milk truck almost standing on its end, discharging most of its cargo to mother earth and blowing its horn for a long time without stopping.

Freddy helped Alec Sykes to get out of his drivers cab and by the time he had done so, the two constables who had pulled themselves together as best and speedily as they could, ran to the front of the pub from the secluded alleyway.

One of the teenage bystanders shouted as loud she could, 'Hey look, Constable O'Donovan's been shagging Constable Wrench behind the pub.'

The two Constables, having ascertained as they approached that there were no casualties, stopped in their tracks to survey the crowd but they were unable visibly to determine the perpetrator of the accusation. They recovered their composure and attended the accident.

Alec Sykes had recovered sufficiently to begin to shout and storm. 'It's that bloody silly wife of yours. She stepped into the road right in front of my truck. I really thought I'd killed her.'

'No, no. You've missed her, more's the pity. She takes a lot of killing does Rosie May. Many have tried but all have failed. Come into the pub and I'll get you a brandy.'

'Just a minute. Just hang on a minute. What's been going on here then?' demanded PC O'Donovan in his best demanding voice.

'A minor matter that we can clear up ourselves, thank you constable. I think we need detain you both no longer,' said Freddy.

'But it's not a minor matter. Look at all the mess in the road. No no, it looks to me like charges will have to be brought. Yes, yes, there's no doubt about it.'

The frustrated young lady, Constable Wrench, kept her own counsel in the matter. She would have preferred to have melted into the distance but O'Donovan was keen and pursued the matter taking out his notebook, flourishing his arms and licking his regulation issue pencil. 'So now then, just exactly what happened?'

There was by now a log jam of other vehicles around the crash site but the Police and everyone else other than the crowd of onlookers were ignoring it.

Meanwhile, across on the green, Rosie May was making slow progress towards the ducks. She was completely oblivious to the chaos that she had caused with the milk truck and was concentrating as best she could on the task that lay ahead. She was having the utmost difficulty focusing her eyes on the ducks. They were continually coming in and out of a foggy haze. Then they kept on moving as well which really was the sole reason for her erratic and rapid changes of direction.

The wise old mother duck observed the progress of Rosie May and realised that she was worse than normal, so she hurriedly reassembled her young chicks in close formation and was then ready to move them quickly as the situation dictated. She had observed Rosie May many times, tripping up, throwing the tray in the air, the food scraps going in all directions, and Rosie May spending ages trying to retrieve her tray. So it was always in the ducks best interest to be prepared. The problem was that the ducklings would not always behave as instructed and she found it most difficult to maintain her flock in a tight formation.

Rosie, by sheer grit and determination, fuelled by an alcoholic fog arrived at the duck pond and the ducks. The mother duck moved her flock back out of range. One chick would not behave and ran towards Rosie May in anticipation of a good feed. The mother duck shouted at the chick to come back but couldn't leave the rest of the brood and the shouting fell on deaf ears. The mother duck screamed at the chick as she observed Rosie May trip and begin to fall forwards, still holding the tray. The chick was still progressing towards Rosie May; the mother duck quacked in anguish and began to run forward to rescue her child. Rosie was still falling, the sky went dark over the duckling, the mother duck stopped running and began to cry as Rosie May hit the ground and the duckling expired this life for ever as it was squashed underneath Rosie May. The tray of scraps took a course of its own.

The mother duck, in her rage, flew at Rosy May quacking and pecking. The other chicks followed the tray and attacked the food. The other grown up ducks came to help attack Rosie May. She recovered her composure, knelt up, told the ducks in no uncertain terms to sod off, stood up, picked up her tray, hit out at the ducks and then wove her way slowly across the village green to the Fox and Grapes.

The ducks stood around the squashed duckling in a little circle, all sad and sorrowful at the parting of one of their number and by such a cruel method of assassination.

The crowd outside the pub, having observed the killing scene were all jeering and booing Rosie May as she returned to the pub.

Meanwhile, back inside the pub, PC O'Donovan, sensing an arrest, which he hadn't had in a long time, was questioning Freddy Whiteside and Alec Sykes.

'So you say that this woman, Rosie May Whiteside, wife of Freddy Whiteside stepped out in front of your truck full of bottles of milk, without looking, without stopping and just marched on in front of you. You stopped rapidly and your unsecured load consisting of more than two hundred full bottles of milk flew into the road smashing beyond recognition and wasting same.'

'Aye something like that.'

PC O'Donovan was now working up to two arrests. Rosie May for causing an accident whilst under the influence of alcohol and Alec Sykes for driving with an unsecured load.

Freddy Whiteside, wanting to settle the matter quickly and without the involvement of the law decided that it was time to play his ace card and put his two pennyworth in. 'Look here Constable, it's a well known fact that you and this lass here…' he pointed to PC Alice Wrench '…were enjoying carnal relations around the back of the pub before the crash disturbed you.'

'We were doing no such thing. I could have you for slander.'

PC Alice Wrench kept her gob firmly shut.

'No you can't, and come down off your high horse. I was watching you out of the back window.'

'Oh well, in that case I'll have you for being a peeping Tom as well.'

'What if I was to tell you that I was not the only one to observe you, and just for your information, you do not know that I am a personal friend of your Chief Constable. I have therefore decided what we will do and if you do not agree, I will pick the phone up and ring the Chief.'

Alec Sykes looked at him but said nothing.

Constable O'Donovan looked at Constable Wrench, who returned his gaze without any emotion.

'Oh. Go on then,' said O'Donovan.

'OK. You forget all about our little accident which Alec and I will sort out between us and you two can have the use of our little back room for an hour and we here will never have known about it. Agreed?'

'Oh yes. Thank you.'

'Indeed, thank you,' said PC Alice Wrench.

The police were shown to the boudoir by Freddy.

'By gum, that were a flaming good idea. You were bluffing about the Chief Constable weren't you?'

'No. I know him quite well. He pops in here for a drink quite often. Right, now then Alec, what's the damage?'

'Well it's not so much the money, although that is very important, but more to the point is where am I going to get replacements from? It's all to deliver yet today, you know.'

'Can't you ring around the local competition to see what they've got spare?'

'Well I can.'

'Come on then, I'll help you. You find the numbers in the directory and I'll phone them and explain the circumstances.'

Just at this time Rosie May stumbled back into the bar. She saw Alec and within seconds her arm was around his waist and she was leaning heavily on him.

'What about my milk bottles?' He asked trying his best to extricate himself from her drunken embrace.

'What milk bottles?' She began to advance on him again.

Freddy intervened and directed Rosie May into the kitchen.

It didn't take long to organise relief milk supplies, then they agreed that Alec would go away and reckon up his costs and damages, then return later in the day to sort it out and settle up. He was just leaving when the kitchen door swung back with a bang and Rosie May trotted in.

'There's, I say, there's, hic, there's a, no, no, there's two. Yes, that's it, two. Two policemen in the back room.' The last couple of words came out quickly and with the greatest of effort.

'Actually Rosie there's a policeman and a policewoman in the back room and they're making love, not war with you, so here take this bread and go feed the ducks.'

Rosie went out of the front door. Alec went with her to make sure she got across the road safely. He suddenly realised that there were over two hundred smashed milk bottles lying in the road that he had forgotten about. So he went back into the pub to get Freddy to come out of the kitchen with a couple of brushes and shovels in order to clear up the mess.

It took Freddy a long time that Saturday to try to explain to Rosie May about the police and the broken glass in the road and for her to keep her mouth well and truly shut.

There were those in the village that chose to comment on the very rare event of PC O'Donovan walking his beat with a smile on his face. A unique happening.

*

Bewdlay's best/worst exploding coach back-fired its way up and over the Pennine hills and down into Lancashire. The passengers were all in good humour and extremely well behaved. The vicar was joining in the conversation, having lowered his ecclesiastical guard, and acting on a mill trip level for the day. Fat Harry was at his foulest and Evans was poking fun at anyone and everyone. There was a right good holiday atmosphere in the coach.

Norris Oakes was experiencing a little difficulty with the coach. Nothing new in a Bewdlay's coach, he always had problems with the gears. They were a new kind known as crash and grind, which he very successfully managed to do at every gear change. Coupled with the exploding engine, it made for hard work driving.

They were rolling along nicely through eastern Lancashire when there came a cry from the back of the coach. 'Stop, stop, I'm bursting for a pee.'

Norris ignored the plea and motored on.

A couple of miles further along and the cry came again. 'Stop, stop, I really am bursting for a pee.'

Norris once again ignored the cry and continued to wrestle with the coach.

The voice came running down the aisle of the coach. Its owner grabbed Norris by the collar and shouted. 'If you don't stop right now, I'll have an accident and you'll have a wet coach.'

The coach lurched to the centre of the road as Norris had his collar felt.

The other passengers were shouting at the man who had been taken sudden to sit down.

Norris growled at the man. 'Fred Armitage! I can't stop now; we're in the middle of a lot of houses. Hang on to it for five minutes and we'll be out in the countryside again.'

'I can't. No way. You'll either have to stop here or I'll do it onto the coach floor.'

Norris looked sideways at Fred to see him standing bent forwards, cross legged and cross eyed, so he applied maximum force to the brake pedal. The lucky occupants of the coach just slithered onto the floor, the more unlucky ones shot forward into the seat back in front of them. Fortunately no one received any lasting injury.

The man waiting to pee hurtled forward, down two steps and headlong into the front window. He picked himself up whilst cursing Norris, dusted himself down, opened the door, jumped off the coach onto the pavement and was faced by a long row of red brick terrace houses. He looked around. On the other side of the street was another identical row. He therefore had three choices. He could pee against the coach in full view of his mates, he could go into one of the narrow passages that ran through the terrace giving access to the back gardens or he could knock on someone's door and ask if he could use their toilet. He chose the middle course and ran into one of the nearest narrow passages.

A somewhat large Lancashire lad was sitting by his front window reading his Saturday morning paper when the coach stopped. It was a rare event, a coach stopping right outside his house, so, filled with natural curiosity, he pulled back the curtains just slightly, and observed part of what was happening, deduced the rest and said to his wife, 'I'm just going to take the dog for a walk.'

His wife couldn't believe her ears because he never took the dog out, but then she also had discovered what was going on outside and she begged her headstrong husband not to do anything stupid.

Fred Armitage, having the pee, was well on with doing what he was doing when the biggest Alsatian he had ever seen bounded towards him, barking growling and snarling. A split second decision was called for and without having time to tidy himself up, he made one, jumping, running and diving for the coach at break neck speed. The Alsatian kept up with him just a hairs breadth from sinking its teeth into his ankles. He literally dived into the coach - the Alsatian followed him. He ran up the aisle to his seat. Someone at the front grabbed the dog's lead. It stood howling and snarling. The dog turned around and emptied its bladder against Norris Oakes's seat.

Its owner stood on the pavement laughing. Norris was not amused and pressed the button to close the door before driving off with the dog still on the coach creating mayhem. The dog's owner went berserk on the pavement and began to run after the coach. The passengers all sat perfectly still and silent not daring to move except for Eustace who had been brought up to be used to handling dogs. He got out of his seat, talked to the dog and played with it, observed that the owner was a little way behind them and motioned to Norris to stop. Norris opened the door and Eustace ejected the dog. Norris closed the door and they accelerated away.

There were many who craved for a relief of internal pressure in the next half hour or so, some almost again at bursting point, including the Fred who became known as Alsatian Fred. But they held on to it with grim determination until the first organised stop was reached.

The landlord of the Duke of Leeds was used to trip coaches descending on his pub on weekend mornings and to selling them a lot of ale. He had specially extended his parking facilities so that coaches could drive through and park without the need for reversing. He had obtained, by using slight financial incentives, and even in one case blackmail, the special licenses required for serving alcoholic refreshments to early morning trips.

Norris pulled their coach into the parking lot at the side of a party of ladies of mixed age from a sweet factory in Dewsbury. The men from Murgatroyd's mill were, without exception, in need of the gentlemen's facilities. The ladies from Dewsbury were in a similar condition. This state of desperation did not hold either side back from a little petting, kissing and cuddling on the way to the toilet block. The landlord, used to these happenings, stationed himself outside the toilets just to make sure that ladies used the ladies and gents the gents, so that there was no untoward extra sexual activity.

Willie, Arthur and Eustace found themselves a table in the corner from where they could examine the carryings on with ease and enjoy their pints in comfort.

Fat Harry had already got his arm half way around the non-existent waist of a buxom lass from Dewsbury and was feeding her with a glass of sherry. Other male members of the trip were to be found in similar positions with some other members of the female trip.

The vicar brought his pint over to join the terrible three.

'I hope this carry on isn't upsetting you Vicar?' Eustace posed the question.

'Not in the least. Don't forget that I worked in a foundry before I took the cloth and I've seen nothing yet that compares with what I saw there at times.'

Four of the men and four of the ladies began to play an eight hand snooker game. Some were playing darts, some dominoes. Small groups of the men and the ladies preferred their own company.

Eustace began to look at his watch and to fidget. 'If we don't go before long, Arthur, we'll be late for lunch in Blackpool. It takes an hour and a half from here and it's a quarter to eleven and by the time we get everyone back on the coach it'll be too late and...'

The Vicar sought to reassure him. 'Don't worry Eustace it will be alright on the night, as it were.'

'Which night?' asked Eustace.

'It's a saying, Eustace. A saying, that's all.'

'Oh, yes.' Eustace stood up and wandered out to the coach where he found Norris Oakes sitting on the wall in the sun, talking to the driver of the Dewsbury coach.

Eustace went straight to Norris. 'Norris, don't you think that we'd better get going again if we are going to make that lunch appointment in Blackpool?'

'Alright for half an hour yet, Eustace. Don't panic.'

So Eustace went back into the pub and joined in the conversation for the next half hour until, he started fidgeting again. He once more decided that it was time to round up all his trippers and get them back on the coach.

'Sit down and enjoy your drink,' said Willie.

'No, I can't, we're going to be late.'

'They'll not be expecting us until at least one o'clock,' said Arthur

'But it's going to take us until then to get there. Will you three please help me to round up the others and get them on the coach?'

But the others were not for going. The landlord didn't help because he was selling ale faster than he could pour it. He had three more coaches in by then, his pub was full to bursting and the atmosphere was brilliant, warm and cuddly. There were two female, two male and one mixed trip and the contents of the coaches were by then, completely mixed up to the point where Eustace was having difficulty sorting out one from the other. It took him another half hour to gather his trippers together, to separate them from new found friends, to get them in and out of the toilets and to get them back onto their coach.

Willie, Arthur and the reverend did eventually lend a hand but it was only out of a sense of duty to help an old friend and not because they wanted to go.

When they did get everyone aboard, some of them began to get off again to go to the toilet yet again. When they finally did close the coach door and Eustace did a head count as they were pulling out of the car park, they had to stop again whilst Eustace asked two ladies, that he found curled up with two of his trippers in the back corner of the coach, to leave.

CHAPTER 11

The coach only stopped fourteen times between the Duke of Leeds and the Golden Cockerel Restaurant. By the time they arrived it was half past one. Very fortunately, most of the journey had been through open countryside which meant that Norris could pull his coach up on the verge, in a field gate or some type of lay-by so the passengers could dive off the coach into the hedgerows and byways to relieve themselves. There were no exceptions to this because they all, at one stop or another, had to get out. Some only once, some four or five times.

At one stop, where there was plenty of room to pull the coach off the main highway, they all descended and opened the luggage compartment to get out some of the bottled ale they had brought with them. At this point, Fat Harry took command, as they were his bottles and he was responsible for them. He kept a tight leash on them all, counting them out and counting them back in again.

When Job Crabtree having drained his bottle, threw the empty over the hedge, just before he belched, Harry set off for him at a canter.

'Go and fetch that bloody bottle back here now. They've all got to go back to the club tonight.'

'You can fetch it if you want it,' slurred a very drunk Job.

Job was a big man, but he was well gone and had not reckoned on the agility, strength, or speed of Harry. As fast as lightning, Harry took hold of Job by the scruff of the neck in a vice like grip and set off at a trot along the side of the hedge, through an open gate and doubled back behind the hedge to the spot where he thought the bottle should be.

This episode had drawn an audience of a coach full plus driver, all shouting, cheering, jeering, falling over with excitement and drink, not to mention emptying bottles at a fair rate of knots.

'Now find my bottle,' shouted Harry at Job who dropped to his knees as the vice on his neck was released. The bottle was not obvious in the long grass and it was not long before half the trippers were on their hands and knees in the long grass, hindering the search for it.

'Harry, is this pantomime necessary?' enquired Arthur, who was sober enough to instill an element of sanity into the situation.

'Yes, very necessary, I'm responsible for the bottles and I have to pay for any I lose.'

'What if we pay for it out of the trip fund?'

But he didn't get a reply as the coach with the ladies from Dewsbury pulled into the parking area. They all piled out of their coach screaming and shouting. Some ran for the field but others just crouched down at the side of the coach in desperation to empty their over full interiors, much to the men's delight. Those in the field, having done what they had to do, jumped onto the men who were still on their hands and knees. Within seconds there was an absolute melee. Arms and legs everywhere, bottles forgotten. There were legs in the air, knickers on display, hands where there should not have been hands, lipstick marks where there should definitely not have been lipstick marks and a general air of drunken enjoyment.

The driver of the ladies coach and the lady in charge, who had tried to retain an air of decorum throughout, were worried about the delay. They had only made a quick stop for the purposes before described and they had to meet their boss for lunch at the Copper Kettle restaurant at one o'clock.

Eustace was worried about the delay and Norris Oakes couldn't have cared less although he was aware he was running late.

Eustace decided to revert to plan C. He didn't know what plans A and B were, but he did know they wouldn't work. As a last minute thought, and as a plan C, he had brought along his football referee's whistle from his younger days in the local football league. He was just about to step into the middle of the affray and blow the whistle loud and clear, when he observed the local police force arriving in their little Ford Popular Panda car.

Two officers exited the vehicle, put on their helmets, straightened them, put their arms together behind their back, did a short knees bend, coughed discreetly and approached the jamboree that was taking place. Observing the two coach drivers and the two party organisers standing back and looking to be on edge, the police came towards them.

Norris, although just a little worried about the delay, was actually enjoying the scene and wondering if he dare join in the orgy that was happening in front of his eyes.

The plod that appeared to be in charge spoke to whoever would listen to him. 'As we proceeded along the highway we observed one of your party urinating in a public place. This is an offence against the law which carries a fine of twenty five pounds, no shillings and no pence, or failure to pay may lead to a gaol sentence of two months.'

Oh hell, thought Eustace, *we've got a right one here.*

Arthur and Willie who had been standing with Eustace cocked a polite ear but did not get involved.

'However in the spirit of friendliness, and as a gesture of welcome to Lancashire, we are prepared to ignore the offence on this occasion providing you immediately get everyone back on their respective coaches and get on your way.'

'Constable! We have been trying to do that for the past quarter of an hour. We're already late for lunch in Blackpool. Do you have your regulation issue police whistles with you?'

'Yes, we do.'

'Well please step into the middle of that lot, blow them with all your might and order all of them back onto the coach.'

The policeman looked at him. 'We can do that sir, but I must warn you that any resistance we encounter will lead to a caution being issued and may then lead to a prosecution being issued, depending on the mood of the Chief constable.'

'Please carry on Constable,' said Eustace with the others nodding their assent.

So the police dived into the middle of the ninety or so bodies that were not all playing at doctors and nurses, but enjoying sitting in the field in the hot sun drinking.

The two whistles were blown long and hard with great relish. The trippers were alarmed and stopped whatever they were doing. Those that found it necessary hurriedly adjusted their clothing and all piled back into their respective coaches. Some of them made an arrangement to meet up again at the entrance to central pier at half past three.

The Murgatroyd trip arrived at The Golden Cockerel Restaurant without further incident, other than a few comfort breaks, and was only half an hour late.

*

Anthony and Margaret Murgatroyd, and their chauffeur plus his wife, had arrived at the Golden Cockerel Restaurant in good time for the lunch. They had travelled over in style in the Rolls Royce purposely taking a different route to the coach. They had parked the vehicle in a car park at Gynn Square and travelled to the Central Pier by tram from where they had walked the couple of hundred yards or so to the venue.

Anthony and the chauffeur had taken a long time to walk the two hundred yards to the restaurant spending ages on the slot machines along the way, examining the stalls selling 'kiss me quick' hats, post cards, Blackpool rock and other novelties that were available to a gullible public. Anthony did not visit Blackpool very often and liked to relive his misspent youth when he did. His chauffeur wasn't complaining, it was costing him nothing. Anthony gave him two ten shilling notes and asked him to go change them for pennies, then they both enjoyed losing them.

The two ladies, on the other hand, walked along the promenade on the far side of the tram tracks looking at all the people on the beach, the donkeys and the ice cream sellers. The chauffeur's wife would have preferred to be on the golden mile with Anthony and her husband but didn't object as she was on a free day out which she didn't get very often.

The men and ladies joined forces again outside the Golden Cockerel restaurant where they mounted the stairs and had a good look around at their surroundings.

Elsie Proops was at the cash desk at the top of the first flight of stairs. She observed the four people, who did not look like a mill trip, ascending towards her and then, instead of speaking to her, they began to look around.

She left her desk and went over to them and in her best affected, high class voice she asked, 'Can I help you? A table for lunch for four is it?'

The chauffeur answered, 'Yes you can and no it's not. We are here for the Murgatroyd trip lunch.'

'Ah yes…' Elsie was lost for words. These four smartly dressed people did not look like your average day trippers. They were not drunk, they were not behaving like animals and they were polite. Elsie began to think that they were going to have a very staid, well behaved and well mannered lunch. Elsie, being used to surprises concerning what arrived in her restaurant, asked the same question of them that she asked any visiting diner, 'What can I get you to drink?'

She realised even more that these were not your bog standard day tripper when Margaret Murgatroyd asked for a Campari and soda, the chauffeur's wife ordered a gin and tonic, Anthony also a gin and tonic and the chauffeur himself a pint of best bitter.

'It's South Shore Best,' said Elsie.

'Wonderful, marvelous. A long time since I sampled the brew. The last time I drank it it was very palatable indeed.'

'Please have a seat whilst I get your drinks.'

They sat down at a table in the panoramic window and admired the view of the roofs of the golden mile and the sea in the distance. They just couldn't see the promenade and the trams.

Elsie returned with their drinks and laid them neatly before them. 'You've not travelled on the coach with the others then?' she ventured to enquire.

'No. We've only just come really for the lunch and then we are going back home. What time to you expect the main body of the party?' Anthony enquired.

'Well, the lunch is booked for one o'clock, but on average, trip lunches are served between half and one hour late. This is because most of the participants have had difficulty in getting here.'

'Why difficulty in arriving here?'

'Because most of them are completely inebriated by the time they get here, many of them are ill of their own making and sometimes we do have problems cleaning up after them.'

'That sounds just like our lot,' said Anthony. 'So where are we having the lunch?'

'Upstairs on the second floor in the function suite. If you would like to go and sit up there until your colleagues arrive and enjoy your aperitifs sitting in our comfortable chairs and admiring the view over the sea and the promenade, it will be pleasanter than remaining down here.'

'You mean we are in the way down here?' asked Anthony.

'No, no, I didn't mean...oh dear, what have I said?'

Anthony laughed aloud, 'Don't worry, Mrs err...'

'Proops.'

'Mrs Proops, it was only my little joke. Yes, we will rise to the next elevation and take in the majestic expanse before us.'

Elsie gave him a peculiar look. 'There is another bar upstairs and I will send someone up in a little while to make sure that you are all alright.'

So the four people, knowing that they might have some time to wait, climbed the stairs to the top floor and sat in the comfortable armchairs watching the world go by on the promenade, the trams passing by and all the holidaymakers enjoying the sea and the beach.

It was almost half past one, and another round of drinks later, when Ken Proops came puffing up the stairs. 'How do all, I'm Ken the proprietor and chef. Any idea what time your lot will be arriving as I'm just beginning to be a little bit anxious about the state of the lunch?'

Anthony Murgatroyd smiled at Ken and replied, 'I think you need worry no longer, if I'm not mistaken that is Willie Arkenthwaite's voice that I can hear coming from somewhere in the bowels of your emporium.'

Sure enough, first one, then another head appeared up the stairs. Eustace, being in command, was in the lead. He saw Ken, came over and shook his hand. 'Well, we've made it. A bit touch and go at times, but we are here. All of us in body, some in spirit, others in spirits.' He laughed at his own joke which was more than Ken did.

Willie and Arthur were amazed that Eustace could even crack a joke. They led him away to the bar.

'No, no, Willie, I won't have a drink just now, not before dinner,' said Eustace.

'Luncheon,' Arthur reminded him. 'And what's the matter with you all of a sudden. Never been known to refuse a drink.'

'No, I've got to make sure that the wheels of catering run smoothly and that there are no problems.'

'Plus of course you've got to remain sober to deliver your speech.'

The other two looked at Willie.

'What speech?' Eustace exploded with incredulity. 'I'm not making a speech. No one said anything about a speech. I'm not Arthur, Willie, not. No, no definitely not.'

'Trip organiser's prerogative. You've got to welcome your guests. You can do it before the meal, or after, it really does not matter.'

'But they're not my guests. They're just workmates on a day trip. Over half of them are so drunk that they'll not know whether I give a speech or the head clown from the Tower Circus gives it.'

'No, Eustace, it is your responsibility as trip organiser to make a speech of welcome,' said Arthur.

So Eustace went to the bar and borrowed a piece of paper and a pen, then went and sat in the quietest corner he could find to compose a few words. He had not been there long, just long enough for the trippers to get a drink, when Ken Proops came over to him and asked him to call everyone to their places at table as lunch was about to be served.

'Why me?' he asked.

'Because you're the trip organiser and I need you to get everyone sitting down as the meal is beginning to spoil. So please put some urgency into it.'

Eustace, being naturally tall, pulled himself up to his full stretched height and began to shout. 'Gentlemen. Gentlemen. Please take your seats for lunch as it is about to be served.' He was a nervous wreck and motioned to Arthur to come over. 'Please go and get me a whisky, Arthur.'

His request for the trippers to sit down had fallen on deaf ears. The noise from the rabble was increasing and it was apparent that Eustace was in charge in name only.

Arthur brought the whisky. Eustace downed it one long swallow and marched over to the bar where he interrupted whatever was going on and asked if they had a gavel he could borrow. They had, and he took it and walked back into the middle of the crowd of drinkers. He hammered the gavel hard, several times on one of the tables and eventually, after more hammering, got the silence he wanted. 'Gentlemen and Ladies.' As he spoke, he saw the two ladies for the first time. He knew they were coming to the lunch but had forgotten. 'Ladies and Gentlemen...'

'You've said that once only t'other way round,' said Percy Cox.

Eustace began again. 'Ladies and Gentlemen...'

'Three times now,' said Percy Cox.

Eustace started again. 'Lunch is served. Will you please make your way to the tables?'

'Is there a table plan?' someone shouted.

'Is there hell as like as a table plan.' This time it was Willie's turn to respond. 'You can sit where you like, just get on with it.' He belched loudly much to the amusement of the trippers.

So the disorganised rabble sat down where ever they could. Mr and Mrs Anthony Murgatroyd, Mr and Mrs Chauffeur, Eustace, Willie, Arthur and the Reverend Clifford Tunstall sat at a round table in the window.

The reverend said to Eustace, 'I would like to say grace.'

'Well I have to say a few words of welcome to our guests, so I'll do that first.'

Eustace stood and banged the gavel on the table and after several bangs managed to restore silence. 'I'm not used to making public speeches...'

'We know that,' shouted Sid Beaumont.

Eustace decided to ignore him. 'But I just wanted to say welcome to Blackpool, thank you all for coming and we hope you all have an enjoyable day. Now lunch is ready to be served, but before that happens, the Reverend Clifford Tunstall will say grace.'

He sat down to wild applause and the Reverend rose to his feet and held his hand up for silence.

'Will you all stand for grace, please.'

'Why, is she coming?' That was Sid Beaumont again.

'No I'm here already,' shouted Mrs Chauffeur, who no one knew.

'If I may continue, seeing that we are in Lancashire and it is an auspicious occasion, I would like to use a good old Yorkshire grace just to teach these Red Rose people a thing or two.' There were wild cheers which subsided and he continued. 'Oh Lord, look down and make us able, to eat all the food that is put on our table.'

There were cheers and more cheers.

The vicar sat down and was congratulated by Anthony Murgatroyd. 'Thank you, Clifford. That was just what was needed to get the meal off to a good start.'

'Yes, well, I do think that it is essential on such occasions to start the meal off with a grace, but I also think it essential not to bore a congregation of the type that we have here with being too ecclesiastical.'

'Oh! And what's wrong with the type of congregation we have here?' demanded Willie. The drink was fuelling his thoughts and his mouth.

The Vicar, recognising a developing situation, replied, 'I meant no offence. It is just that when people have been drinking, they do not always readily accept a lot of religious mumbo-jumbo, so I like to keep it on the light side of things.'

'Ah yes, thank you Vicar.'

The vicar knew that Willie didn't have a clue as to what he had been saying, but he was relieved that Willie had accepted it with good grace.

The soup had been served and enjoyed and diluted with yet another pint of beer. The roast lamb had just arrived, when Dennis Haigh kicked the underside of the table with his right leg so hard that he sent glasses flying, beer flooding all over and four plates of roast lamb and three veg, into orbit. George Schofield being seated in the wrong place at the wrong time received a lapful of beer, roast lamb, vegetables and gravy.

'Bloody hell, Dennis, what you gone and done that for? It's all over my best flannels. The wife will kill me when we get home.'

'It's cramp, cramp in my leg. For heaven's sake give up eating and come and help us.'

'Yes, but it's my best trousers, ruined, look at them, not fit to walk around Blackpool this afternoon.'

But Dennis was taking no notice of him as he was sitting there, moaning, his face contorted in agony and kicking the underside of the table regularly. His mates, eventually, through their alcoholic haze, realised that something may be amiss and went to Dennis' aid. But before they got to him, Dennis had tried to stand up and had fallen back into his chair. They helped him to stand up and tried to get him to put both feet on the floor at the same time. Here he refused and began to howl in agony.

The Vicar decided that it was time to render succour to the ill of the parish of the Golden Cockerel and so he walked over to Dennis' side.

'Don't you think it may prudent to attempt to put both feet firmly on the ground?'

'You a parson in charge of doctoring as well?' asked Dennis still howling.

'No, no, just trying to give moral support,' replied the reverend.

'I thought not,' said Dennis, 'most of your patients would be dead by now.'

The reverend decided to remove himself gracefully from where he was not welcome and returned to his meal.

By now the table had been cleared and re-laid by Susan Proops and her helpers, and with Dennis rapidly returning to normality, the meal was recommenced with gusto.

The treacle sponge went down a treat and coffee or tea was served.

Willie was having problems of a personal nature. Pressures were building up inside him in all directions and he did not know what to do or how to control himself. Finally, he could control the situation no longer and erupted in a thunderstorm of acute intensity.

The whole room looked at him and the Vicar said, 'Amen to that,' silently to himself and no one else.

Anthony Murgatroyd stood up, banged his wine glass with his dirty pudding spoon and called for silence. After a few more bangs on the glass he achieved his objective.

'Ladies and Gentlemen, I think we should just thank Eustace Ollerenshaw, Willie Arkenthwaite and Arthur Baxter for organising this most splendid of trips, so please put your hands together to salute them.'

There was prolonged applause and cheering.

Anthony Murgatroyd did not sit down and Arthur turned to whisper to Willie. 'What now?'

Anthony continued, 'Now, we at the mill have not contributed anything to this event other than paying for a round of drinks, and as there is no further organised event I decided that we should give each of you some money to buy your next meal. So Margaret has a pile of pound notes and is going to give each of you five as a present to help the day go well.'

There were cheers and more cheers.

*

After lunch, when most of the trippers had departed, Anthony Murgatroyd congratulated the terrible three for a job very well done and then took his leave of them.

'Are you going to the Pleasure Beach, Mr Anthony?' Willie enquired.

'No, Willie, sadly not. But we are going to Stanley Park for a game of bowls, even the ladies are going to join in, and then possibly a row around the lake. After that, afternoon tea in the park café and then home. So thank you once again, do enjoy the rest of your day and please don't forget to come home tonight.'

As soon as Mr Anthony had departed, 'What was all that about not forgetting to come home tonight?' Arthur made a general enquiry.

'Memories of a Blackpool trip during his father's time when some of them didn't make it home for a few days,' said Eustace.

'I know nowt about that,' replied Arthur.

'I only know because my dad told me all those years ago and it's not worth going into just now, and anyway, it couldn't happen again. So let's go see Elsie Proops and pay her whatever we owe her and then we can go and enjoy ourselves.'

They made their way to the pay desk on the floor below and sure enough there was Elsie Proops behind it looking just like she had been waiting there for ever for them.

Eustace handed over a paper bag that he had been keeping in his jacket pocket since he had left home earlier that day.

'I think you'll find it's all there, Mrs Proops, I counted it twice last night, just to make sure.'

She opened the bag and looked into it. Thank you, Mr Ollerenshaw, it looks to be about right, I'll count it later. Have you all had a good meal?'

'Yes, it's been a right good do. Thank you. I think it fair to say that everyone has really enjoyed it. Right you lads, let's be having you. Blackpool here we come.'

CHAPTER 12

Eustace, Willie, Arthur, Fat Harry and one hanger on by the name of Reverend Clifford Tunstall walked over the tramlines, leaned on the railings and viewed the sea. Willie was the first to speak, 'By gum this is grand.'

'Yes, we have a lot to thank the Good Lord for.'

Willie continued, 'Now then Reverend, you are very welcome to come with us but we do not want a load of religion all afternoon.'

'Sorry Willie, I was just marveling at the beauty of nature. I mean to say, just look at that sea, it is fantastic, not to mention the beach, the people, the donkeys, the ice cream sellers, the jugs of tea for the sands, the...'

'Vicar, Vicar, please give over. We've heard enough of it now,' said Arthur.

'Yes. Sorry. I'll try not to do it again.'

Eustace changed the subject. 'Can we go on the pier and ride the humpty cycles?'

'Aye, come on,' said Willie, 'I might have more luck with them than I did last time we were here.'

'What's a humpty cycle?' enquired the Vicar.

'Nay, Vicar,' Willie replied, 'don't you know? It's a bicycle without pedals.'

'How can one possibly ride a bicycle without pedals?'

'You shove the seat up and down with yer arse.'

'And then what?'

'It goes.'

'What do you mean it goes?'

'Come on, I think we'd best take you onto the pier.'

So the five friends made their way along the promenade in the general direction of the pier. They paid their two pence entry fee and headed for the humpty cycles where Arthur espied the owner of the bikes whom they had met on their previous visit. Arthur had not forgotten their previous meeting so he shouted, 'Hoi you!'

The proprietor looked up and stared at Arthur, then Willie, and then Eustace and a smile crossed his face as recognition hit him. He came over to the fence that surrounded his small domain.'

'You said you'd come back. It's right glad I am to see you, where was it you was from?'

'Grolsby,' said Arthur, 'and here's a couple of new customers for you, Harry and our vicar.'

'Not wearing a dog collar I see.'

'No, but I can if you want me to preach to you. I have brought it with me.'

'Nay lad, don't bother, there's enough nut cases around here without adding to them.'

'I'll take it that's a no then, shall I? Can I have a go on one of these humpty cycles? It looks jolly difficult to me.'

'Well we three are having a go,' said Eustace, 'so what about you Harry?'

'You wouldn't see me dead on one of those things. Anyway, I'm going to the end of the pier to see what I can find.'

'He'll be off womanising,' said Willie.

'Oh, I don't think he'll be...'

Willie cut him short, 'Of course he will. Use your brains, Vicar; you're supposed to have more of them than us poor common folk. That's all that Fat Harry does. Drink and womanise.'

'Ah, I see. A bit of a hobby with him is it?'

'More than a hobby, it's a science. He's studied it for years. Mind you, he's never made much progress with it, but he's tried, by gum he's tried. He should have a degree for trying.'

'He's trying alright,' said Arthur, 'he's been trying us for years.'

'Well, are you lads coming on theses cycles or not? There's a queue developing, so are you having a go?'

'Yes, come along boys, let's be having you,' the Vicar shouted at them.

They each gave the man a shilling and took a bike from the stack.

Having had previous, if but brief, experience of riding the humpty cycle, Willie, Arthur and Eustace managed to start off even if they failed to get very far without falling off. The Vicar however, being not a practical sort of human even though he could ride a bicycle, was having no success at all in even moving the bike. Willie being the youngest and most agile of the four men did eventually begin to make substantial progress and began to enjoy himself. Eustace had limited success but Arthur and the Vicar were hopeless. They struggled for the remainder of their ten minute slot but were delighted when the owner rang the bell for a changeover.

'My arse is sore,' said Willie.

'I don't want to know,' said the vicar, 'mind you Willie, you did very well.'

Arthur was worried. 'I think we'd better go and find the fat one, you never know what trouble he might have got himself into.'

They ambled along the pier. They stopped a while to watch the Punch and Judy show, they looked at all the side shows, but of Harry, there was no sign. Arthur was getting more agitated about Harry's whereabouts as he was concerned that he could not look after himself properly. They went right to the end of the pier and turned to look at the aspect of Blackpool.

'A wonderful sight,' said the Vicar.

'Yes, Vicar, you are right,' Eustace replied, 'God's gift to us all, with a little help from mankind.'

Willie and Arthur looked at one another, then at Eustace, and then at the vicar, and then without a word, set off walking back towards the promenade looking for Fat Harry.

'I can hear him,' said Eustace. They were half way back along the pier, but of him there was no sign.

'You bloody Trollope. Charging all that for nothing.' They had heard him again but could not see him.

They heard a ladies voice but could not determine where it came from. Then Arthur pointed to the tent of Madam Zsa Zsa - Palms Read and Fortunes Told.

The canvas curtain was pulled across but they entered in force and surveyed the scene. Harry was sitting with his hand in Madam Zsa Zsa's, outstretched palm uppermost and he was staring into her eyes.

'What the hell do you lot want,' he shouted.

'It sounded as if you were in trouble, we could hear you shouting from miles away.'

'Yes, she's done me fair and square. A whole half crown to be told nothing that I didn't know already. But isn't she beautiful?' And he went on staring into her eyes.

'Come on, let's be having you out of here. Put the young lady down and leave her alone. Her husband will probably kill you if he gets hold of you,' Arthur observed.

Harry rose to come with the others, but Madam Zsa Zsa refused to release his hand.

'Sorry, good people, but can I tell you your immediate fortune,' she said. 'You are going home without this young man tonight. I am claiming him as my prize for today.' She held Harry's hand even more tightly.

'But my bus leaves at six,' he said, 'and I've got to get back to open the club tomorrow morning.'

'Sorry,' she replied, 'I'm keeping you here to live with me, forever.' They continued to stare into each other's eyes.

'Madam,' said the vicar, 'you cannot forcibly keep this man here against his will. To start with it is imprisonment, which is against the law, and secondly, it is morally indefensible.'

'Shut your gob and bugger off out of it, all of you.' Harry began to stand up to go with his friends. 'Not you sunshine, you're going nowhere.' She held his hand even more tightly.

'We'll see you on the bus,' said Arthur as they left.

When they had reached the promenade again, Willie said, 'I don't like leaving Harry alone with Madam Zsa Zsa.'

Arthur looked at him, 'Harry's a big boy and he can look after himself.'

'Well he might be able to back at home, but not in Blackpool, and not with a man eating specimen of the human race like her.'

'Well,' said Arthur, 'we'll just have to hope he turns up for the bus.'

'I'll just say a silent prayer for him,' said the vicar.

Eustace, who had not said anything of the debacle so far, aired his views on the matter. 'I think this might be a good thing for our barman. He's had a lonely life so far. I know he's got Alice who comes into the club on occasions and helps him but really he does need a good woman in his life. Mind you, he's got Cybil Peace now, if she's permanent.'

'You've hit the nail on the head there, lad. It's a good woman he wants, not the trollop he's sitting with right now. Anyway, which way are we going? Tower to the left? Pleasure Beach to the right?' Willie posed the question. 'We can't stay here worrying about the fat one all afternoon.'

The general consensus of opinion fell on the right turn option and they wandered off in the direction of South Shore.

They strolled slowly along the promenade but then crossed the tram lines and the road to look at the side shows, the novelty shops, the food shops, the hotels and the main one, the pubs. They called in and had a round then called at another hostelry, and had another round, and finally they walked into the pleasure beach.

'Big dipper?' asked the vicar.

'Not for me,' said Eustace.

'Or me,' Arthur agreed.

'Come on then Vicar,' Willie said and away they went to join the long queue.

'I fancy a gentle ride on the miniature railway,' said Eustace.

'Yes, come on,' said Arthur.

So they joined a short queue and waited for the arrival of the train from its current journey. Because the train track wove its way in between all the existing rides, they could not see it to check on its progress, but soon it was pulling into the station. They boarded it along with the rest of the throng, which only gave the driver enough time to just stretch his legs, and they were off.

Eustace, being quite tall and having long legs coupled to a short body, was very uncomfortable with his shins wedged firmly against the back of the seat in front of him. Arthur on the other hand, being of average everything, was sitting very comfortably.

The journey lasted all of five minutes, and Arthur thoroughly enjoyed his trip, but Eustace was very fidgety trying to get comfortable. 'By gum, I'm glad that's over,' he said when they were standing on the platform again.

Arthur said, 'Oh I really enjoyed it. Are you sure you don't want to go again?'

'No, certainly not. Let's go to the big dipper and see if we can find the other two.'

They found them still standing in the midst of a long queue.

'Come on, Arthur, let's go to the river caves.'

'That sounds good to me, Eustace. These two are going to be at least half an hour yet.'

So away they went into another almost non-existent queue and jumped into the first boat that they came by. They very slowly meandered through the fixed tableaux depicting various areas of the world. It was quiet and peaceful with only the lapping of the water against the boat and the background music to disturb the silence.

Eustace was looking around admiring the various scenes. 'My words this is much better than the train.'

'Good, but not better. Just the same,' replied Arthur.

'Yes, but my legs are much more comfortable in here and it's fascinating how all the other countries of the world look. The elephants and deserts and wild animals in Africa and the mountains and rivers in South America and all the ice and icebergs and glaciers in Antarctica and the jungles and lakes and mountains in Asia and New York and all the cattle and the Red Indians in North America and then Europe, Paris and Spain and the Fjords in Norway and everything and everywhere, oh how I wish I was rich and could visit them all.' Eustace sat back and took a deep breath.

Arthur looked at him half in wonder and half in admiration. 'How on earth did you manage to remember all that lot from such a short trip in a slow moving boat?'

'Well, Arthur old friend, I'm not just a pretty face. You know all that time when Joan was shouting at me and making my life hell, I used to read books and magazines about geography. I studied the continents and the rivers, mountains, cities, people and animals of the world. I know quite a lot about it now and I do wish I could visit some of it.'

'So why don't you save up and take your Joan to Paris at next year's holiday week?

'I couldn't. Could I? I could, but there'd be the expense and the language and, and...'

'Go on, do it. Take the bull by the horns. It strikes me that you are quite capable and you know a bit about it. You could get one of these new fangled French language courses that they're always on about. They are supposed to be easy to learn. You can get them on gramophone records, I've never had one but I've seen them advertised in the newspaper.'

'Well it might be worth thinking about. I did do a little bit of French at school and so did Joan, but we've neither of us ever been there, and anyway we've not got passports, either of us.'

'Well that's no problem, you just go to the post office, get a form, have your pictures taken then take it back to the post office with your fee and Bob's your uncle. Talking about the language, you could always go at a night class at the Mechanic's Institute.'

'Do they have night classes at the Mechanic's Institute?'

'Oh yes, I'm certain they do.'

'I really wish I was as clever as you Arthur, I really do.'

'I'm not clever, I just read a lot including every word of the local rag each week and I have a good memory, and talking of good memories, where are those other two people that we have forgotten about.'

By now, they were standing in a position where they could see the top of the Big Dipper tower as well as the queue.

Eustace, who was sharp eyed, said, 'they are not in the queue now. Oh there they are, just going around the top of the tower to begin the long downhill.'

'So we'd better wait for them by the exit, they'll not be long before they're back here.'

It wasn't long before the two revelers arrived laughing and joking out of the Big Dipper exit.

'By gum, you should have come with us it were real,' said Willie.

The Vicar was in an equally jovial mood. 'Oh yes, you should have, it was worth the wait. In fact, if there hadn't been such a long queue, we would have gone again, wouldn't we Willie?'

'Oh by gum, yes we would and how!'

'Has it given you a new theme for your Sunday sermon tomorrow Vicar?' asked Eustace.

'Not yet, but you might just have given me food for thought, something along the lines of flying through the air near to heaven. You will all have to attend to see what materialises. And talking about food, is it time we were spending our tea money, the bus leaves at six and we need to get back to the bus pick up point and eat as well. We can't travel on an empty stomach.'

'We passed a right good looking fish and chip shop just before we came into the pleasure beach,' Arthur enthused.

'Well I fancy a horse on the Kentucky Derby before we go,' said Willie.

'Do you, Willie? Do you?' asked Eustace.

'Yes I do. Come on, it's on the way back, it'll only take a few minutes, so let's have a go. Are you all game?'

They were all more than game, so they got four seats side by side, paid their money and under starters orders they began to roll the balls. The horses set off at a gallop and soon Willie was well ahead of the field and heading for victory. He was first past the post and the stall holder offered him a selection of prizes.

'I'll have one of them big teddy bears for the wife.'

'Sorry cock, they're only for five wins and anyway I don't take wives in part exchange, I've enough bother with Mrs Never Wrong.' He pointed to his chief assistant. 'Anyway, this is the selection down here what I already showed you.'

'There's nowt worth having there,' said Willie, 'it'll have to be one of them other little stuffed animals then.' He was presented with a cloth animal that bore no resemblance to anything alive or dead. 'A fat lot of good that is to anyone. Still, I'll give it the wife as a present from Blackpool.'

The vicar, who liked to be punctual, was getting worried about the time. 'We should be going you know, we've got to eat yet and if there's a queue…'

'Do give over worrying,' said Willie, 'the bus'll not go without us.'

'Are you sure?'

'Aye, don't fret yourself, there's two reasons why it can't go. To begin with we've got the passenger list and we are definitely in charge, and secondly, there's never been a trip bus yet that left anywhere dead on time. So where is this fat-hole that you were on about Arthur?'

'It's a couple of blocks further along the prom, just past South Pier. We will be there in a few strides. Look there it is, Happy Harry's, there's a big sign outside.'

They joined a short queue and soon were shown to a table by a grumpy looking frump of a woman. 'You can sit here,' she growled.

'How to make your customers welcome,' observed the vicar, 'I think I shall say a silent prayer for her to hope that when she is reincarnated she comes back as a frog.'

'That's very uncharitable of you, Vicar,' said Arthur.

'I think in her case it's well deserved.'

'Do you believe in reincarnation then?'

'Not normally, but for her I can make an exception.'

The waitress arrived to take their order. Now here was a different case, she was young, beautiful and all her equipment was just in the right place.

'I think its fish and chips four times and four pints of beer, please' said Eustace.

She gave them a radiant smile. 'Sorry gentlemen, it's tea or coffee or soft drinks, we're not licensed.'

'Not licensed?' There was shock horror.

'No. Sorry.'

'But we're on a trip,' Willie explained just before he farted.

'Yes, I know. A lot of our customers are but we're still not licensed. So what's it to be? And by the way, sir, will you please refrain from making those noises and smells in here, it disturbs the other guests.'

'I don't think I've disturbed them, they look like they're disturbed already without my help.'

Eustace decided that he had better cool things down a little. 'Tea all around?' he looked at the other three.

'No, I'd prefer coffee,' said the vicar.

'So that's three teas and one coffee please. I knew you'd be different.'

'No, I just thought I'd have coffee for a change.'

216

The young lady went away to get their order.

'It's funny we are in Happy Harry's,' said Arthur, 'I wonder how our fat friend is going on?'

'Well, he'll either be doing well, coping, getting what he wanted and enjoying himself or he'll be dead scared and trying to escape. Whichever it is, it's his own fault for trying,' Willie replied.

*

Back on central pier, Harry had really enjoyed himself for a while. As soon as the other four had disappeared, Madam Zsa Zsa had hung the closed sign on the outside of her canvas shed and returned into the arms of Harry where, for a while, he began to think that all his birthdays had arrived at once. After a while, when the initial euphoria had subsided, Harry said. 'What shall I call you?'

'What do you mean?'

'Well I can't call you Madam Zsa Zsa now, can I? Not now that we're on such intimate terms.'

'Cynthia.'

'What?'

'Cynthia. Cynthia Pearson.' At this point, she removed her long black wig and hung it up on a hook on the tent pole, at the back of the room.'

Harry examined the prospect in front of him. She had gone in seconds from a somewhat sophisticated good looking lady with an exotic name to what he thought might be just another scrubber with an ordinary name and short mousy grey hair. *Mutton dressed as lamb*, he decided, and he thought, *time I was going*. So he started to prepare for his departure.

'Well I think it's time to go and catch up with the lads now. They'll be wanting to have their tea before we get back on the coach so, if it's alright with you, I'll say goodbye, thanks for the fun, it's been nice meeting you.' He stood up and turned towards the door.

'Sit down and shut up. You're going nowhere except home with me. I haven't shut the shop this afternoon for nothing. First of all when we get to my house, we'll have some real fun and then, if you've been good, we might think about some tea.'

Harry began to get worried and stood up again to go. She placed a hand on his shoulder and forcibly pushed him back into the chair. She then got her coat and her bag, grabbed his wrist with a vice like grip, and pulled him forcibly out of the door which had a snap lock. She walked away down the pier pulling Harry and said, 'Now walk with me as if it's just natural or you'll suffer badly later.'

Harry cringed. He was beginning to be really afraid. She was strong, common, and horrible in fact, not the delightful creature that he had first fallen in love with on the pier and he didn't know how to get out of her clutches. Oh how he wished he had ridden the humpty cycles with the others.

They soon arrived at her back street dump that was reputedly her home. He was thrust inside once the front door was opened, the door was locked securely behind him and the key removed. Cynthia climbed the stairs, ordering Harry to go before her. She shoved him into a back bedroom and told him to wait there whist she prepared herself for him. She disappeared out of the room. Harry, in a state of blind panic, looked out of the dirty window, observed a half height sloping roof just below it and tried to open it. It rose with ease and he leaned out, had a look and dived out onto the sloping roof. He didn't know where he was going but anywhere was better that what the future according to Madam Zsa Zsa foretold, even though he had not heard it. He rolled down the sloping roof and dropped a long way onto the ground below in her back yard. He didn't stop long enough to find out if he was alive or dead, he just picked himself up, went through the open gate into the lane behind and ran, faster than he had run in many a long year.

*

Huge plates of fish and chips, mushy peas, bread and butter and a giant teapot were served to the four trippers.

'Well look at this,' said the vicar, 'I've not seen a plateful like this since the Bishop came to the confirmation last year.'

Arthur enquired, 'What has the Bishop and confirmation got to do with a huge plate of food?'

'Well you see, every time we get the higher ups at a Church function we have to provide a lot more food than we would for a normal event because they eat like horses. In order to save money, they eat very little at home, saving their appetites until they descend on us poor providers. You should see them open their mouths, like huge coal pits that can take in a plateful at one swallowing. We have difficulty in filling the present Archbishop, and if he brings his ecumenical entourage with him, well, we've had it. We just cannot satisfy them. Anyway enough of my problems, shall I say just a little grace? I think I should before we gourmandise.'

'Go on then,' Willie agreed with him.

'We thank the good Lancastrians from Blackpool for providing us with such a marvelous feast. Amen. Right come on, tuck in, it's going to be cold if we don't.'

So they did and they really did enjoy it.

'Well...' said Willie when he had finished giving a demonstration of eating in company with his knife and fork and fingers to help. He did lick his knife a couple of times but did not dare to lick his plate '...that has been a real good meal in a nice little café with good company and I really have enjoyed it. What are we having for pudding?'

'I wasn't thinking in terms of a pudding,' said Arthur.

'No, but I was,' said Eustace, 'I saw some rather good looking Knickerbocker Glories being taken past a little while ago and they really did whet my appetite.'

'Yes, I must say that we do like to finish off a meal with something a little sweet at the vicarage. So I say we all have a Knickerbocker Glory. Are you joining us Arthur?'

'Aye, come on Arthur, give over being your usual miserable self and spend some money,' said Willie.

'Oh go on then. It won't do a lot of harm just this once.'

So the Vicar gesticulated to the young lady and he gave her their order.

Willie squeezed the young lady's bottom and she grinned with pleasure at him. Then he belched loudly and she threatened him with being sent out, so he squeezed her bottom again and she forgave him.

'I have already forgiven your sins, Willie, seeing that I observed them take place.'

'Nowt to forgive, Vicar. I only fondled her arse a bit. No more than any self-respecting tripper would have done and anyway she enjoyed it because she were asking for it.'

'How do you know she was asking for it?'

'Nay Vicar! You've nobbut to look at the lass to know that.'

When the young lady returned and served the four sweets, she asked the vicar, 'What are you staring at?'

He didn't answer.

'Hey you, I'm talking to you. What are you staring at?'

The vicar came out of his trance. 'What? Sorry, Pardon. I was in another land.'

'But you were staring at me.'

'Was I? Well now fancy that. I was miles away, not seeing where I was looking, so if I have offended you, I apologise, but I was not conscious that I was.'

'Well alright then, but I don't like people who do nothing but stare.' She departed.

'My words, that was a close shave Willie, but I was trying to look at her to confirm what you said and I can't for the life of me believe that she would enjoy being manhandled.'

Willie was about to comment again on the vicar's naivety when Arthur intervened, 'I'm still worried about Harry; he should have been here with us in a restaurant that bears his name. I wonder where he is?'

*

If they had turned to look out of the window, they would have seen a half dead, petrified apology for a human being almost on his last legs, running for all he was worth down the road at the side of the fish restaurant, across the main sea front road, without looking, across the tram lines, again without looking, and onto the promenade where he leaned on the railings with his back to the sea and began to recover his breath. He faced the land because he figured that he would see Cynthia Pearson if she approached him and he was sure she would, but there was no way he was getting into her clutches again. He would kill her if necessary, for a spell in His Majesty's pleasure would be better than being snared by Madam Zsa Zsa again.

He didn't know what to do next; his breathing was laboured, his chest hurt from running too far too fast, his brain would not focus and he had this overriding dread of that woman coming after him. But she was not in his line of sight and so he decided to rest where he was for the time being until his legs stopped feeling like jelly and he could think straight.

*

Back in Happy Harry's the four customers paid their bill and walked out of the café, across the road and onto the promenade.

'How shall we get back to the bus?' enquired Eustace.

'Well after all that food it would do us good to walk,' replied Arthur.

'But we haven't time,' said Willie.

'We haven't now,' said Eustace.

221

'What do you mean?' enquired Willie.

Eustace pointed in the direction of the sea and they all looked to where he was pointing.

'Bloody hell. What's that? What on earth has happened to him? Come on we'd best go to him as quick as possible.'

They ran the one hundred yards or so to where they had observed Harry. When they got there he was so overcome with emotion he had the greatest of difficulty in getting any words out at all.

'Am, am, am I glad. By gum, I am glad to see you lot.'

'What's happened to you?'

'Where have you been?'

'What have you been doing since we last saw you?'

'Where's Madam Zsa Zsa?

'Have you eaten?'

Harry's situation finally got the better of him and he sank to the floor holding his head in his hands. He was a little while before he could bring himself round to speak, and when he did his voice was very emotional. 'By gum, but it's good to see you all. I never thought I'd see you again. Oh what an afternoon I have had. I wish I'd stayed with you and ridden the humpty cycles.'

None of the other four quite knew what to say, even the vicar was somewhat tongue tied.

'You see, she wouldn't let me go. She wouldn't let go of my arm. She hurt my arm; she's a grip like a vice. Didn't let go once until she got me to her hovel. It was awful, horrible and her, when she took her hair off and all the fancy clothes, she was ugly, plain, mutton dressed as lamb. I've never had such a bad experience ever and I never want another.'

'What do you mean she took her hair off?' Arthur asked.

'A wig, you know, a bloody great wig. When that had gone there was nowt but a bit of mousy hair. She were almost bald, by gum my side doesn't half hurt.'

'Why does your side hurt Harry?' asked Eustace.

'Well, it was when I jumped out of the bedroom window and rolled down the roof and fell off the low building, I landed on it. But I wasn't going to stop, no fear of that, I just ran and ran to here until I could run no more. I need a brandy.'

Willie suggested they should go across the road where there was a hostelry residing between two amusement arcades and where they could enjoy a small libation before rushing to the bus.

So they pulled Harry to his feet and, for the second time that day, he was dragged across the promenade and the tram lines. One large brandy and five pints of South Shore bitter and Harry, not to mention the others were all feeling much revived and ready to face the world once more. Not that the other four had any reason to need the comfort of a drink, but it just helped a little under the circumstances.

'Have you had owt to eat Harry?' Willie enquired.

'Owt to eat? Owt to eat? I've had nowt except a near death experience and that nearly killed me. Mind you, that brandy and beer has revived me so I could possibly just manage a bloody big fish with a mountain of chips.'

They set off towards the meeting point for the bus and called in to the first fish and chip shop they came across and helped to bring a smile back to Harry's face.

CHAPTER 13

At the coach pick up point it was already a quarter past six, none of the passengers had returned and Norris Oakes was doing his nut. He should have been away from there fifteen minutes ago. Almost all of the other coaches had loaded and departed on or about the due time, but there was one other waiting like he was. Norris having recognised the other coach as the one they had met earlier at the half way stop in the morning, and later at the comfort break which was bringing a trip of ladies from Dewsbury, went over to have a word with the driver.

'You having the same trouble as me?' asked Norris.

'What, waiting for your passengers?'

'Yes. A bad lot, a mill trip. All from our village but a right drunken hoard. How about yours?'

'From Dewsbury. Ladies section of a working men's club. Mind you there's not a lady amongst them, a right load of, well you know. All as right as rain when they're at home with their husbands, but get them out without their men and no other men are safe. They don't bother me though, I've driven them for years, but God only knows what time we'll get home tonight. Probably after they've drunk Lancashire dry and interfered with one half of the Lancastrian male population.'

'Same with my lot, although other than a few of them, I don't think the female population will be in any danger. But there's no doubt about it that the brewery drays will be in great demand tomorrow to restock Blackpool. What time does the superintendent come around and give us a ticket for overstaying our welcome?'

'Oh, he'll be here in a few minutes I expect, but don't worry about him. I've been here before. My boss sends him a special bottle of beer, it's here ready for him. Fancy a fag?'

He got a packet of Three Castles out and offered Norris one.

'My words those are expensive cigs.'

'Yes, I don't smoke these regularly. It's just that I was wandering around Blackpool, like you do, and I saw them in a shop window display. So I thought why not, you only live once and they'll have a collection on the bus going home for me, that will pay for these cigs. That is if they're sober enough to find their money.'

'Well I won't have one but I will have a pipe.' Norris took out his pipe and tobacco and filled the pipe, then lit it and sat on the bottom step of the Dewsbury bus, chatting away to his new found friend.

*

Sid Beaumont and Richard Dodson had had one hell of an afternoon. They had left the Golden Cockerel restaurant not sober, but not drunk, and they, like so many of their fellow trippers, had walked across the promenade to look at the sea and then they had made their way into Talbot Square where there were a number of establishments that were designed to sell the maximum amount of drink that they possibly could to gullible trippers.

So the two friends had found themselves in a beer cellar where there was a snooker table and there they had stayed drinking and drinking and drinking and even more drinking. Eventually when they were getting so rowdy and argumentative that they were becoming a nuisance to the rest of the customers, the barman cum door man helped them out into the fresh air.

The air hit them, as the air does, and sent their senses reeling. Richard had just enough wit about him to know that they needed food. He had no idea what time it was, but he knew that they would have to eat. So he looked around for a food shop, saw a fish and chip shop, and took Sid with him. They bought fish and chips twice and took them outside wrapped in newspaper. They walked unsteadily towards the sea. Cars jammed on their brakes and hooted their horns as they walked straight out into the road without looking, and then they carefully stopped at the tram lines.

'Is there any trams coming?' asked Sid.

'Don't know. Can't see any. No. No. None. No that's right none. Come on let's go.'

So off they went, the tram driver having seen them slowed a way back until they had cleared the tracks. They reached the edge of the promenade just where there were a set of steps down onto the beach and so they just kept on walking and fell down the steps onto the sand below. They picked themselves up, no worse for the experience, and plodded on through the sand towards the sea. They walked straight through a sand castle that a little boy had spent all afternoon constructing, destroying it as they went. The little lad's father jumped up to remonstrate with them but, as soon as he approached them, he realised that he was wasting his time and he returned to console his son.

A little further towards the sea and Richard got his foot stuck in a hole in the sand. He fell over forwards, Sid fell on top of him and there they remained for a while. Once they had picked themselves up, they sat on the sand, and ate their sand crusted fish and chips which by this time were well on their way to being cold. When they had finished, Sid looked at his watch.

'It's six.'

'What is?'

'It's bus time.'

'Is it? What bus.'

'The bus back home. You know the one we came in.'

'Oh that one.'

'Yes.'

'Where is it?'

'I don't know, up the road somewhere. Past the Tower, I think. Come on, we'd best go.'

They tried to rise to their feet and made it at the third attempt, and then began the slow trudge back to where they thought the bus was. They had not gone far when they came across a hoard of donkeys being taken home after a hard day's work ferrying the children up and down the beach. Somehow they managed to get tangled in the middle of them and everything ground to a halt. The donkey master was none too happy at the situation because he was late finishing, he was hungry and more important he wanted to pee. However he decided to turn the situation to his own advantage and realised, that having got themselves wound around the donkeys harness, unless he released them they were there to stay, he said, 'Just mind the donkeys for me for a couple of minutes whilst I make a call of nature.' It being somewhat urgent he didn't wait for a reply but went.

'What we going to do now?' Sid asked a donkey called Arthur.

Having received no sensible reply he decided that the only way out of the situation was to unfasten any clip he could find and so he did just that. Soon both he and Richard were free and so were all the donkeys who wandered off in every direction under the sun.

Sid had fallen in love with a donkey called Charlie, the reins of which he took hold of and began to walk it towards where he though the bus was. Richard followed him patting the donkey. The food and the rest had helped to sober them up a little but not enough to not take the animal and so the three of them headed for the coach.

*

Job Crabtree, Roy Duckworth, Lewis Earnshaw and Dick Jordan had decided on the coach before lunch that they were going to have a game of bowls in Stanley Park that afternoon.

So after lunch, having walked over to look at the sea, they found the local bus and took a ride to the park. They dismounted at the park gates and walked along the drive to the bowling greens. Dick and Lewis both bowled for the club team back at home and so they began to teach Job and Roy who were novices at the game. They were progressing quite nicely, it was quiet and they bowled in an atmosphere where the learners could learn without worrying about any distractions, when suddenly there was a cacophony of sound. They looked up to see half a dozen of the women that had been on the Dewsbury bus, whom they had already met earlier in the morning, advancing on them, arms waving and shouting.

'Oh hell,' said Dick.

'Just what we wanted,' agreed Lewis. 'Lesson over for the time being. Sorry lads, but we appear to have visitors.'

The ladies walked, and in some cases waddled, onto the green straight over to the fellows and wrapped themselves around them, kissing and cuddling and generally being amorous fuelled by a surfeit of alcohol.

The green keeper came over and remonstrated with the group and Lewis pointed out that all they wanted was a quiet game of bowls. One of the ladies, a rather large buxom wench, hit the green keeper with her handbag, spilling the contents all over the green. The other bowlers, of which there were not many, came over and shouted at everyone to clear off and leave them in peace. Fortunately other park keepers came along just at the right time and cleared all ten of them off the green.

'But we've paid to play,' said Dick. 'We just want to be left in peace to have a game of bowls. It's not our fault that these floozies landed here.'

'Look now, lad, you get rid of these badly behaved women, come back when you have, and we'll let you back on for another game.'

But the ladies were having none of it and demanded that the men take them for a row on the lake. The men protested but were ushered along to the landing stage and resistance was futile. The ladies insisted that the men should pay for the rowing boats and again it was impossible not to because the large lady offered to put her hand into Job's trouser pocket to get out the money and he was having none of it. So two rowing boats with two men and three ladies each cast off and made their way slowly around the lake.

The ladies were becoming more and more amorous with the men and the men were becoming more and more miserable. In the middle of the lake, the fat lady stood up in one of the boats and began to rock it.

'Sit down, now!' commanded Lewis who was rowing and therefore the captain and the voice of authority in all maritime situations.

'Shut your cake hole,' she replied.

'Madam, if you do not sit down immediately I shall have you clapped in irons and flogged before the mizzen mast.' He ran out of nautical expressions.

'Do be quiet you insignificant little twerp,' she replied but continued to stand and sway.

Dick, being Lewis's friend and the other male member of the crew, leaned over and grabbed the lady's leg, more to pull her down than anything otherwise. She looked at him with a twinkle in her eye and pounced on him. This action had the unfortunate consequence of turning over the boat and throwing the occupants out into the water. The ladies screamed, the men cried out and they all thrashed about for their lives until they realised that the water was only about two feet deep and they could even kneel up in it and keep their heads above water.

The two men righted the boat and jumped in. They had rescued the oars and away Lewis went, rowing for all he was worth back to the jetty where they left the boat with as little fuss as possible and walked away from the boat keepers hut as fast as they could with dripping wet clothes.

The ladies who were in the water shouted at the men to take them back in the boat, but Lewis told them to wade back to the bank of the lake and get themselves out.

Job rowed their boat back to the jetty as fast as he could, but he could not keep up with Lewis who was in a bit of a hurry. The ladies in their boat shouted at them to help rescue their friends but Roy told them to be quiet or he would put them into the water and so they quietened down again. As soon as they docked, the ladies made a bee line for their friends who were still struggling to get out of the lake half way round and out of sight of the jetty.

Fortunately, it was a bright, hot, sunny day and Lewis and Dick soon began to dry out. Job and Roy caught up with them and they hurried towards the park gates and the bus back to Blackpool.

'What are we going to tell our wives?' asked Dick

'And our fellow trippers,' replied Lewis.

'You could always tell them the truth,' said Roy.

'What and get killed, dead? Not likely.'

'So what then?'

Roy came up with a possible solution. 'Tell them we had a terrific rain storm. A cloud burst in fact.'

'And we were the only ones that were out in it, were we? I don't think so.'

By this time it was about half past four and Dick suggested they walk back into Blackpool so that they could dry off because he didn't fancy sitting in his wet clothes in a bus or later in the coach for that matter.

Lewis began to moan about the fact that he would go to his death with a terrible cold by this time next week, and there was no way he was ever going near Dewsbury again if that was how the women behaved.

Dick said, 'when I grabbed the woman's leg it was like a tree trunk and then she looked down at me and smiled, it was horrible, awful, she was ugly and just for a moment I was terrified. I thought my end had arrived.'

So they walked, briskly and soon they were sitting in a café just behind the Tower, having their tea before returning to the coach.

*

Hubert Gormley and his brother Jason, Dennis Haigh, Joshua Johnson and John Sidebottom, having as did everyone else, looked over the railings at the sea, decided that in order to have a cheap afternoon they would walk to Bispham and possibly back depending on the time available for they had absolutely no idea how long it would take them to get there.

They ambled along at leisurely pace past the Tower, past the North Pier, past Derby Baths, past Gynn Square and finally they arrived near to Uncle Tom's Cabin where a refreshment stop was requested by all five of them. They found a little pub jut off the promenade, down a side street, and went in.

'Five pints of your best South Shore Bitter please Landlord,' Hubert requested.

The man behind the bar informed them that he was not the landlord, just a serving wench, and asked Hubert for the full amount.

All five of them looked with curiosity at the man who had described himself as a wench then Hubert informed him that they were all paying for their own.

'Paying for your own? Paying for your own? How the hell do you expect me to sort that out?' He said in his own peculiar light coloured voice.

'We've got a right one here,' said Hubert.

'Aye, well, my advice is to stand facing him,' said their Jason. 'Anyway lad, here's t'brass for mine and if you don't like it you can shove it right up your...' he checked himself realising who he was dealing with '...chuff,' he finished.

'Aye, and if you don't sort it out, we'll come round there and help you shove it.'

'Ooo, the pleasure would be all mine,' the serving wench said with a huge smile.

Somehow or other they managed to pay and escape to the outside of the pub where there were some seats. They sat and watched the world go by. The sun was blazing down and beginning to scorch John Sidebottom's bald head. So he took out his somewhat soiled pocket handkerchief and tied a not in each corner. He then put it over his head and declared that it was a vast improvement.

'It's not done a lot for your looks though,' said Hubert. 'You'll never get a new woman with those bits of dried up snot resting in full view of everybody.'

'They might think it's a pattern,' said Jason.

'Pattern be buggered, anyone can tell its snot,' Hubert roared with laughter. 'Anyway, I'll tell you what, there's an old lady just coming up the street, we'll ask her.'

'We will hell as like,' replied John.

But Hubert wasn't having any of it and as the lady arrived opposite them, he asked her, 'Hey missus what do you think of John's new hat?'

The old lady stopped and stared for a few minutes then said, 'Very common,' and she walked away.

Just then the wench came out collecting dirty glasses. 'Oh my words, how fetching. Just what I've always wanted ducky. Why don't you come inside with me and we can rearrange it.'

'I wouldn't bother its covered in snot,' shouted Hubert.

'Oh well, on second thoughts…you can't win them all, but one occasionally would be nice.'

'Time we were going, the afternoon's progressing and there's no way we're going to manage to walk to Bispham and back and have our tea. So the choice is let's walk to Bispham, have our tea and get a tram back to the bus or walk back to the bus from here and have our tea on the way.' This came from Dennis Haigh who was blessed with just a little bit more common sense that the others.

They took a vote and adopted the latter course of action.

They walked back up the street, over the tram lines and into the sunken gardens. They made their way slowly towards Gynn Square and were almost there when John Sidebottom said, 'I want to pee.'

'Well there's nowhere to go just here, so you'll have to hold onto it for a while.'

'I can't, it's come on sudden like and I'll have to go now.'

'But there's nowhere to go. But hey up, hang on a minute. You'll have to go into that hotel over there and use the gents.' Hubert pointed to the Crown Hotel, a big imposing building across the main road.

'I can't go in there; I've never been into nowt like that in my life.'

'Well there's always a first time. Off you go; we'll follow you and wait inside there for you so that you won't get lost.'

'Well owt's better than nowt when you're hungry,' said John and he took off at a gallop heading for the revolving front door of The Crown.

He went through the door as quick as his legs would take him, hurrying some other clients of the hotel out a little faster than they had anticipated. He ran in and stopped dead. He could not believe his eyes. He was in a huge entrance lobby that towered up several stories. It was furnished with big armchairs and settees and coffee tables. The floor was covered with a thick pile carpet and the curtains at all the windows were heavy, colourful and homely. But the important bit, the gents was nowhere to be seen.

A porter had witnessed the man, who was smartly dressed except for the fact that he sported a knotted handkerchief on his head, enter the hotel and who did not quite fit in with their image, so he set off towards him. John saw him coming and went towards him.

'Where's the gents lad? I'm bursting for a slash.'

'I'm sorry sir, our gentleman's toilet is only to be used by bona fide guests.'

'I don't give a monkeys who it's for lad. If I don't get there bloody quick, there'll be a bloody enormous great big puddle right where I'm standing.'

'Follow me, sir.' The porter had enough common sense not to create a scene in front of their normal guests, so he took John to the gents. 'In there, sir.'

'Ta lad.' John went inside the gents and did what he had to do. When he had finished he looked around and could not believe the opulence. There were big sinks with big bars of soap attached to metal rods that projected from the wall. There was a big pile of clean white towels and a bin for the used ones. The whole room was done out in black and white marble and the floor had a big patterned tile cover. John washed his hands, rubbing them all over the big soap bar.

John came out of the gents and came face to face with the porter who had waited for him.

'Have you managed, sir?'

'Yes, thanks lad. Sorry about that, but I was bursting.'

'Allow me to escort you to the front door, sir. Just so that you will not get lost on your way you understand.'

'Oh aye, I understand alright. Anyway thanks again.'

He was taken back to the front door, all the other guests staring at a man with a knotted handkerchief on his head, and one covered in snot at that, being escorted from the premises.

The others were sitting on the front wall waiting for him.

'We thought we'd not come in,' said Dennis Haigh.

'You should have done, it was like nowt I've ever seen before. The gents were far better than our bathroom at home and the furniture, right posh it were. Mind you one of them toffee nosed flunkeys took me to the gents and then threw me out when I'd done. But it were a good experience.'

Hubert looked at him. 'I think that if you'd taken that snot ridden handkerchief from your head before you went in there you might have fared better. I did shout at you across the road to get rid of it but you mustn't have heard me.'

'Right, where are we going for us tea and what are we having? I'm fair hungry now that I've had a slash.'

'We'll see what providence will provide us with,' said Hubert.

'What?'

'Come on let's walk towards Gynn Square.'

It was there that they found a nice little café where some of them had, as was only to be expected, fish and chips.'

After tea they walked quickly back to the coach arriving just in nice time to be a little late.

*

The remaining passengers of the trip had passed the afternoon in a very similar way. Some had visited the Tower and walked along the promenade or visited the various attractions of the Golden Mile. Some had taken a tram trip to Fleetwood, and some had visited the Winter Gardens, so that when six o'clock arrived and they had all had a good tea, they were ready to return to the coach, get a bottle of beer out of the stock and have a good sit down in the almost comfort of Bewdlay's clapped out coach.

*

Charlie the Donkey and his two new friends, Sid Beaumont and Richard Dodson, headed slowly towards the coach. Charlie was pleased with his new friends, they didn't keep on shouting at him, they just talked to him and one of them had given him some cold chips, and he loved cold chips. So he walked at a fast pace for him, keeping up with his new humans and soon the coach was in sight.

No one stopped them, no one asked them why they had a donkey, and so, with Norris Oakes still sitting talking in the Dewsbury coach, the Blackpool Corporation Transport Superintendent having been and received his inducement, Charlie arrived at the coach.

Now he wasn't sure just what this place was that they had brought him to, but it certainly looked and smelt better than the broken down hovel that he was normally taken to each evening. So without further ado, and with a lot of help from Richard and Sid, he mounted the steps and was led towards the back seat. The present occupants of the seat agreed to change places and Charlie was pushed into place, hidden behind the seat in front and along with Sid and Richard. One of their friends went and fetched three bottles of beer from the stock and they had one each and poured one down Charlie's throat. Charlie was beginning to like it here; he had not drunk beer before, the people were very nice and it smelt much pleasanter than the dump he usually stayed in.

There had, as was only to be expected, been a modicum of opposition to having a donkey on board from some of the more sober passengers, but they were in a large minority and were instantly overruled by an animal loving, fairly well drunk majority who didn't know or care whether it was a donkey or a camel.

Sid and Richard finished their beers and called for another and one for Charlie. He guzzled it down and thoroughly enjoyed it. It was at this point that Charlie decided he liked it here, even though his new quarters were a bit cramped, he was with friends, the drink was good and he was stopping for a while.

*

The terrible five of Arthur, Eustace, Fat Harry, the vicar and Willie arrived back at the coach in a fairly sober state. They took a couple of bottles each from the stock in the luggage compartment and took their seats near the front.

'There's a funny smell in here,' said Eustace.

'Well it's not me,' said Willie, 'I haven't done nowt, but I will do...' and he did.

'And there's a surprise,' said Arthur.

'And I can assure you that it is not me brethren,' added the vicar.

'Well there's something, and I don't know what, but...' Arthur cut him short.

'Give over worrying about nothing. We are on a trip. Relax. It does pong a bit but there's been a lot of drinking today and its no more than is to be expected and it will go when the coach starts up and the draught blows through it.'

'Where is our driver?' asked Eustace.

'In yond coach full of women from Dewsbury,' came a voice from half way down the coach. 'No he's not, he's here.'

Norris Oakes climbed aboard. 'Is everyone here and accounted for?'

'Yes,' said Eustace.

Norris shouted, 'There's a funny smell. Who's shit themselves on my coach? Still never mind, whoever it is will have to live with it, it won't affect me, I will be downwind of it.'

So at six forty five the coach banged and spluttered its way into life and began its journey back to Yorkshire.

CHAPTER 14

Blackpool was not far behind them when Charlie the donkey decided that it was time to stretch his legs and take a walk down the coach. Sid and Richard tried to restrain him, but he was having none of it. He was going exploring and there was nothing that anyone could do about it. He took his time, stopping to look at everyone as he passed by. Some gave him sweets, which he enjoyed, but none gave him a drink and he had enjoyed his beer. Yes, he really had enjoyed the beer. It was a new taste; one that he had not experienced before and one that he would most certainly like to try again. As well as that he was feeling just a little bit happy, nice, at peace with the world and ready for another bucket full.

Most of the trippers knew he was on board and played with him on his route to the front.

Charlie got as far as the vicar. Richard, who was following him and trying to get him back, leaned forward and tapped the reverend on the shoulder, who turned around and came face to face with the unexpected. He looked at Charlie, then at Richard who motioned to him to keep quiet.

Harry was sitting opposite the vicar and he was also motioned to to keep quiet. Harry had a stock of beer, so Richard asked him quietly to hand over a bottle. Harry took off the top and Richard indicated that he should pour the beer down the donkey's throat. Harry was somewhat put out at this waste of beer, but Charlie had seen the bottle and was pushing his mouth towards Harry's hands. Harry, having already observed a row of donkey teeth coming towards him and having had enough trouble already for one day, poured the golden liquid into Charlie's throat.

Charlie was very appreciative of the beer and he began to nuzzle Harry for another. So he got one, and another, but then Harry decided that enough was enough and, instead of opening yet another bottle, he smacked Charlie on the nose with his hand. Charlie decided that he had had enough of these people and went forward, investigating. He looked at Willie and Arthur and Eustace, but received no encouragement to stop by them. It was about this time that his bowels decided they also would like some exercise, so seconds later, there were Arthur, Willie, Eustace, Harry and the vicar sitting and staring at a pile of fresh donkey doos resting in the middle of the isle, on Bewdlay's best Axminster floor covering.

'Who's dropped one?' roared Norris. 'Because whoever it is can get some windows open and let some fresh air into here before I pass out.' Norris looked into his rear view mirror that showed the interior of the coach of which he looked at very infrequently. All he could see to start with was a greyish something or other that was completely obliterating his view.

'Whichever idiot that is that's blocking my view, just sit down now, please, I can't have people standing up and walking around whilst we are traveling.'

Norris turned his attention back to the road, and Charlie turned his attention to Norris' head and particularly his ears, as his head was lower down than everyone else's due to the location of the driver's seat.

The next thing Norris knew was that his left ear was being licked.

'Stop that and go and sit down you daft bugger,' was his first reaction.

Charlie licked Norris's ear again and his neck, just for good measure.

'If you don't stop this minute, there's going to be one hell of an upset the next time I stop this coach.' Norris lashed out with his arm and hit Charlie on the chest.

Norris thought to himself that whatever he had come into contact with did not feel quite right, so he quickly turned his head to look, just for a split second, so as not to disturb the driving.

'What the bloody hell!' The brakes slammed on. People fell from their seats, beer bottles rolled all over and Charlie took off landing on top of Norris.

Charlie began to bray, just like the donkey he was, and he would not be quiet. He was drunk, he wanted his mummy, he was hungry and he decided that if this was how humans carried on he was better off at his hovel.

Luckily, they were almost at a big lay-by and when Richard and Sid, ably assisted by twenty or thirty pairs of eager hands, had managed to separate Norris and Charlie, Norris pulled the bus in to it and parked up.

Norris stood up at the front of the bus, brushed himself down and shouted at the top of his voice, 'Right! Which bloody stupid lummock has brought this animal onto my bus?'

'It's not a bus, it's a coach,' Willie shouted.

Norris was ready for battle. 'And you Willie Arkenthwaite can shift that pile of horse shit out of my coach before I drive it one yard further. And who the hell's brought this four legged article onto my coach and what on earth are we going to do with it?'

'It's not my donkey and I haven't got a shovel. I left my bucket and spade on the beach and I didn't bring it onto the bus, so I'm not shifting it.'

'It's a coach, not a bus,' said Norris.

'It smells more like a bus than a coach to me,' said Willie.

'Aye well, if you don't shift that shit we're going no further.'

'Not our problem, it's your coach, you shift it. I'm getting off for a James Riddell,' retorted Willie.

There were shouts of 'suits us' and 'come on let's get off and have a drink.'

So the coach emptied as quickly as it was possible to shove Charlie down the steps back to mother earth and the trippers to follow.

The beer was soon flowing and Charlie was consuming far more beer than was good for him. He was enjoying himself again both drinking and being petted by all and sundry.

It became noticeable that Charlie was beginning to stagger a little, to look just a little bit glazed in the eye and to be wandering aimlessly. The more beer they poured into him, the worse he was going.

Eustace called a quick management meeting.

'Now what are we going to do about this here donkey, then? If murder was legal, I'd just put Richard and Sid to an early end.'

'Why don't we just push it through that gate into that field, get back into the bus, sorry, coach, sharp, and bugger off home?' suggested Willie. 'Somebody will find it sometime and it'll have plenty of grass to eat.'

'Might I utter a word of caution here?' said Arthur. 'There's bound to be repercussions, you know?

'What sort of repercussions Arthur?' enquired Eustace.

'Police, legal experts, we might all end up detained during His Majesty's pleasure.

Willie interrupted, 'Well you're going to find out now, here come the rozzers.'

A black, police, Riley car pulled into the lay-by and the two police people, who had dealt with the disturbance just before lunch and were on their way back to the station to go off duty, got out and surveyed the scene.

Charlie, espying two new arrivals that might have some more beer, staggered over to them and leaned on their car; their spotlessly clean, shiny, polished car.

One of them kicked Charlie, but he did not move as, just at that moment, he could not because it was time to exercise his bowels once again, all down the side of the spotlessly clean, shiny, polished police vehicle.

'Look at that, just look at that. We'll be in right bother now when we get back to the station and we'll have to stop late and wash the bloody thing. Someone here's going to suffer for this before we leave and no mistake.'

Willie intervened. 'I say you constables, we just stopped for a quiet drink and this donkey came amongst us from nowhere. Unfortunately it would appear to be somewhat poorly.'

Charlie was by this time nuzzling one of the constables who fell backwards under the pressure of Charlie's nose.

Just at that second there was divine intervention as the coach from Dewsbury, full of well intoxicated women, pulled into the lay-by. The ladies tumbled out and hurried behind the hedge in the field. At least those who could wait so long, those that could not wait performed for the constables right in front of them.

'Right, that's it,' shouted the constable that appeared to be in charge. 'Let's get their names and addresses.'

'May I enquire as to what the charges might be?' asked the vicar, 'because as a man of the cloth I look upon your intervention with disdain.'

Now the constable neither knew nor cared what disdain meant so he ignored the vicar's remarks and carried on shouting.

'Well if you are a man of the cloth, then I am Gunga Din. Now you will all be charged with making water in a public place. Drunk on the public highway, being in possession of a stolen...unhand me this instant or else...'

He got no further as the trousers of his police uniform were removed by several pairs of Dewsbury hands and his wedding tackle began to be interfered with. His companion took fright as the ladies advanced on him and he ran into the police car and locked himself in.

Charlie was having a whale of a time. He was getting more and more intoxicated and he was staggering from one beer bottle to the next.

Norris Oakes decided that enough was enough and he began to order his passengers into the coach one by one. Most of them obeyed him without question and those who did not were threatened with a good punching if they did not, so they did. However some of the more worldly wise, drunk and randy trippers, before getting on the coach, arranged with the ladies from the Dewsbury coach, who had by this time finished relieving themselves and slecking their thirst from the on coach supply, to meet them at the Dog and Duck for a convivial get together.

The passengers were almost all seated in the coach again, they were all on board, but some were queuing for another bottle of beer or two, when the Policeman who had been debagged by the ladies then retrieved the bottom part of his police uniform, realised that he was losing the perpetrators of the crime of bringing a seaside donkey to the inland and abandoning it and he stood in front of the coach. Then in true police tradition he put his hand up to indicate that it may not move until such time as he directed it to.

Norris Oakes was by this time in the right frame of mind to run over the police constable but restrained himself and sat placidly staring through the front window.

The policemen walked over to the car and ordered his mate out to assist in the massive arrest that he was about to make. But his colleague would not unlock the doors.

'No, no, I can't come out. I want to go home. Come on, get in, let's get back to the station. I'm hungry and thirsty and I don't like these women.'

'Get your big soft butt out of there and come help me arrest them all. I can't do it all on my own, and anyway, I've got them under control now. They'll all get a good long sentence for this lot you know.' The constable was already visualising himself in a sergeants uniform for the good work he was about to do. He was power mad but his mate was most definitely not.

So it was with the utmost reluctance that the soft hearted constable got out of the car and, accompanied by the jeers and shouts of the ladies, he entered the coach belonging to Bewdlay's Transport following his mate who was already there.

'Right everyone sit down, now, immediately.'

'Shut your face and bugger off,' was the reply he got from one of the trippers who was patiently waiting for Fat Harry to open a bottle of brown ale.

'Right, that's it, take his name and address constable.'

The other constable opened his notebook, licked his pencil and asked the person's name.

'Alouicious.'

'How do you spell that?

'T.H.A.T."

'No, no sir, I meant how do you spell Alouicious?'

'How the hell should I know?'

'But it's your name.'

'Aye, but I don't use it.'

'So why tell me about it?'

'You asked.'

The policeman wrote A.

Have you any other names, sir?'

'Yes, a lot.'

'So, what's next?'

'Brugman."

'What?'

"Brugman and don't tell me you can't spell that, a highly educated piss pot like yourself.'

The policeman followed the A with a B.

'Any more, sir?'

'Coreolanous.'

'Spell it.'

'Put C.'

'Next.'

"Donizetti.'

'I think you're having me on. Hey look here...' he shouted to his mate who came to look.

'Have you ever seen anything like this bloke's name?' He looked at his mate's notebook.

'All it says is ABCD.'

'Yes it's Alouicious Brugman Coreolanous Donizetti.'

'You dozy twonk. Go and sit back in the car, I'll sort it out myself. Right now, I'm prepared to ignore the charges of making water in a public place, being drunk on the King's highway and exhibiting yourselves in such a lewd manner as being likely to cause a breach of the peace.'

There were shouts of 'Hurray' and 'For he's a jolly good fellow' from the trippers,

He continued, 'But I am not prepared to ignore the fact that you stole a donkey from Blackpool beach and then attempted to abandon it in the countryside. So someone is going to be charged with stealing this donkey named Charlie. So would the criminal person like to own up?'

"It were all of us,' said Willie.

'I cannot believe that it was all of you, so I will ask the bus driver.'

'It's a coach,' said Willie.

"It smells like a bus to me, a bit like the late night Saturday bus, but it's not late enough for that just yet. So, Mr bus driver, who brought this donkey onto your bus?'

Now Norris who was fed up with his crowd of trippers was even more fed up of the policemen, so he said, 'I don't know, I wasn't there, and anyway, as Willie says it's a coach.'

'What do you mean you were not there? A bus driver must at all times be in charge of his vehicle.'

"I'd gone for a piss. I must have, it's the only time I wasn't there. Am I not allowed to answer a call of nature?'

There was not a lot of love lost between any of the trippers and Norris, so from somewhere down the coach came the cry. 'You bloody liar, you were sat on your arse in the other coach having a pipe of baccy. We all saw you.'

The policeman turned his attention to where the voice came from. 'And what do you know about it?'

'Nowt lad, I were just saying.'

The policeman realised that he could stay there all night and get nowhere. So he took the only course open to him. 'Right, I've taken the name and address of the coach proprietor and we will be in touch with him very shortly. You may go.'

The policeman dismounted and Norris rammed in first gear, the coach coughed and spluttered its way back onto the road bound for the Dog and Duck.

Sid turned to Richard, 'Well that was a piece of luck, we got away with it and we didn't have to take the donkey back to Blackpool. I just wish it hadn't crapped in here, it doesn't half pong.'

They turned to look out of the back window to see the policemen fighting off an army of drunken women and a very poorly donkey.

*

Norris Oakes concentrated on his driving and took the coach to the Dog and Duck which is always a good stopping point for Yorkshire bound Blackpool trippers on the return journey, for a couple of hours or more.

On the journey, Eustace turned to Arthur and Willie. 'What are we going to do about the donkey?'

'What about the donkey?' asked Willie.

'Well, we might all be in terrible bother over it, next week like.'

'No, no, we shall never hear about it again. Them two buffoons that arrived will have it to deal with and then they'll be in right bother when their super gets hold of them.'

Arthur said, 'Their Superintendent might never find out about it and anyway it'll be Bewdlay that's in bother not us, because Oakes should not have let the donkey onto the coach in the first place. He's responsible for security, it's all his fault. Sid and Richard can't help it if the donkey followed them onto the coach. Oakes should have been guarding the coach door instead of being sat on his backside somewhere else.'

A voice came from in front of them. 'I heard that. I'm not taking the blame for nowt. You lot are going to get well and truly into right deep and deadly trouble over this lot. You'll have to pay for cleaning up the mess on the carpet and getting rid of the smell.'

Willie looked towards where the voice came from. 'It smelt like the backdoor of a brothel when we got on it this morning and we were promised the new coach, not this clapped out wreck of a bus that belches and farts more than it runs, and we were promised a decent driver and not the idiot we've got, so it's going to cost Bewdlay a fortune when we put our claim in.' Willie belched out loud just for good measure.

'How far to the Dog and Duck?' Arthur shouted to Norris.

'About half an hour and then I'll be rid of you for a couple of hours, thank the Lord, and I'm locking the doors so that you can't bring any elephants, manure, strange women or anything else in here behind my back.'

*

Just as Norris had said, within half an hour the coach pulled into the huge car park of the Dog and Duck that was already almost full of coaches. There were still a few parking spaces left and it was not long before the coach was empty, the trippers were in the pub and Norris was in the gents wetting a cloth to try and wash the donkey doo stains from the carpet before Bewdlay saw them tomorrow morning.

Most of the trippers had been there before, many times, but to those who were having their first visit it was a revelation. It was vast; there were people everywhere, hundreds of them. The bars stretched as far as the eyes could see and were staffed by gorgeous young ladies, loads and loads of them. This was Eustace's first visit and he was mesmerised. He just stood and stared and had to be awakened by Willie who pushed him along towards the bar. Fortunately there were enough young ladies to cope with the deluge of humanity that faced them in regular droves across the bar counter and in no time at all, all the trippers were served.

Finding somewhere to park themselves was another problem altogether because the place was full to overflowing and seats were just not available. Fortunately, Arthur espied a chap he knew who was secretary of a bowling club in the next village to Grolsby that the Club played matches against, so they went to talk to him and the other bowlers that they all recognised.

They had not been seated long, just long enough to get nice and comfortable, before they became uncomfortable and yet another trip to the gents was called for before they came back and got comfortable again. Suddenly, there was a commotion at the door and fifty well inebriated ladies of indeterminable age from Dewsbury entered the pub and turned it into a scene reminiscent of Fred Cano's Circus. They were everywhere and anywhere. They had consumed so much drink that they made Randy Andy from Tony Pandy look like a beginner. They were on top of the men, underneath them; drink in one hand, man in the other.

Eustace, Arthur and the vicar were not enjoying the situation and took their drink outside to sit on the wall. But Fat Harry was taking a different view altogether. He wasn't exactly sure just exactly which view it was that was staring him in his almost focusing eyes, but it was one of those moments when he thought that he had arrived in Utopia.

Willie just sat where he was, enjoying the performance that was going on before him, feeling very mellow and just avoiding getting dragged into the melee. The people round him were rolling about and beginning to get a bit near for his liking, so he took the only action that was available to him which was to get a bit of air and a bit of freedom; he farted, long, loud and horrible. Although this action did not clear the air it did clear the air space and Willie was soon enjoying his drink sitting comfortably and watching the goings on. Fat Harry cursed Willie for having spoiled some of his fun, but Willie ignored him and carried on drinking.

*

Outside on the pub wall the conversation was a little bit slow, a little bit dull and very boring.

'I can't understand why anyone could get themselves into such a state as what them women have. They're beyond paralytic. Goodness only knows what their husbands will be thinking when they get home,' Arthur observed. 'Mind you, I suppose they're used to them by now.'

Eustace replied, 'I just can't understand them at all, how about you Vicar?'

'Well, I've said it before and I'll say it again, the Good Lord works in mysterious ways his wonders to perform. It amazes me how they can get themselves into such a state as they do. No morals, no sense of decency, no religion, in fact nothing. Nothing at all.'

'Why don't you go back in there and wade into the middle of them and do a bit of bible thumping, so as to get them more respectful?' said Eustace.

Arthur looked at him.

'Well I would, but in the state they are in, it would seem to me to be absolutely pointless as I shall make no impression at all and probably end up being debagged or something worse. So I think I'll give it a miss just this once. I realise that this is probably a dereliction of duty but, on this occasion, I think that I am justified in remaining derelict.'

'It's not been a bad day out though,' Eustace said. 'I've really enjoyed it, the lunch, the pier, and the pleasure beach.'

'The donkey,' said Arthur.

'Yes, the donkey,' said the vicar. 'Do you think there might be some repercussions over that matter?'

'I don't see why,' said Arthur, 'it was nothing to do with us. It was Sid and Richard and they should have known better.'

'Aye, but it was the drink,' said Eustace.

The vicar said, 'Yes, but I cannot see a high court judge accepting a plea of "it was the drink you honour." I think we might all face the consequences of Sid and Richard's actions and it will not look good with the Bishop if this does happen.'

'It all depends on the Two Stooges,' said Arthur.

'Who?' asked Eustace.

'Those two completely useless representatives of the Blackpool Constabulary and I wouldn't worry about them at all Vicar because by the time those women from Dewsbury had finished with them, they would have lost the donkey and their dignity and would have been glad to escape with their uniforms intact. I am sure that by now Charlie has disappeared into the undergrowth and is enjoying his freedom and those two coppers are head down somewhere trying to decide how best to explain their dirty car to their superior officers. Anyway, if you are so worried, just walk into the pub and ask one of those women what happened. Just to put your mind at rest.'

'I think I'll worry, thank you. Anyway my glass is empty so I think it's time for a refill.'

'Yes, me too,' said Arthur. 'How about you Eustace?'

'No. No thanks, Arthur. No, it's my bladder you see, it's full again now and it's filling very quickly all the time. So I'll not have another just now, give it a bit of breathing space for the journey ahead. And talking of journeys ahead, isn't it time we were thinking of making a move towards home, it's been a long day. Let's go inside, because as I was saying, I need a piss.'

'Here here,' replied two other voices.

*

As the three unwilling revelers walked back into the pub they were met by a scene of utter carnage. There was a pile of bodies, some male from Murgatroyd's mill, some female from Dewsbury. Some of both denominations from other places, all heaped together in such a way as to make it impossible to determine t'other from which. They stared in disbelief at what was before their eyes. There were heads up, heads down, legs down, legs up, body parts exposed that should not have been, mouths where they definitely should not have been, in fact a huge non-stop orgy.

'That's Fat Harry's foot there but where's the rest of him?' asked Arthur.

'I don't know, but just exactly what Horrible Hector is doing to that lady I am not quite sure,' said Eustace

'Well I think it is absolutely disgusting,' said the vicar and I am about to have it stopped.' He marched smartly over to the bar and sought out the landlord. 'I am the Very Reverend Clifford Tunstall, Vicar of St Cuthbert's on the Hill, Grolsby, and I demand that you put a stop to this orgy at once.'

The landlord looked at him, 'Yes mate, no dog collar, pull the other one it's got bells on it. Anyway, don't worry, it's ten to nine, Sergeant Cummins and his lady assistant Big Barbara will be here at about any second now, they call in every Saturday night and sort out the good from the bad if you know what I mean. Oh, dead on time, here they are now, wait for it...'

The three trippers turned to observe a large, savage looking uniformed officer with three stripes on his arm and an even more savage mountain of a uniformed lady officer, without stripes, just placing a regulation police issue whistle into each of their mouths. Sergeant Cummins gave a signal and they both blew their whistles together as loud as they could.

It went quiet, it went still, nobody moved and nobody spoke. Then Big Barbara, who was exceptionally well named, picked up Horrible Hector by the scruff of the neck, pulled him out of the melee single handed and frog marched him out through the door into the car park. 'Stand there and do not dare to move.' She had put her face right up to Hector's as she spoke these words to him at about one thousand decibels and the halitosis that hit him at one and the same time paralysed him to the spot. He was frightened of Martha at times but Big Bertha was in a different league altogether.

Back inside it was still quiet. Sergeant Cummins looked at them and waited for Big Barbara to return.

'Right you lot, outside all of you, single file, orderly, stand next to that specimen that I just ejected. Keep quiet, in line, don't move.'

The two police walked over to the bar and the landlord gave them a glass each.

'Thanks for turning up again and quelling another riot.'

'No problem, we'll deal with them in a minute when we've just enjoyed this small libation.'

The vicar opened his mouth, 'should you be drinking on duty officers?'

Sergeant Cummins turned his attention to the man who had just dared to question his actions, 'And who the hell might you be?'

'The Very Reverend Clifford Tunstall, Vicar of St Cuthbert's on the Hill, Grolsby.'

'Where's your dog collar? You with that lot? Your Bishop know you're here?'

'No.'

'Well he bloody soon will do if you open your mouth again. Now, we'll just let that lot starve to death out there, finish our drinks and go and dispatch them. Or at least Barbara will, her breath, her halitosis, it has to be sampled to be believed.'

Willie walked over to them. 'Where have you lot been?'

'Outside having a drink where it was peaceful and quiet. How did you manage not to get involved in this here orgy?' asked Eustace.

'Easy, I just kept belching and farting and sitting watching the proceedings, no one bothered me.'

'Right, I think it's time your bus was leaving,' said Sergeant Cummins, let us all go outside. Goodnight Reg.' He turned and smiled at the landlord who thanked him profusely yet again.

They laughed when they observed the scene that met them in the car park. There were over two hundred and fifty people all lined up in three straight rows not daring to move, by now quite cold and all wanting to use the toilets.

'Right,' shouted Big Barbara, 'I have no doubt that you'll all be wanting a piss. Well hard chuff, you can stand there and wet yourselves for all I care. Now you can all use the pub toilets as I release you one at a time. You go in there quietly, orderly, you do NOT have a drink, you do what you have to and you come back and get into your bus. You do not, NOT, relieve yourselves in the car park, you hold on to it until your turn comes. Any of you who do relieve yourselves in the car park will be arrested and charged with "making water in a public place." Do I make myself clear?'

There were nods throughout.

'Finally, those of you who go first will, by the time all the rest have been, want to go again. Well hard lines, you'll have to hold on to it. Right, good, we will start here at this end.' Big Barbara who had brought her halitosis with her leaned forward in front of the first in line, breathed heavily, opened mouthed over him and said, 'You may go.'

Each of them grimaced at the offensive cloud that hit them but did not dare complain for Barbara was big, ugly, menacing, strong and an entire police force on her own.

Sergeant Cummins stood to one side and smiled and nodded to each tripper in turn as they returned to their respective coaches.

Norris Oakes looked at his passengers and observed that some of them were shivering, some wanted to go again and some were so drunk they didn't know what they wanted.

'Right, that's it, homeward bound now. I'm not stopping this coach again until we're back at the club.' He pulled out into the main road again and pointed the coach towards Yorkshire.

The men were waving to the ladies from Dewsbury who were also on their own coach and the ladies good humouredly returned their waves.

*

They had not travelled far when two different cries were heard from the interior of the coach; the first one was the inevitable one, 'Stop the coach I need to go, now.' The second one was, 'Norris, put the heater on its bloody cold.'

'No good, the heater doesn't work and anyway it's plenty warm enough for the time of year and I can't stop here, it's nowt but houses.'

'Well you'll have to stop or else you'll have a wet coach.'

So Norris pulled up and several bodies piled into some Lancastrian family's front garden and their front wall got wet.

It just so happened that the man of the Lancastrian house was just returning home from having taken his pet, savage, Alsatian for a walk, espied the carryings on in his front garden and quietly slipped the lead off the dog. Seconds later a huge ball of fur landed amongst the bladder relievers and began to chew his way through them.

The coach filled with bodies again, even faster than it had emptied. Norris shut the door on the snarling animal and he set off again with the man of the house hammering on the side of the coach.

They had not gone far when a voice came from afar. 'You'll have to stop again, I got rudely interrupted.'

'I'm not stopping this bloody coach again until I get back home.'

'Well I'm going to do it here and now,' and he did.

'Right. That's it!' said Norris. 'I'm going to phone Bewdlay.'

So Norris sought out the next telephone box, stopped the coach and dismounted to phone his boss. He did not return for a long time.

A lone voice from within the coach shouted out loudly, 'Can anyone drive this contraption?'

'Yes, I can,' replied a rather well inebriated Jasper Collins.

'Well, come on then, we can't wait for Oakes, get into that drivers seat and get us home.'

So whilst Norris Oakes was in the phone box, he heard the pip pip pip of the coach's horn. He looked around to observe fifty pairs of hands gesticulating at him and the coach chugging away leaving him stranded in the nether regions of Lancashire.

The coach steered an erratic coarse at a fast pace, narrowly avoiding several other vehicles, lamp posts, pedestrians and sundry other items that should not have been in the way of a drunken coach.

Norris Oakes had finally got through to Joseph Bewdlay who was not very pleased at receiving a transfer charge call and particularly late on a Saturday evening when he was passing a convivial time with good friends and was well and truly drunk.

'Joseph. That you, Joseph? Is it Joseph, is it you?'

'Yes Norrisorris is that you, because it's me here.' He laughed and giggled. 'What do you? What? Do you know we're having a right good time? A right good time. Thank you for calling. He he he.'

After replacing the receiver, Joseph walked back into his lounge and looked at the other five well inebriated people that were there. 'That was. Who was that?'

'Who was that dear?' asked his wife just before she belched.

'It was. Yes it was.'

'No, I asked you, who was that?'

'It was Norrisorris.'

'Who's Norrisorris, dear? Pardon me'

'Why?'

'Why what?'

'Don't know.'

'What?' She laughed a little, then fell asleep.

*

Meanwhile in a telephone box somewhere in deepest Lancashire, an abandoned Norris Oakes didn't know what to do next. So he did the only thing he could do, he dialed the emergency number hoping that they would answer as he had no money.

'Emergency. Which service please?'

'Police.'

There was a brief pause and then. 'Police, can I help you?'

'It's my bus.'

'What about your bus?'

'They've taken it.'

'Who have?'

'The trippers.'

'Which trippers?

'Murgatroyd's mill trippers.'

'So where are you?'

'Somewhere near North Manchester, but I don't know exactly.'

'Where is your bus?'

'I don't' know, the passengers have taken it?'

'Why have the passengers taken it?'

'Because I got out to phone for help.'

The emergency operator turned to her mate and said, 'I've got a right one here.'

'I had one not long ago.'

'So where is the bus now?'

'I don't know, it was heading for Yorkshire the last I saw of it, probably well towards Rochdale by now. Bewdlay's going to kill me.'

'Who's Bewdlay?'

'The chap who owns the bus and he's as drunk as a skunk just now.'

'Is he driving the bus?'

'No, one of the passengers is.'

'Name?'

'Norris Oakes.'

'So a Norris Oakes has stolen your bus and has driven it away.'

'No. I'm Norris Oakes.'

'So who is driving your bus?'

'I don't know. One of the trippers has stolen it. Look, would you like to get it back for me and get me away from this God forsaken hole that I find myself in, because it's bloody cold and I'm hungry.'

'Right, sir. So the bus belongs to whom?

'Bewdlay's Transport Company from Grolsby, West Riding of Yorkshire. It's one of the first villages you come to after crossing the Pennines.'

'Registration number of the bus?

'It's V H seven three four two.'

'Right, I'll alert the patrol cars to be looking out for it.'

'What about me?'

'I'll ask the nearest patrol car to you to come collect you. Are you on the side of the main road?'

'Yes.'

'Right so give us the number of the phone box that you are calling from so that we can ascertain your correct location, then please replace the receiver and we will collect you shortly.'

Norris walked out onto the pavement and stood there shivering for about ten minutes until the patrol car arrived and carried him off towards the local police station.

*

The coach, with Jasper Collins at the helm, had ricocheted its way from off the moors and into the suburbs of North Manchester. It had broken every traffic law that had ever been legislated and some that had even yet not been thought about. It neatly passed through three sets of traffic lights at red, making a series of other vehicles narrowly avoid a multi-car smash then it went round a roundabout the wrong way, negotiated its way erratically through the ornate gates of a local memorial park and drove itself head first, straight into the memorial fountain from where it could proceed no further.

The passengers disembarked, getting rather wet in the process as they had to wade through what remained of the memorial pond and opened the luggage compartment so as to have another drink or two sitting on the park benches at midnight.

CHAPTER 15

Eustace sat bolt upright in bed. It took him a few seconds to enter the land of the living.

Joan said, 'What on earth? Oh I know, Oh, what are we going to do?'

'I don't know, but, oh dear what a mess. What a disgrace. What time is it?'

'Eleven. ELEVEN,' she screeched. 'It can't be!'

'It can. Don't forget it was four o'clock when we got to bed. I'd better get ready and go see Arthur and Willie. Bewdlay's going to go mad, completely mad. Just fancy, coming home in a Black Maria. There's a first, but at least they made sure we got home. But Bewdlay's clapped out coach, head down in a Lancastrian memorial fountain, probably a write off, he'll never speak to us again. Then there's Jasper Collins, detained overnight at Manchester nick, they'll charge him with stealing a coach, dangerous driving, I don't know what, but one thing's sure, they'll throw the book at him.'

'Perhaps I'd better come with you, two heads might be better than one in this case.'

'No love, not just now, I think the others will be at the club.'

*

About the same time, Arthur was having a rather different conversation with Jess.

'You'll end up behind bars, you know, and don't come running to me for help when the day of reckoning comes. You've brought it down on your own heads, you and Willie and Eustace. You were the organisers; you were the ones who instigated all of this mess. Just fancy, leaving a coach in a pond in North Manchester, most of the passengers too drunk to know anything about it than to go paddling and drinking in public, then to cap it all, you turning up here in a Black Maria. Oh the disgrace, the shame of it, I don't know what the neighbours will say or think…'

Arthur had heard enough, so he cut her short, 'That's sums it up right nicely, that does.'

'What?'

'More concerned about what the neighbours might think than how are we going to get ourselves out of the mess we are in. It's about time you gave over feeling sorry for yourself and concentrated more on me.'

'Well, Arthur Baxter, if that doesn't take the biscuit. You keep me sitting up here waiting for you to come home until four o'clock this morning, worried out of my skin nearly, then you arrive in a Black Maria and I wonder what on earth is going on, then you tell me you've stolen and drowned the bus…'

'It was a coach before we killed it.'

'…that you've left in a duck pond somewhere near Manchester, Jasper Collins is in jail charged with driving a coach under the influence of alcohol, stealing a coach and dangerous driving and what else. How we'll ever live this down, I do not know. So what are you going to do now?'

'I'm going to go to the club and get horribly drunk.'

He stood up, put his cap on and walked out of the house to the tones of, 'Well, well I never, well!'

*

At the Arkenthwaite's it was yet another story. Willie was sitting in the front room, with Thelma and the children, keeping them enthralled with his tales of humpty cycles, donkeys and coach crashes.

Peter kept on saying again and again, 'Come on Dad tell us again how the coach ran into the fountain. Did it smash the fountain? Was anyone injured or killed? Where's the donkey now?'

Thelma said, 'Oh Peter, do let your Dad have a bit of peace. He had a long tiring day yesterday and I suspect he might have another day of it today.'

'Yes, you're right, and I'd best get to the club and see what we can do about it.'

*

'Bloody good day out yesterday,' said a very bleary eyed steward as Eustace entered the bar of the Grolsby Working Men's Club.

'Good! Good! It was an absolute disaster.'

'Nay, you can't say that, it was just the last five seconds that might have been a disaster and then the four hours afterwards, but the first part of the day was superb, except for my brush with Madam Zsa Zsa. Wasn't it Arthur?'

'What was?' asked Arthur who had just arrived. 'Give us a pint.'

'You look as if you need it, been giving you an ear bashing has she?'

'You could say that.'

'Your fault that the bus crashed, was it?'

'You could say that as well.'

'Thought so, you look like a man that could use a pint.'

'What are we going to do, Arthur? What, are we going to do, Arthur, what?'

'Eustace, control yourself.'

'Yes, sorry Arthur, sorry, I'll try not to do it again.'

'Nothing at all.' They all turned to look at Willie. 'Give us a pint; I've a thirst like I don't know what.'

'What do you mean nothing at all?'

'Not our problem, nothing to do with us. We weren't driving the coach. We didn't crash it. We didn't abandon the coach and go off crying to Bewdlay. In fact, we should ask Bewdlay for our money back because his driver abandoned us in the wilds of

Lancashire. Anything could have happened to us out there you know.'

'What time is it?' Asked Eustace, who never wore his watch.

'Eleven forty five by a good chronometer.'

They all stared gob struck at Harry then Arthur ventured to ask, 'Where did you learn such a big word as that Harry?'

'What do you want to know what time it is for? And chronometer is just one of the words that I learned as part of my superior education.'

'We were not aware that you had actually been educated, Harry,' said Willie.

Harry ignored him. 'So why do you want to know what time it is?'

'Well the reverend will be just saying goodbye to his parishioners, so you'd best pour him his first pint ready, he'll be here in a couple of minutes.'

'Yes, and he might be accompanied by my wife's relation Bewdlay who is one of his regular worshipers,' said Eustace.

True to form the Very Right Reverend Clifford Tunstall MA appeared dead on time and alone.

'Not brought Bewdlay with you Reverend?' Asked Willie.

'No, like you people he hasn't worshipped this morning. May I have a pint, Harry, please?'

'Certainly Vicar, it is always a pleasure to serve someone with manners. Someone who says please, unlike this other collection of ne'er do well's, hangers on and latter day saints that stand before you.'

'So where is Bewdlay then?' asked Eustace.

'Well, rumour at church has it that he was seen fairly early this morning loading his truck with welding equipment and various tool kits, ready for a trip to North Manchester. That was after the police had arrived.'

'Police?'

'Well, of course, the police are bound to be involved. A coach crash, a coach that must be almost a write off, a wreck that has to be recovered and removed and bear in mind that from where we abandoned it last night or in the early hours, it will take a lot of recovering. A damaged memorial gardens, dead ducks, dead swans, flower beds set asunder, plants all over, a ruined memorial, a small lake that at this moment is devoid of water, and the entrance gates smashed to smithereens.

Then there's Jasper Collins, drunk in charge of a public service vehicle, stealing a coach, kidnapping all its passengers, fighting with the police, breaking the speed limit, going through three sets of traffic lights at red, driving the wrong way around a roundabout, damaging the memorial gardens.

Then there's Norris, abandoning a coach full of passengers, and that was just the few tit bits that I picked up at Church this morning and you question as to why the police were early visitors to Bewdlay's garage.'

'So,' said Arthur, 'do we assume that it is safe to stay here and drink, avoiding the wrath of one Joseph Bewdlay, coach proprietor of this village?'

'I think that it is probably a safe bet for, as you already know, I believe him to be in deepest Lancashire at this very minute attending to his wrecked coach.'

'Not quite,' said a voice from behind them. They all turned aghast to see Joseph Bewdlay looking grim, or even grimmer than usual. Then he smiled, laughed and said, 'Can I buy you lads a drink?'

There followed a very pregnant silence.

'A drink?' Arthur enquired. 'I thought you'd want to hang, draw and quarter us before feeding the remains to the dogs.'

'Not so.'

'How come?'

'Well, it's like this. What you don't know is that you've actually done me a big favour.'

'How come?' Arthur repeated himself.

'To begin with, let me say it's been a particularly difficult morning. Tell you what; we'll start at the beginning, this being later on last night. We'd had a bit of a party at home, just a few of us, but we'd drunk so much wine and spirits that when Norris Oakes telephoned me from the phone box somewhere the far side of Manchester, and I now know exactly where it was, I was so pissed that I didn't make any coherent conversation with him and I put the phone down on him. He tried again and the same happened again and that was when he rang the police. So anyway, I woke about five this morning, bursting for a piss, and I don't know why, but I began to think about a peculiar phone conversation I'd had last night and somehow or other I got worried about the coach.

Now, I could not remember the gist of the conversation at all, but something was nagging at the back of my mind. So at about half past five I was at the garage and there was no coach. I went round to Norris' house and there was no coach there either. The curtains were all drawn and I didn't want to wake them but, as I turned to come away, a police car came up the road and discharged Norris outside his house.

So then I got two tales. One from Norris about the fact that the bus had been stolen, that he had phoned me from a roadside phone box, without success because I was drunk, and that he had been charged with abandoning the coach to the detriment of his passengers. The other from the police telling me the whole sorry story. So I thought it best to go to Lancashire there and then to look at what remained of my coach.

The roads were very quiet, the sun was up and it was a very pleasant trip. I found the coach. There was no one around, the police had obviously retired for refreshments, and I realised that the coach was a write off, but that there was a lot of valuable stuff in it, including a crate or three of ale and some valuable bits that I could do with at the garage before the local vandals and looters got to work. So I drove as quick as I dared back to the garage, got the truck out, loaded it with some gear, drove back, removed all the equipment I wanted, under the watchful eye of the local plod and I've got anything that is anything back to the garage. So there are seven full crates of ale outside that just want bringing in. So here I am and what do you all want to drink?'

They all shouted their order and Harry obliged. Then he said, 'Before we get any further I think we should all go outside and bring a crate of ale each back into here.' So they traipsed to the front door and each returned with a crate.

Harry said, 'I thought that there should be a few more full crates than what we've brought into here.'

'Well that's all I could see, the rest are probably either buried in the wreck or the police supped them whilst they guarded the coach during the night.'

Harry looked at him with a knowing look but Joseph just stared him out with a very innocent look.

'So what about the empties?' Harry asked. 'Because I'll have to account for all this lot to the brewery.'

'Don't worry about that just now,' said Joseph, 'the insurance company will sort out that lot for you. The club is insured I assume?'

'Oh aye, but it's all the clerical work involved that's going to get me.'

'Harry, give over worrying, I'll get the bookkeeper from the garage to help you.'

Arthur intervened, 'So I still haven't figured out why you don't want to skin us alive for wrecking your coach.'

'Well you see, as soon as I got up and began to get a picture of what had happened, I phoned my insurance man and he was so alarmed about what had happened that he went and met me at the scene of the misdemeanor on my second visit. Mind you, he was justified in being alarmed, because it's going to be a big, big claim. There's the coach, which is a write off, there's all the personal belongings of the passengers and there's the recovery of the coach to a scrap yard then there's one memorial garden destroyed including the ornate front gates, one set of traffic lights knocked down and no doubt some other items that have not come to light yet. So altogether quite a princely claim. I doubt that he's celebrating like we are.'

'Yes but,' said Arthur, 'after all that I cannot see why you aren't mad as hell at us.'

'Well I am, but out of it is coming two really good things worth celebrating.'

'What?'

'I've already sacked Norris Oakes. I've been looking for a good excuse for a long time and he gave me one on a plate. But better even than that I'm going to get a brand spanking new coach.'

'Blimey.'

Willie asked, 'So we're not in bother then?'

'Not at all. Mind you, Jasper Collins is, and you lot will have some explaining to do to Anthony Murgatroyd tomorrow morning.'

'So where is Jasper Collins right now?' asked Fat Harry, because he is usually in here at this time on a Sunday.'

'Well as far as I know the Police at Manchester still are detaining him.'

'Wrong again,' said a voice they all recognised, but still turned around to confirm their suspicions.

'What on earth have you done with my best coach?' asked Joseph Bewdlay.

'Best coach? Best coach? The worst, most clapped out, knackered rust bucket that I've ever had the misfortune to drive and I've driven a few in my time.'

Joseph laughed and infected all the others. When the turmoil subsided, he asked, 'Now tell me Jasper, what exactly happened and I mean, exactly?'

'Well it was like this. That first rate idiot driver Norris that you employ…'

'Correction, employed, in the past tense.'

'…abandoned us in the middle of almost nowhere, in rural Lancashire and went into a phone box from where he did not emerge for a long time. We was all getting fed up of waiting for him...'

'Yes, that was my fault,' interrupted Joseph.

'So anyway, some body shouted, "can anyone drive this coach?" and I could, so I got into the drivers seat and drove away. We all waved bye bye to Norris and I just drove. I remember the houses going past us very quickly but I don't know where we went and I can't remember a lot about it. I do remember a lot of shouting at some traffic lights and a problem at a roundabout, then a big crash at some gates and then we stopped quick and there was water everywhere. I think I went to sleep then and I don't remember anything more until I woke up in a cell in the police station.'

'So what have they charged you with?'

'Taking a coach without consent, but they may throw that out, depending on what you say Mr Bewdlay. Then there's driving whilst being under the influence of excess alcohol, driving without due care and attention, defamation of a public place and making water in a public place. Added together it will probably mean loss of license for three years and a fairly hefty fine. Other than that I'm going to get off with a clean record.

But I'll tell you what, from what I can remember, I didn't half enjoy it, particularly smashing the park gates, that was something else. My words, the speed we hit them at, it was fantastic, they disintegrated and went everywhere. I have vivid flash backs of that instant. I remember a bit about drowning the coach, but not a lot. Sorry, Mr Bewdlay, it was your coach I know, I wasn't trying to glamorise the event, but oh, the thrill of clouting those park gates.'

Joseph Bewdlay walked around and put his hand on Jasper's shoulder. 'Jasper, my dear boy, you'll never know what a favour you did me last night. I will be going to get a brand new coach out of this debacle and as far as I am concerned, the charge of taking the coach without consent will never apply and

I am quite prepared to come to court and put in a plea of mitigation.'

Willie looked at him. 'A what?'

'A plea of mitigation.'

'What's one of them then?'

'It means that I shall go to court and tell them that it wasn't Jasper's fault, it was all down to Norris Oakes. He abandoned you all and you had to do something. The fact that the only bloke that could drive the coach was well fuelled with alcohol was very unfortunate and helped to get him arrested, but possibly my plea may save the day for him. By the way, I detected a distinct farmyard type aroma in the coach. Anyone know what that was all about?'

'The Lord moves in a mysterious way his wonders to perform,' said the vicar.

'And just what exactly do you mean by that Vicar?' asked Joseph.

'I was just wondering how there gets a farmyard aroma in a coach that is sitting in a fountain, washing its tyres.'

'Had you not detected this smell then, whilst you were on the coach?'

'Well, now that you have mentioned it, there was a somewhat farm yardish smell at times.'

Arthur intervened, 'Donkeys. It smelled of donkeys.'

'Not first thing in the morning, I hope,' said Bewdlay.

'No, no, much later in the day than that, in fact it was after we left Blackpool that I smelt it.'

'Funny,' said Bewdlay, 'Norris Oakes was mumbling about a donkey that fell on him and started all the trouble, but I just dismissed it as the ramblings of a deranged driver at the time. But still, it makes you think doesn't it?'

'Aye, it does,' replied Arthur.

There followed a very pregnant silence until Willie pointed out that his glass was empty and Joseph did the honours yet again.

'Well I'm away for my Sunday roast,' said Arthur being very glad, despite the free drinks, to be able to get away from Joseph Bewdlay unscathed and not incriminated.

The other drinkers returned to their respective homes for their Sunday lunches.

*

'Well what happened?' Joan was straight at Eustace before he had even had time to remove his hat.

'Not a lot. Cousin Joseph came and bought us all a few free drinks and that was about it.'

'So what about you all going to goal, for stealing his coach and damaging it?'

'Well you see, it's all sorted out. Norris Oakes has got the sack for abandoning the coach and passengers in the first place. Then the insurance have already been and agreed to settle all claims including a brand spanking new coach and Joseph is going to help Jasper Collins get off as best he can. So all taken into consideration it has not been a right bad do. Is dinner ready?'

'Yes it is love. Go was your hands and sit at the table, I'll go and serve it up.'

Eustace washed his hands and sat at the table as asked. He had a non-obvious smile on his face as he told himself, 'a right good outcome and life is almost perfect.'

*

Arthur Baxter walked in home to silence. He washed his hands at the sink in the kitchen then turned to look at Jess.

'Is my dinner ready?'

'Your dinner ready? Your dinner ready? And you having murdered Bewdlay's best coach. I make no wonder they've let you come home. I thought I was going to be a trip widow for the next five years whilst you were detained at his Majesty's pleasure.'

'Don't worry yourself, woman. Bewdlay's been and bought us all a few drinks. He's right suited that we've got rid of his old coach for him.'

Jess started up again, 'I knew I could smell drink on your breath. How dare you come home for your Sunday dinner reeking of stale ale? What the neighbours and the folk around here will think I do not know.'

Arthur had had enough. 'No and I don't bloody well care. NOW,' He began to stand up and started to raise his voice, 'for the second time of asking, is my dinner ready?'

Jess made a hurried move to serve dinner. She had seen Arthur in a foul mood like he was in right now only a few times in their long married life, but she understood enough to know that about now was the right time to keep calm, behave and feed her man.

*

Willie walked into Cutside cottages and sat at the table. He had met the children playing on the canal towpath and they also went with him to sit at the table. Thelma and Josie came out of the back kitchen with a feast fit for the King. They knew better than to ask Willie to wash his hands.

'What sort of a morning have you had love?'

'Real. Everything's being sorted out by Bewdlay's insurance company and he came to the club to see us and brought us a couple of rounds of drinks. So all in all, it's been a right good trip.'

CHAPTER 16

At about ten o'clock on Monday morning, Mr Anthony Murgatroyd entered the mill dyehouse at a brisk rate of knots and made a bee-line for Arthur and Willie.

'Be outside my office at eleven thirty prompt.' That was all he said before turning about and hurrying on his way to some other part of the mill.

Walter Smith, the foreman dyer, was seething with rage. Mr Anthony always came into the dyehouse about that time of morning and he always, but always, spoke to Walter first before he acknowledged the presence of the other labourers and minions that worked under him. He usually asked about the cloth that was being dyed, how many pieces there were today, had they sufficient raw material, were there any problems and all manner of other questions. But today it had been different, he had been slighted by Mr Anthony, ignored, all because of that bloody trip that he hadn't been on anyway. He was a foreman, much superior to those that worked under him, they were labourers, he did not mix with them and they were far below his station in life. So his thoughts were that those two were going to suffer for his problems, and he walked over to them.

Before he got there Mr Anthony returned to the dyehouse and this time walked over to Walter. 'I forgot to tell you. Arthur and Willie have to be outside my office at half past eleven prompt.'

Once again he walked out of the dyehouse and left a more than upset Walter standing almost shaking with rage. Without it appearing that he was rushing, Walter almost galloped over to Arthur and Willie.

'My words you two are for it. You've got to be outside his office at half past eleven. In a very nasty mood he is. Shouldn't wonder if he doesn't sack you when he gets you up there and that's less than you deserve for what you lot have done. Never

271

seen him as mad as that, just looked like the Grim Reaper, death warmed up, he was. It's obvious that the disgrace you have brought on the mill is having a bad effect on him. I'd best start looking for two replacements for your job and I'll tell you this; I'm having two blokes that can do their job properly and well, not like you two useless, no good layabouts.' He turned and went back to what was described as his office. Actually it was an old chair under a plank of timber balanced on the steam pipes on which he kept his paper work.

Willie was ready to go and knock seven bells out of Walter, but Arthur urged caution until such time as they had been to see Mr Anthony.

'I think you could probably kill him dead then murder him after that because I don't think he's Mr Anthony's best friend. So just bide your time until our turn for revenge arrives, and it will.'

'Do you think that Eustace will be at the meeting?' asked Willie, who proceeded to rock the building with a fart of immense proportions.

'I am sure he will,' replied Arthur ignoring Willie's minor explosion.

What they didn't know was that Mr Anthony had visited the teazing room as soon as he had left the dyehouse and told Eustace to be at the meeting.

Eustace was slowly becoming a jittering wreck.

Mr Anthony had left the teazing room and as soon as he was out of sight of the building he began to smile and said to himself, 'Well that's put the cat amongst the pigeons,' and returned well satisfied to his office.

*

At twenty five past eleven a pair of very nervous people were standing outside Mr Anthony's private office at the top of a long flight of stone steps. They heard Eustace coming slowly up the stairs puffing and panting, partly from the condition of his body and partly from nervousness. He eventually arrived and started talking. 'Hello Arthur. Hello Willie. Are we going to get the sack? Are we Arthur? Willie? Do you think we are? I daren't go home and tell my Joan, I daren't, no I daren't. I'm scared about what might happen, I am Willie, Arthur.'

Arthur attempted to calm him without much success. 'Now calm down and take control of yourself Eustace. I am sure that Mr Anthony will not deal unfairly with us.'

'So what will he do Arthur? Willie?'

'I do not know. We will just have to wait and see.'

A couple of Willie farts later it was dead on half past eleven and the private office door opened. Mr Anthony stuck his head out.

'Please come in.'

He showed them to a plain table at one side of the room with four chairs around and nothing else.

'Please sit down,' he invited them.

They sat, quietly and meekly.

For quite a time nothing was said. They all looked at one another, then at the table, and then Mr Anthony said, 'Well?'

'Err, well what, Mr Anthony?' Arthur ventured to enquire.

'Well what exactly happened after we had left you all at the Golden Cockerel Restaurant. Margaret had only been saying, on the way home, what a nice, well mannered, orderly bunch of people work at the mill and that you were all a credit to the business, and then as soon as our backs are turned you go and destroy more of Lancashire than The Wars of the Roses succeeded in doing, and to cap it all, you almost put Bewdlay out of business. Will someone please tell me exactly what happened?'

So, Eustace, who was theoretically the originator of the trip idea, began a long slow droning blow by blow account of the whole of the proceedings leading up to the drowning of Bewdlay's clapped out coach.

Whilst he was talking, Arthur listened intently and Willie stared and stared at Anthony Murgatroyd.

What none of them had realised was that, whilst Mr Anthony had met them with a very cross expression on his face, he was by now having huge problems to stop himself howling out loud with laughter. Suddenly he said, 'Eustace, let me please interrupt for a couple of minutes.'

Eustace stopped, glad of a break.

'Willie, why are you sitting there staring at me so intently?'

'Err, who me, Mr Anthony?'

'Yes, you Willie, you have been staring at my face ever since you sat down. So why? Have I grown two heads or something?'

The other two laughed out of politeness or it could have been embarrassment.

Willie decided that it might do no harm to make a clean breast of things. 'Well, it's like this, Mr Anthony. Walter Smith said you had a face like the Grim Reaper, but I can't see it. You don't look like death to me.'

'Thank you, Willie, I'll just store that reference in my head and deal with it later. Please continue with this fascinating account Eustace.'

So Eustace carried on with his monotonous account of the trip and Mr Anthony continued with the utmost difficulty to listen and not burst out laughing. Eventually he could contain himself no longer and he descended into fits of uncontrollable mirth.

The other three looked at him and awe and began to wonder just what fate awaited them.

Eventually, he stopped laughing and picked up his phone. He looked at the other three. 'I've got a new telephone. I'm not sure just how it works but it has a loud speaker that I am going to attempt to switch on for the very first time and with a bit of luck you can all hear my conversation.'

This explanation meant nothing to any of the other three as they were not familiar with the use of the telephone. However they listened very carefully to what happened.

The handset was built onto the top of a polished wooden cabinet which had several rows of switches and a loudspeaker on the front. Mr Anthony took a little time to select the correct switch. He depressed it and soon they all heard a ringing noise form the loudspeaker. The ringing stopped and a female voice was heard.

'What the hell do you want? Don't you know I'm serving dinner?'

'Ah, Martha.'

'Sorry, Mr Anthony.'

'Martha, Willie, Arthur and Eustace are with me and they will be a little late for lunch today. Will you please keep it warm for them?'

'No. Tell them to bugger off.'

'Thank you Martha.'

He was about to replace his handset when Martha carried on talking. 'Have you sacked them yet? We are all eagerly waiting to see them walk down the yard for the last time.'

'Not yet, Martha. Thank you for your observations. Please continue serving lunch.' This time he did replace the handset.

Eustace began to talk again, 'You aren't going to sack us are you, Mr Anthony? Are you? Are you?' He began to visibly tremble and the other two were looking very worried.

Mr Anthony decided he had better get on with it before he had three human wrecks to deal with.

'Now gentlemen, to your punishment.'

They began to fear the worst.

'It comes in two parts. Part one, I order you to organise another trip to Blackpool next June.'

'Eh?'

'You all heard, and part two, I order you to continue to run the Christmas club until at least next Christmas.'

'Well I never did,' said Arthur, 'I really thought that we were for the long drop.'

'Well you see, Arthur, the more I hear about this trip the more I like it. We did enjoy ourselves. But then hearing about Harry in the clutches of Madam Zsa Zsa, and then the donkey falling on Norris Oakes, oh how I would have loved to have seen that. Finally, all the little bits in between, but destroying the memorial gardens and drowning Bewdlay's clapped out coach, I have really enjoyed hearing about it. There is just one further third part of your punishment.'

'Anything, Mr Anthony,' said Willie.

'Put my name down as your first passenger for next year. Now you had better go and face Martha.'

Arthur made a small speech. 'Thank you very much, Mr Anthony. We all three did think we might get the sack. So thank you once again.' They left to go to the canteen.

*

The three very relieved friends mounted the canteen steps and opened the door. The servery hatch was closed so Willie banged loudly on it.

'Bugger off,' it said.

'Come on, open up, I want my dinner.'

The hatch did not open but it did reply, 'You can bloody well wait. You've inconvenienced me and because you no longer work at the mill you can be inconvenienced yourselves.' Suddenly the hatch was opened with ferocity. 'So what the hell are you doing here demanding food when you've been sacked?'

'We haven't been sacked,' said Willie. 'No, actually we've been promoted.'

'Promoted? What you three? Pull the other one; it's got bells on it.'

'We have. We are now officially Murgatroyd's Trip and Christmas Club organisers.'

The whole of the canteen erupted in a bout of cheering and congratulations.

Martha however did not cheer. She just continued in the same vane. 'I shall have to have a word with our Anthony. He must be going senile. Fancy not sacking you. That was the least he could have done I would have thought.'

Whist she was talking, three plates of resurrection appeared on the servery counter and a big jug of gravy.

'Can you manage to put your own gravy on or has this promotion gone to your heads?'

'What sort of meat is it?' Willie enquired.

'It's meat, from an animal,' she said.

'Well, that's nice to know.'

They paid for their dinners and, to yet more applause and cheering, made their way to their usual table in the far corner where Dick and Lewis were just getting the cards out having finished their meals.

'What happened?' They both asked together. 'We didn't realise that Mr Anthony had sent for you.'

Eustace began to talk, 'Well, it seems he quite liked what went on. He was very sorry he had missed the donkey falling onto Norris Oakes and he wished he'd been there to see Bewdlay's old coach destroy the memorial gardens, and he's ordered us to run another trip to Blackpool next year, and he's leaving Margaret at home and coming on the coach with us and we've to continue running the Christmas club.'

'So all's well that ends well,' said Dick.

'It looks a bit like it,' Arthur agreed.

But it wasn't quite, because immediately Willie and Arthur returned to the dyehouse, Walter Smith got onto them. 'What the hell did you two dozy lummocks go and say about me to Mr Anthony?'

'Why, has he said something?' Willie asked.

'Been down here and given me a right bollocking about saying he looked like the Grim Reaper. What do you want to go telling him that for?'

'Well, it were a bit delicate like,' said Willie.

Arthur thought he had better explain to ward off any further nastiness, so he did and that ended the matter.

*

Arthur arrived home to find Jess still in the same mood she had been on Sunday.

'Well, you're not home early, so I assume you've got to work a weeks notice and not be out of a job immediately. Have you given any thoughts to where you might get another job from?'

'Do give it a rest woman, we got promoted.'

'Promoted? Promoted? What do you mean promoted?'

'Just what I said. Me, Willie and Eustace are now Murgatroyd's official trip and Christmas Club organisers.'

'How come, and do you get any extra wage for it?'

'Do you know, I was so suited at not been given the sack that I never thought about extra money.'

'So what made him promote you then?'

'Well, he so enjoyed hearing about what went on that he has asked us to organise next years trip and he is coming with us and he is pleased that we are running the Christmas club again.'

'Coming with you? Mr Anthony?'

'Yes, he's leaving Margaret at home and coming on the coach.'

'Not Bewdlay's?'

'Yes Bewdlay's. The new coach that hasn't arrived yet and this time I hope he is going to drive it himself.'

*

'Three pints as usual is it?'

'No,' said Willie, 'we thought we'd have Harvey Wallbangers for a change.'

'You'll have what? Never heard of it, and anyway you can go and...'

He got no further as Eustace said, 'You can't make it because you haven't got the ingredients.'

'How do you know?'

'I do know, anyway, as you said, we'll have three pints.'

So whilst Harry dispensed the evening medicine he continued to talk, 'Anyway, what you lot doing here on a Monday? You never come in here on a Monday unless it's a life and death matter.'

'We're celebrating the success of our trip,' said Willie.

Harry ignored them and went on talking, 'by gum I had a right lucky do with that Madam Zsa Zsa, you know.'

'Yes, you could have been locked away for ever and we'd never have had the pleasure of your scintillating conversation and company ever again,' replied Arthur.

'Shame you escaped,' said Willie.

'You'd have missed me if I hadn't come back with you.'

'Wrong again, there would have been huge celebrations. Is my pint ready yet? I'm parched,' asked Willie.

'Anyhow, rumour in the village has it that you three have got the sack.'

'Well now sorry to disappoint you, Harry, but we have in fact gained a promotion.'

'A promotion? Don't talk so daft. Who the hell would promote you three? Only somebody that was brain dead or a zombie. What to?' he added quickly.

'Mr Anthony, and for your inside information,' Arthur beckoned Harry to lean over so that he could whisper in Harry's ear, 'you'll have to buy a copy of this week's Grolsby Trumpet on Thursday. Until then our lips are sealed.'

Harry appealed to the other two to inform him of what the promotions might be but he was told to buy the Trumpet.

'Fine friends you lot are keeping your secrets, not telling anybody anything about anything, I don't care see if I don't, it doesn't matter to me anyway, I shan't ask you again, you can all sod off for all I care, yes, you can sod off as far as possible and that's a long way.' Harry looked up to see that he was talking to himself as the others had gone to sit at a table as far away from the bar as they could. 'And I'm talking to myself and you lot don't care, and I don't care that you don't care, and I'm not bothered and, and, and...' He sat down behind the bar and made the biggest sigh ever heard.

'What's the matter with the fat one?' asked Arthur.

'Oh nothing,' said Willie, 'we've just upset him a bit. I don't really know why, but we have. He'll be alright tomorrow. Any of you ready for home. I fancy an early night, it's been quite a day one way or another.'

'Yes, yes I'm ready to get home to my Joan. I even look forward to it these days.'

Arthur took the other view. 'I think I'll just sit here and be miserable with the Harry. It'll be a happier occasion than going home to her indoors.'

'Still your fault is it?' Willie enquired.

'What is, Arthur, what is your fault?'

'Shut up Eustace and take Willie home.'

So Willie and Eustace went home and Arthur joined Harry in a pint or three or seven or...getting into even more trouble when he got home, but he was so inebriated as to not care.

*

Eustace returned home to have a friendly relaxing supper with his Joan before retiring for the night.

Willie sat chatting with Thelma about how good the Murgatroyd's were and how they both enjoyed working for them. Just before they went upstairs to bed, they went together into the back garden to look at the pigeons. Willie could contain himself no longer and farted so loud that he woke all the pigeons and the neighbours. The night air was pierced once again by Thelma shouting, 'Willie!'

Thank you for buying and reading

Murgatroyd's
Mill Trip

We hope you enjoyed it.

If so,
We would be honored if you leave a review on the
Facebook page

https://www.facebook.com/murgatroydsmilltrip

Or at

www.smashwords.com

www.amazon.co.uk

Murgatroyd's Christmas Club by Stephen Bailey

Skint! Broke! Pennyless! Hard-up!
Willie Arkenthwaite, an ignorant, rude and terribly crude dyehouse
worker in Murgatroyd's Mill is feeling a bit poor after his Christmas break
and returns to work a troubled man. Not only does he have to put with the
nagging mother-in-law at home, but he has a family (and pigeons) to look
after and he fears next Christmas will be just as tight.
Until one day this normally docile and inarticulate man does something
he's never done before – he has an idea. Willie wants to start a Christmas
savings club.
So what does he know about running a club? Nothing.
What does he know about setting up a committee? Nothing.
Has he ever saved before? Definitely not.
Luckily his best friend, Arthur Baxter, who has visions of grandeur, is a
little bit more organised and is able to help Willie along and before he knows
it, he's the Treasurer.
What does he know about being a Treasurer? Nothing.
So how on earth will this man be able to collect his wits about him and
make next Christmas better for everyone? Well, with the help of his
whimsical friends and workmates, a kind and generous mill boss and a
eclectic local Yorkshire village community (and not forgetting his tolerant
wife), he might just be able to pull it off although you can guarantee, where
Willie's concerned, there's bound to be some mishaps on the way.